Hat Man Harvest

Talia Greer

Content Notes

This story contains elements that might not be suitable for all readers, including sexual content and very dark humor used as a coping mechanism. Please visit my website for the full, detailed list of content warnings. If you feel a warning is missing, please reach out.

Specific Note: This story includes brief but emotionally intense scenes involving suicidal thoughts. Chapter 23 portrays a panic spiral, a flashback to a past suicide attempt and hospital care, and a separate moment of self-harm behavior by another character. These pages are intense but brief—please take care of yourself and skip as needed.

To Sleep Token,

This book would not exist without "Dangerous" — the song that singlehandedly fueled this book's unholy levels of yearning, and made it about 30% hornier. You knew exactly what you were doing. I hope you're proud of yourselves.

CONTENTS

Chapter One

Mia

Mercurial // "Still feel off-track? Align your goals with the stars. Who were you before you gave up?"

If you would've told me six months ago that I'd be wrapping up my third cleaning service as a topless maid for Coral Key's most expensive penthouse assholes with huckleberry milkshake dripping down my chest, I would've laughed in your face.

But whether I like it or not, it's my reality now.

The milkshake in question is cold and sticky as I glare up at my client in disbelief. He's the last before lunch. I was *almost* done.

He's an incubus, a nasty, devilish thing—pun intended. Like most of the clientele here, he's all glamour and claws, wings and warning signs, dressed up in expensive cologne. Because he's handsome, a six-foot slab of scarlet-skinned muscle and luscious black hair, I might've even given him a pass for being rude. Or convinced myself the spillage was an accident.

The shit-eating grin on his face tells me it was anything but.

"Sorry!" he cries. "My hand slipped."

I'm used to normal supernatural shit, but honestly, it's times like these I wish I was anything but human. I want to punch him in the face so bad. Unfortunately, since he's a demon and I'm not, that would probably end up with him tossing me out the window of his twenty-sixth floor apartment.

I might have wanted to die a few months ago, but I don't currently, and I'd like to keep it that way.

I stand, dropping the rag I'd been using to polish the expensive tiles on his bathroom floor. He's leering down at my bare breasts. I look away.

What I *should* do is plaster a simpering customer-service smile to my face and pretend everything is fine. Instead I give him my meanest glare.

"You're a fucking dick."

The words are quiet, almost polite, but they taste sharp on my tongue. His grin stutters just enough to give me an opening. I scoop up my bag, shrug my jacket over milkshake-sticky skin, and step into the elevator, ears popping on my way down.

It isn't much, just a scrap of control. But right now scraps are what I live on.

The penthouses are technically part of Coral Key, but they jut out on their own little strip of glamoured land across the bridge—separate, shinier, and enchanted in a way that makes most locals squint if they stare too long. Everyone just calls them the Spires, like that makes the whole thing less absurd. This one sits near the top of Spire Three.

I clench my phone in my hand until the plastic case creaks. With sharp jabs of my finger, I bring up the MaidForYou Cleaning app. This service gets marked as incomplete, and with extra glee, I tab over to the Report screen, ding him for harassment, and flick the toggle to indicate I will not be accepting any requests from this client again.

The elevator beeps, dumps me out into the lobby, and I storm outside to my security car. The air smells like salt and ozone and something faintly sweet—some kind of magic that always clings to this town like mist.

Tulgan is waiting for me in a low and sleek black sedan around the corner. The massive orc has one green hand dangling out the driver's side window while the rest of him slouches in the seat.

"Mia?" he says with a start, his deep baritone voice rumbling out the window. "You're early. What happened?"

I toss myself into the car and slam the door behind me. The interior has never felt like more of a sanctuary. "Let's go."

Tulgan twists to look at me, gingery hair falling across one deep green eye. He frowns so deeply his brows nearly brush the gray tusks jutting from the corners of his mouth.

As my assigned security through the maid service, my wellbeing is quite literally his job. I can't hide this from him no matter how much I might want to. Sighing, I open my jacket to show him the topmost part of the damage.

"What the fuck? Did he—"

"No, he didn't jack off onto my chest. He spilled a fucking milkshake on me. On purpose."

Jaw working, Tulgan glances back toward the apartment building. "Want me to kill him?"

"*Tulgan.*"

"I'm only half-joking."

"It's fine," I assure him, shaking my head. "He's been reported on the app. I just want to get cleaned up now, ok?" But my tiny subletted apartment is clear across town, a far cry from the Spires, where all my clients live. The thought of having Tulgan drive me all the way back home just to change uniforms over lunch is almost enough to make me scream. "Know anywhere I can hose myself off? A car wash, maybe?"

He purses his lips, which is a ridiculous expression on a hyper-masculine orc with tusks. "Come on, you gotta give yourself more credit than that."

I just blink at him. I'm not in the mood to entertain any positivity right now.

He sighs. "My gym isn't far. I could buzz you in with my card, let you have a shower."

"That'll work."

The entire drive, I studiously avoid eye contact with him in the rearview mirror. He doesn't push me.

As promised, he swipes me into his gym—with loud electropop blaring—and I lock myself in a shower stall. Only then, once I'm alone, do the tears come.

I feel ridiculous crying here, in an upscale shower stall made of pale sage marble. I strip, aim the nozzle at my chest, rinse away the milkshake—and break.

It's not the topless maid thing. I don't mind that—it's honest work. I like cleaning, I have great tits I'm not afraid to show off, and my clients are, for the most part, perfectly respectable.

I just feel so lost. This isn't what I imagined for myself. But then, I never imagined the collapse, either.

Three months ago, I had a corner office, a title, and a life I thought was secure, running a startup I built right out of college with people I thought were my friends. I'd done everything right—aced the degree, skipped the safe desk job, and poured myself into Mercurial. That stupid, flashy little personal finance app with its immaculate vibes and astrology tie-ins became my life—even as App Store reviews crucified us and called it a cursed love child of Venmo and Headspace.

Mercurial was everything. My job, my identity, my future.

Until it wasn't.

Until they forced me out over one simple mistake.

I was such a high achiever before everything cracked. Before *I* cracked.

If only the Mercurial girls could see me now.

With the milkshake rinsed off, I slide my uniform back on, then my jacket over top. It's all cheap, silky fabric, the kind you'd get at a discount Halloween store—a stereotypical maid costume in black and white, with pink accent threads, and a halter-neck top with a button at the nape of the neck for easy undoing. It's much too hot outside for a jacket, but I refuse to walk around town in just the costume.

Back outside, I flash Tulgan a quick smile and duck back into the car.

The rest of my shift is routine. Standard. No one else dumps any milkshakes on me, thank God.

Back over the bridge, away from the gleaming towers, the real Coral Key reappears, quirky and colorful and alive. Most folks pretend the Spires aren't part of the town at all. Honestly, they're kind of right.

Tulgan drops me off at my place just after 7pm. While I can tell he wants to say more, I refuse eye contact, so he lets me off the hook.

The building is three stories, with external staircases and vines climbing the side walls like curling fingers. Once-white brick has faded to yellow beneath the constant onslaught of heat and sun. As I unlock the door and step over the threshold, the entire place shivers.

Some people say Coral Key lets you in only if you're weird enough, broken enough, or already halfway magical without realizing it. Reika always claimed the town had a mind of its own—that it chose who got to stay. Most tourists never notice anything strange. But once you see a minotaur buying beef jerky at the gas station or a hellhound chasing birds in the park, you're either in—or you aren't.

Maybe Coral Key let me in because I was unraveling, burnt out, and broken. Maybe it liked that I didn't flinch.

Really, it was Reika's fault. She scooped me up after I tried to disappear for good, told me I could crash at her place as long as I needed. She said it fast, like it was nothing—like she hadn't just handed me keys to a door most people never notice. By the time she had to leave the country for her own emergency, it was too late. Coral Key had already pulled me under, and I'd already seen too much.

Immediately, a text from Reika pops up on my phone.

Reika Tsukino:

> *Proof of life?*

What she means is, *did you try to kill yourself again? Please don't do it in my apartment.* I send her the emoji of the woman dancing in response.

After—well, everything—Reika was kind enough to offer me her apartment for a few months. She needed an emergency sublet, and I needed a cheap place to crash while I figured my shit out. Reika, who's half-siren, was unexpectedly called away to help a relative in Japan. As a tattoo artist, she had that freedom.

And her apartment is her cool, art-girl essence boiled down to a few design choices—temporary wallpaper in saturated blue that depicts the ocean's waves undulating at waist-height. Feline-safe potted plants placed on every available surface. Thick rugs strewn across the cool tile every few feet, soft yet textured like sinking your toes into warm sand. The apartment is a box. One bed, one bath, a kitchen big enough to stand in, and a living room with just enough space for a two-seater sofa. But it's all I need.

Reika Tsukino:

> *This is also your daily (friendly) reminder to feed Kiki.*

As I glance over the new text and dump all my stuff near the doorway, Kiki herself, a fluffy orange cat, comes strolling up to me with her yellow eyes wide and her tail straight up.

Mia Williams:

> *you don't have to remind me of that. I'm fresh from the psych ward, not an animal abuser*

Besides, even if I didn't feed her, I doubt the apartment would let Kiki starve.

Reika Tsukino:

> *Still. Friendly reminder.*

Smiling, I bend to let Kiki head butt my hand. I will almost immediately have to wash it, given that I'm allergic, but it's worth it. Reika's good-natured and persistent concern, even from multiple oceans away, along with Kiki's gentle acceptance, have done wonders for my mental health in just the few short weeks I've been here.

Hopefully, I won't be here long. Just enough to get back on my feet, figure out what's next. Once you've been a CFO, and your golden parachute's been slashed to shreds, there isn't really a whole lot waiting for you on the way down.

I'm not trying to build a new life, not exactly. I just want to stop hating the one I had before—endless work, endless expectations, and a high-strung, high-achieving friend group that showed its love like a noose around my neck.

I need to figure out what I'm doing with my life beyond the pressure cooker of Mercurial.

Kiki's dander works its way into my nostrils, and I sneeze my way into the kitchen. I pop a frozen box from Trader Joe's into the microwave—yes, I *am* going to eat about fifteen chicken tikka samosas and call it dinner, thank you very much—and snatch up my phone out of habit.

I've been away from my high-pressure job for a while now, but I still can't shake my habit of constantly checking my goddamned fucking email.

My samosas cook. I scroll through meaningless spam, sales offerings from clothing companies I can't afford to patronize right now, and the occasional newsletter.

Then I see it.

An email from Imani Brooks, from a few hours ago.

Imani, Chief Technology Officer of Mercurial, where I no longer work.

On instinct, I click it. My heart contracts and sinks at the same time. Within the cheery black and orange square is an invitation to the annual Halloween party. Also known as my favorite event of the year. Or at least, it used to be.

In the mood to poke at old bruises, I scan the names in the recipient line. Yep, all the usual suspects. The whole gang. And even me—my name, normal and right, on a list I don't belong to anymore. Why did Imani even invite me? Pity? We're barely friends at this point.

The email feels like seeing a car crash on the highway. I can't look away, even though I know I should, that I'm only making things worse—

The microwave dings. I dump my sad dinner into a bowl, and not even bothering to change out of my uniform, park myself on Reika's couch. I've developed a routine, something small to keep me from tumbling into my darkest thoughts.

Work. Dinner. Netflix. Benadryl, because of the cat. Sleep.

I don't think. I don't engage my mind. I stare at screen until screen go blurry, until eyes go tired. Then I sleep.

I'm not intending tonight to be an exception. Turning on some horrific true crime documentary, I shovel samosas into my mouth.

But my attention keeps flickering back towards my phone.

Finally, I snatch it up again, go back to the email. I should've looked before, but I was too chicken. Now I read the names more carefully.

Selene Vega is also on the invite list.

Of course she is.

I toss my phone to the other side of the couch, where it slips into a crack between cushions. Kiki tosses me an affronted look from her perch on the coffee table.

Whatever. I'll grab it later.

There's no fucking way in hell I'm going to that party if my bitch of an ex-girlfriend will be there. I mean, I wasn't planning to go before, but I'm definitely not going now.

It's tempting, sure. Even though I quit the startup, some of those people are still, in theory, friend-adjacent. It might be nice to see them—to see anyone besides Kiki, my weird inhuman cleaning clients, and the too-sentient interior of Reika's apartment.

But I know how we work, how that group works. The party isn't just a party—it's a showcase. They'll all be showing up with new boyfriends and girlfriends, the keys to a new house, new and expensive haircuts, new tattoos. They'll all have something to show for their time.

Me? All I'll have is myself, and the fact that I'm still here after desperately trying not to be.

So why the fuck would I put myself in that situation?

The bite of samosa in my mouth goes cold. My appetite is gone. I force down the rest of the bowl anyway, because I've already lost too much weight recently, but it all tastes like cardboard now.

There's a quiet ache in my chest as I picture the party, the vibes, the sense of belonging I felt in the past. Selene at my side, surrounded by all our friends, feeling like we could take on the world.

I never needed to find direction because I was always surrounded by people who did it for me. First my mom, then the Mercurial girls. And now I don't know where to turn, what to do. Just to keep moving forward, one shuffling step at a time.

I know I should go to the party. The thought of seeing Selene makes my stomach knot, but not going would almost feel worse. If I don't show my face, it's just more proof I've vanished, that they were right to erase me.

But isn't that what burned me out in the first place? Building my life atop a series of bricks labeled as "shoulds"?

I try not to think about it. I take my Benadryl for the night, watch the documentary mindlessly as I wait for it to kick in.

Just as I feel it starting to hit, the apartment dims its lights, ever so slightly.

I roll my eyes. "I get it, ok? I'm going to bed."

I shut off the TV, go brush my teeth and wash my face. I slip into a giant T-shirt and crawl into bed. It is 8:30pm. I feel no shame.

Even as I doze off under the Benadryl haze, I am still thinking about that dumb fucking party, imagining myself showing up and knocking everyone's socks off with how great my life is now—somehow showing them I am trying to claw my way toward something better.

Only, I don't know what.

Chapter Two

Nate

Clouds gather across the night sky, thick and eerie as the curdled milk I accidentally poured in my coffee this evening. I catch myself imagining the drop through the glossy windows—what it might be like, if I were capable of ending things that way.

The thought almost tempts me. Almost. But immortality's a cruel joke: this job is killing me, and I can't even die.

Hands in my pockets, I turn away from the windows with a sigh, rein in my scattered focus, and return my attention to the conference room. Twelve nightmares in corporate suits stare back.

"Right. Sorry. Got distracted." I clear my throat and gesture at the PowerPoint projected on the screen. I had an intern mock up some moodboards for me this morning, all eerie images of mirrors and haunting sorts of reflections. "As I was saying, the concept is a looping nightmare. I'm picturing the dreamer trapped in a room of mirrors, only each reflection is subtly wrong. The reflections age while the dreamer doesn't. They start moving out of sync. When the dreamer cries, one of the reflections smiles."

I pause, glance around. More blank-eyed stares as usual; ignoring this, I push ahead.

"We could tweak it any way you like. More horror or more unsettling. But the angle I had was that it's not gore—it's existential. It's the idea of identity decay, of watching yourself vanish in real time and being helpless to stop it."

The idea struck me the other night, wandering through the city. I'd strayed into the neat cobblestone charm of Old Town Coral Key—past the beachy tourists, past the cheerful, glamoured dryads slinging crystals. There was a folk art installation in the park that had passersby—supernatural and human alike—stopping in their tracks for a good long gander.

Stacks upon stacks of mirrors, all enclosed in different frames, creating an eerie and compelling tower of sorts. And all *types* of mirrors, too, some very clear, some whose reflections were warped beyond recognition. I stood in front of one, dropped my glamour, and watched my own shadowy form in the distortions. It was, quite literally, nightmare fuel. So I thought it might work.

Clicking through a few more slides, I show them the remaining moodboards. Then, because I can feel everyone getting bored with me, I wrap it up.

"It's simple. Clean. Not too flashy, so, probably won't cost too much. Maybe a 5-10 minute dreamscape, max."

The silence that descends after I bring my presentation to a close is so unbearable, I start thinking about flinging myself out the windows again. The board takes their time in responding, conferring with each other through a series of loaded and meaningful looks and quiet side conversations. Eventually, each one of them taps notes into their provided tablet.

Director Krell, my boss, is seated at the far end of the table. The distance yawns between us like a chasm. He collects the notes on his own tablet and finally meets my eyes.

"A for effort as always, Alston," he rasps. Krell is a wraith, technically dead but still functional and refuses to disappear. He speaks in a voice like an old vampire from a movie. "But I'm afraid the board isn't quite...*on board*. The mirror concept is too abstract. Dreamers won't be afraid, they'll be confused. It'll be a slow burn, not a spike. Too resource-heavy, and certainly not cost-effective."

Heat prickles under my collar. I can't tell if it's shame or fury, only that I want to peel my skin off. This is the third presentation of mine they've rejected in as many months. I keep trying, but I don't understand what I'm doing wrong.

No, scratch that, I *do* know, I just don't want to admit it—I'm much too artistic for what these people want.

I used to think nightmares were poetry. Now they're just quarterly metrics.

"I understand," I respond, low, clipped.

"We love your creativity. You just gotta keep it focused, dial it in on the objective—profit."

Nodding, I stare at the floor. "Yes, sir. Of course."

I hate this. I want to flee. And as soon as Krell dismisses the others, I gather my own tablet and try to do exactly that. But he corners me. This close, he smells like printer toner and funerals. His gray pinstriped suit is impeccably tailored and faintly translucent, as always. Above it, his mottled blue-gray skin reminds me of moldy bread.

"Alston, a moment?"

It's not as if I can say no.

I linger at the corner of the table. If Krell can tell by me angling my body toward the door that I'm ready to leave, he doesn't comment on it, and probably doesn't care.

"Listen," he ventures gently, but the stern set of his jaw tells me what's coming isn't gentle at all. "You know we all like you around here, right? It's nothing personal. We all respect the work your father put into Obscura."

Translation: I'll never be more than the founder's disappointing son.

They'll never say it out loud, but I'm only here because of my father. And they'll never let me forget I'm not him.

And I don't want to be. Fuck my father. All he ever did was crush my ideas, the same way Krell and the board just did. My father encouraged my creativity only as a trick to lead me toward what he wanted—becoming a clone of him. I'm not sure I'm ready to admit that Krell is likely doing the same.

My free hand tightens into a fist at my side.

"And I hate to do this, kid, but numbers are numbers." *Kid.* As if I wasn't nearly as many centuries old as him. "Your last three concepts tanked. Not one converted. The board doesn't care about artistry if it doesn't sell. Your father built Obscura on nightmares that worked, nightmares that made people afraid. And you're not living up to that legacy. I've been covering for you because I like you, because I know how hard you try. But I can't keep doing that—it's my ass on the line too, understand?"

Is he firing me?

Holy shit, this is going to be humiliating.

I stare at him. Through gritted teeth, I force out, "So, what? Am I being fired?"

"No, of course not. Nothing of the sort. But I need you to step it up. Get your performance metrics back on track by Halloween, or the board's going to make me re-evaluate you. Put you on a performance plan."

"A performance plan," I repeat, feeling hollow.

"Come on, don't look at me like that. It's not so terrible as you think. And it can all be avoided—just get those numbers up. You've got almost a month."

He claps me on the shoulder like we're buds. Like we're human jocks who just finished a good-natured game of basketball. Then he strides from the room, leaving me alone in the conference room as if he hasn't just nearly shattered my entire life.

A fucking *performance plan*?

My shadows twitch, restless, like they want to lash out on their own. I can't handle this right now. My calendar is packed today with meetings I don't care about. I'm not due anywhere that matters.

So I head for the nightmare chamber instead, too fragile and furious for small talk. The glamour drops like armor sliding off, leaving me raw beneath it, a sudden riot of shadows.

A chamber tech glances up from his laptop as I breeze in. "Hey, Nate, how—"

But I ignore him and slam myself into a stall, sliding the lock home with far too much force.

"O-*kay*," the tech says from outside.

"Let's just get this over with," I bite out.

"Of course."

I'm not supposed to be in the field anymore—pitching new creative ideas is my job. But my concepts keep bombing. Nothing seems to appease the board. At Obscura Group, performance metrics are everything. If the board won't respect my ideas, then fine. I'll prove myself the only way they seem to care about—by harvesting fear with my own hands.

The stall is a metal box, much like a human bathroom stall, only without the toilet. It provides us a private space through which to dream walk and build our landscapes. Once the tech hits the button, I enter Obscura's cloud-based dream software and am randomly assigned to a sleeping human. Then I enter their dream, make it a nightmare, and Obscura collects the raw power of their fear.

The stall pulses once, twice, a low thrum like a room full of computers. The slate gray metal flashes.

"Sequence commencing in 3...2...1..."

And I'm in.

The stall falls away.

I'm standing in a small bedroom. An apartment, maybe. An air-conditioning window unit hums away in the corner. Through thin walls, I hear the tenant in the next apartment, or a roommate, watching loud reruns of *Grey's Anatomy*. The person in the bed before me is slender and pale-skinned, with a swath of bright green hair swept across their forehead and an open-mouthed snore.

I let all of my frustration from the meeting earlier simmer to the surface. It makes my shadows darker, deeper, more eerie. Poised in the corner of the room, stretched to my full height, I am everyone's worst nightmare.

Too impatient and pissed off for my usual theatrics, I snag the edge of this person's dream beneath my fingers and *tug*.

They jolt awake mid-snore. The green-haired dreamer looks frantically around their dark room. Most of them have no idea I'm even here, not until they spot me —the too-tall shadow silhouette in a trench coat and wide-brimmed hat, a figure out of nightmare folklore, lurking patiently in the corner.

Fewer still know what I really am—a shadow entity, a thing that haunts nightmares. Or, as the internet likes to call me, The Hat Man.

The dreamer spots me. Their eyes go wide. They snatch their sheets up to around their chin, as if that'll keep them safe.

"Oh, fuck," they mumble.

I strike.

It takes me very little effort to paralyze a dreamer, to keep them physically trapped in that hazy space between asleep and awake. Most of the time, their own fear does it for them—pinning them to the bed, muscles locked, unable to flee though their mind is sounding the alarm about an uncanny danger.

Now, as I hover menacingly next to this dreamer's bed, I reach out a hand. In this form, those hands have too many fingers, and each is much too long. It takes only the briefest brush of my fingertips against the dreamer's hair to give them full-body trembles, their mouth falling open into a little 'o.'

And then their fear hits me. Others describe it as sweet or savory. Some of us nightmare creatures discuss human fear with the same reverence as wine connoisseurs waxing poetic about the perfect vintage. But the scent, the taste, is consistently underwhelming to me. The others will talk about a rush of energy they feel after a particularly good feed. Like a high, almost.

Me? I feel nothing. The thrill has gone stale.

I siphon dream-fear from this green-haired dreamer until I've hit my minimum, then back away.

Fear doesn't keep me alive—not technically. But it keeps me whole. Too long without it and my shadows start turning inward, eating away at me until I'm brittle. Most of us learn to manage a steady diet.

I've never been good at moderation.

The fear drains into Obscura's servers, stripped down to raw data and sold by the gigabyte to the advertising industry. Agencies swear it makes their campaigns irresistible. Humans keep paying to be told, over and over, that they're not enough.

Plenty of other emotions out there, yet this is all we're told to harvest. No one at Obscura even talks about joy, or calm, or want. It's all fear, all the time.

The dreamer's eyes slip closed, and soon they're asleep again. Maybe they'll remember this, tell their friends about a wild nightmare. Maybe they won't say anything at all.

With just a thought, I'm back in the nightmare chamber, enclosed in my stall. Mission complete. Box checked. I did my bare minimum. But it didn't fix anything, didn't make me feel better.

It doesn't even matter.

A glance at my tablet shows a calendar crammed with meetings. Strategy updates. Status reviews. Pointless noise. For all its talk of efficiency, Obscura is addicted to wasting employee time. And I've already wasted enough today.

Krell will notice if I disappear. But after that performance-plan speech, I'm already on his shit list. So what difference does it make if I cut out early?

For appearances' sake, I shoot him a quick message.

Obscura Group Internal Chat - 02:55 A.M.
Nathaniel Alston: *Not feeling well. Heading home.*

It's a lie, obviously. We don't really get sick, not in any way humans would understand. Most of us are damn near immortal and rarely susceptible to illness, human or otherwise. Saying I'm "not well" is shorthand for *I can't stand another minute here.* Krell will know it. The question is whether he'll let me slink away.

A moment later, he simply reacts to my message with the thumbs-up emoji. I wait for a response, but it doesn't come.

Perfect. Not only does he know I'm lying, he doesn't care.

I should be furious. But instead, the fury collapses into nothing. Everything just...dulls out.

With my mood spiraling, I leave.

It's still the middle of the night—3am maybe—and much earlier than I would usually get home. Obscura operates 24/7, perfect for accommodating all sorts of creatures with all sorts of schedules. And I don't need to sleep, not really, so I never have much of an excuse not to work.

But I couldn't stand being in that office for another minute.

As soon as I step into the apartment, my mood blackens further. What looks like fluffy white clouds are strewn all over my open-plan kitchen and living room. My eyes dart to the couch, where a large chunk has been ripped open in the back. A curious and telltale rustling comes from inside.

"Molly!" I thunder.

Molly, my three-headed hellhound puppy, bounds out of the bowels of the couch with one of her mouths full of cushion stuffing.

"Leave it," I growl at her.

To her credit, she lowers all six of her ears, gently releases the mouthful of stuffing, and slinks away to her dog bed in the corner. My eyes slip closed. I pinch the bridge of my nose. I'm angry—with her, with myself for not anticipating my puppy doing normal puppy things—but after the day I've had, it's like everything is coming at me from a distance, through thick fog. It doesn't quite touch me. What would've sent me into a rage yesterday now only has me sighing and dropping to the floor with my head in my hands.

I can't keep up with puppy-proofing my apartment. Molly keeps destroying things I don't have the time to clean. At least the puppy pads are self-cleaning—they vanish in a puff of lavender smoke the second she's done using them. One less thing to deal with.

I work too much. I have no hobbies to speak of, nothing else to pour my time into except work, so it's expanded to fill *all* my time, and as an immortal, I have a lot of it.

And it's embarrassing to need help keeping things tidy. I don't know what I was thinking, getting a puppy when I'm already overwhelmed at work and not doing well performance-wise.

But I can't bear to get rid of her.

I let my hands fall. Crawl pathetically over to Molly's dog bed—which is enormous, practically the size of a bathtub—and curl up next to her, soaking in her animal warmth and faint sulfur scent. Two of the three heads rise to lick my face; one is still upset and turns away.

I rest my head on the soft and expensive fabric and look out the window. From here, I can see almost all of Coral Key—its postcard-perfect main streets and pastel rooftops giving way to deeper shadows, stranger corners. My high-rise is one of the few in town, jutting up from the Spires like a knife between two worlds. Lights glitter below. The ocean stretches out, vast and hungry, a dark and desolate blue.

It's a view most people would kill for. But it just leaves me feeling hollow—and wondering when I'll feel anything close to vibrant again.

Chapter Three

Mia

MERCURIAL// *"It's been 18 days since your last login. That's okay. Your ambition's still here, waiting for you to come back."*

Two days later, and I am still thinking about that stupid fucking Halloween party.

I tried to take my mind off of it. Really, I did. It's just that I have so little in the way of distractions these days. I even downloaded one of those silly story-based home renovation mobile games onto my phone—rife with microtransactions—in the hopes of snagging my mind on something else. But the allure of Imani's invite email keeps sucking me back in.

I find myself opening my inbox in between cleaning clients, not to *actually* check my email, but to open the invite, glance over it, mark it again as unread, and click away.

By now I've memorized its contents: `Costumes, cocktails, and questionable decisions—come celebrate the spookiest of nights with us at The Gilded Orchid! October 31, 8pm till midnight. Costume required. RSVP below.`

It's just an invitation. To an event I don't even want to attend. At a Miami club I hate, less than twenty minutes away, beyond Coral Key's glimmering borders.

And I'm ruminating, I know that now. For a week or two, right after I got out of the hospital but before my employer-sponsored healthcare through Mercurial ran out, I saw a therapist who helped me put a name to my worst mental spirals. She told me I had a tendency to chew on negative and distressing things like a dog gnawing on a giant bone.

Which is correct.

Which is why the party won't get out of my head.

Fuck. Get it together.

Giving myself a little shake, I glance up at the rearview mirror. Tulgan's moss-colored eyes dart back and forth as he drives, navigating us back toward the area surrounding the Spires. In a fit of desperation to stop thinking about the email, I booked myself more clients than usual over the next few days, and all in this area.

On this side of the bridge, the tips are better.

"Hey," I ask him. "After I finish this job, want to swing by Moon Doggies for late lunch? I'm in the mood for a greasy hot dog."

The enormous orc eats more than anyone I've ever met. In the front seat of his car, he keeps a small cooler and two large lunch boxes stocked with snacks and more substantial food. I once asked him what he does while I'm in and out of houses and he's waiting in the car. "Eat," he'd said. "Lots of eating. And otherwise reading celebrity biographies on my ereader."

Tulgan's eyes light up in the mirror, just like I knew they would.

"I think you already know the answer to that."

We both laugh as he pulls the car up alongside the entrance of another sleek high-rise. Honestly, they're gorgeous, but they all start to look the same after a while.

"I'll try to be quick," I promise him. A glance at the MaidForYou app confirms this client has only booked a 1.5 hr surface clean. "Hopefully this miserable supernatural bachelor isn't as messy as the last few."

Tulgan shoots me a quick grin. As I shut the car door behind me, I already hear the telltale sound of him ripping into a bag of potato chips.

Inside the glossy lobby, I flash my phone at the doorman—the app handles all entry credentialing, and can even facilitate access for an additional fee, which most clients take advantage of—and am quickly ushered into an elevator. The doors slide shut with a near-silent *snick*, and then I'm staring at my own reflection in their polished black surface. My maid costume is hidden beneath my mid-thigh-length beige coat, and my ultra-comfy black sneakers complete the ridiculous look.

The elevator has *carpet*—sumptuous, rich carpet the color of red velvet cake. We rise higher and higher, the speed barely perceptible. As the steady beeps tick off each floor we pass, I try my best to empty my mind. Get in the right headspace. All I need to do is pop in my earbuds and lose myself in the routine of cleaning.

The doors open and dump me out right in front of a tall black door. I scan my app on the keyless entry portal, the door clicks open, and I step inside.

For a moment, it's utterly quiet. All I can hear is my own breathing and hesitant heartbeat. I'm always a little nervous cleaning a new client's place for the first time, and this is no exception—

There's a sudden scuttling, the sound of claws on tile, and a formless black shape comes scurrying around the side of the counter island. I don't have time to see what it is before it rushes at me. Panicked, I shriek and drop to the ground, throwing my hands in front of my face. But no attack comes. Instead, there's just a rush of hot breath, the sound of heavy, canine panting, and the faintest scent of rotten eggs.

Slowly, I lower my arms.

The creature before me is the size of a small horse, with three heads and no spatial awareness. It's pitch black, its fur incredibly matte, so dark it seems to repel shine. It has all the trappings of a dog—four legs, excited little pants, a long tail that wags, whipping back and forth across the floor like a windshield wiper.

But.

The three heads.

One head has brown eyes, the other yellow, and the other blue. And *all* of them are looking at me like I'm the most interesting thing to come through that door in weeks.

Dimly aware of my heart racing, I swallow. The dog doesn't look like a threat. All of its snouts are round, its eyes big and soulful. In fact, I'd say it was a puppy if the thing didn't nearly reach my waist.

"Um. Hi?"

The dog wags its tail harder. Now that I know it's not trying to kill me, and mostly seems to have normal dog vibes, I slowly push to standing and take in my surroundings.

"I'm here to clean for...whoever your owner is. Are they home?"

The tail stops wagging. A dejected whine comes from one of the heads, and they all slump towards the ground. It damn near breaks my heart.

"I'm guessing that's a no. Fuck. I'm sorry."

What sort of asshole leaves their freakish three-headed puppy home alone all day? And doesn't bother to tell the hired help that said puppy has three fucking heads?

Cursing this nameless dickhead, I move around the counter.

The kitchen is stylish but impersonal—state-of-the-art appliances that look barely used, a stretch of marble counter scarred with faint claw marks, and a spotless black sink.

Beyond that, against the blinding backdrop of a wall of windows, lies a living room: a sleek couch with stuffing ripped out of the back, a coffee table positioned like a showroom piece. The view is breathtaking, Coral Key glittering below like something out of a postcard—but the whole place feels staged, like no one really lives here.

"Okay, soooo." I speak aloud, trying to orient myself. When I move to the living room, the dog follows, all three heads trained expectantly on me. "Your owner isn't here." Which is strange. Most clients who book a topless maid want to *watch* us work, if you know what I mean. "He...wasn't prepared for the responsibility of dog ownership, I suppose? Is there anything else you've destroyed that I should know about?"

The dog looks away and lowers all three of its heads.

"Great." Just one more thing to be on the lookout for. Whether the client is present or not, they paid for their service, and that's what they're going to get. And although I feel completely ridiculous stripping down to my maid uniform and undoing the top halter to get my tits out, especially with a three-headed dog staring at me, that's my job. "Time to get to work, I guess."

All MaidForYou clients are required to purchase a starter pack of cleaning supplies, which are delivered prior to their first scheduled clean and resupplied on a subscription basis for as long as they use the app. On my end, as a cleaner, they pitch it to us as "the easiest clean you'll ever do." All we have to do is show up in uniform, use the provided supplies, complete the service, and leave.

It's the same kind of glossy, elevated, treat-yourself type service we always tried to spin with Mercurial—make people feel like they were buying empowerment, when really they were buying into a giant scam. And now that I've been on both sides, I see it for what it is.

Speaking of Mercurial, I need to delete it from my phone. I keep getting their stupid notifications and each one feels like a guilt trip I didn't sign up for.

The MaidForYou app guides me with a blue locator beacon to where this client has stashed their starter pack. Everything's tucked into an empty cabinet beneath the sink. As I grab the basket of supplies, the scent of bleach flits by, and my chest goes tight—the old map of panic tracing itself across my ribs.

I shake it off. Not thinking about that now. I pop in my earbuds, crank up the old-school P!nk, and get started.

First, I polish the scuff marks off the bottoms of the cabinets. I can't do anything about the claw marks in the marble, so I skip that. The trash can is full of couch stuffing already, so the owner must have done their best to try and clean up after the dog's latest misadventure. A quick once-over of the back of the couch tells me there's really no saving it without replacing an entire panel of fabric, which is well beyond my pay grade, so I simply tug the gaping edges as close together as I can and move on.

Apart from the obvious puppy disarray, the place is otherwise fairly clean. It's a little dusty, sure. But there are no dishes overflowing, no rancid hand towels, no rotting food in the fridge. I find a few odd mugs and water glasses lying around in weird corners—near the window, on the floor by the couch. There's a stack of mail on the coffee table, piled neatly, but untouched. As I give the kitchen counters and coffee table a perfunctory once-over with my rag and some disinfectant, the dog gets a whiff of the fluid and retreats to its massive dog bed, where it curls up and simply stares at me.

To the left of the kitchen is a short hallway leading to the bedroom and bathroom. The bedroom has sleek white tiled floors, an enormous king-size bed neatly made with luscious black blankets, one fluffy black rug that's missing a chunk out of the corner, and a floor-to-ceiling wardrobe with shining black doors. The curtains are drawn. A peek outside reveals a door to a balcony that wraps around to the living room.

Curious, I also peek inside the wardrobe—row after row of designer suits in black, brown, and navy, each of them likely more expensive than my rent, and neat rows of designer shoes lined up along the floor.

Frowning, I shut the door. This guy clearly has money. He couldn't afford a dog walker, at least?

The bathroom is one luxurious spill of gray marble the color of a thundercloud. Sink, toilet, shower; the fancy kind that has only a slab of glass as a door. Hand and bath towels hang from racks, all high-end materials I'm almost afraid to touch. Shrugging, I wipe down all the surfaces. Even if there's very little for me to actually clean, the fresh lemony scent should be proof enough that the service was completed.

It's all strange. Somehow the place is both spotless and *un*lived in, like a stage set someone forgot to pack up.

I'm still musing on this, bobbing my head along to "Don't Let Me Get Me," as I return to the living room, looking for more things to clean. Suddenly, the dog bolts upright and charges for the door.

And I freeze with a rag in my hand as something incredibly unnatural steps inside.

The figure isn't human, that's for sure. It's too tall and stretched too thin, woven out of darkness, stitched with something heavier than shadow. Its skin is black and matte—not fur, not human skin, something smooth but utterly non-reflective. Like looking at a hole cut out of reality. A trench coat and a hat float along its frame like half-forgotten ideas.

For one impossible second, it stares at me—featureless, hollow—and then, with a sudden ozone and burnt sugar smell, the thing snaps like a rubber band and collapses into a man.

Pale skin. Sharp jaw. Coldly handsome. Normal clothes—stylish dark khakis, a navy button-down with the top button undone. Shaggy black hair and bone-white knuckles pulling the door tightly shut. He blinks once, revealing deep, crystal blue eyes.

His gaze flicks over me—lower, then up again too fast.

And I almost believe he always looked like that.

Even if it's just a glamour, he's stupid hot. And I'm stupid for noticing.

"Hello," he says, rather normally.

At his feet, the dog is throwing an absolute fit—whining, crying, jumping on his legs. He gives it a long pat on the head and continues to stare. He's too still. The air around him *bends*, just a bit.

I am not really sure what to say. Sorry I saw your shadow form before you realized I was here?

"Hi."

He looks me up and down, swallows. His eyes drop to my breasts and stay there a moment too long before returning to my face. There's a strange, fractional pause—like he's trying to remember the script for human interaction.

"You're the maid? From the app?"

"Yes."

"You're...topless..."

"Also yes."

His mouth opens and closes a few times. "I didn't realize it was that kind of app."

"I didn't realize you had a dog with three heads."

As if remembering her again, he glances down at the dog, who is now sitting at his side and gazing up at him with unconditional love. "Oh, you don't have to worry about Molly. She's harmless. But I do apologize. I imagine she must be a bit...startling...for a human."

His voice is low and rough, like he hasn't used it much lately—and isn't sure he wants to now. And there are no human stutters or filler words in the way he speaks. Just deep, calm syllables, dropped into the air like weights. He sounds like he's been built out of smoke and broken promises. Stupid voice. Stupid everything.

Since Selene, I haven't so much as *looked* at anyone. Not in that way. It's like a part of me shut down, entered survival mode. And this absolute weirdo is the first one to change that? Ugh, why am I like this?

To distract myself, I ask, "What *is* she?"

"A hellhound."

"Of course."

The opening notes of Taylor Swift's "I Knew You Were Trouble" start playing in my earbuds. I forgot I was wearing them. Forgot I was listening to anything at all, actually. And I absolutely do *not* want to hear this song right now! It's too on the nose. I scramble for my phone and shut off the music.

We stare at each other some more. My heart is *racing*.

"I'm Mia," I blurt. "By the way. Not that it matters."

He blinks again. "Nate." A pause. "Mia? Is that short for anything?"

"Yes," I nod, very seriously. Fuck, why am I so nervous? "Amelia Mignonette Thermopolis Renaldi, Princess of Genovia."

Nate tilts his head to the side. "Really?"

"No. God." Heat floods my cheeks. *Why* did I say that? "Nobody ever gets my references." I clutch my rag like a lifeline. "I should get back to...cleaning. What you paid for. On the app."

Nate nods. Very slow. Very serious. Like I've just announced a treaty negotiation instead of basic dusting.

"We'll stay out of your way," he says. He hesitates like he might say something else. Then doesn't.

Without another word, he stalks off down the hall, Molly trailing happily behind him with all three tongues lolling out.

I exhale a shaky breath and return to the kitchen. I'm going to pretend to clean out the fridge, though I have a sneaking feeling nothing's in there. Yanking it open, I peer inside like it holds the meaning of life.

Just as I thought—empty shelves. One sad bottle of sparkling water.

Perfect.

If I focus really hard on pretending to reorganize his nonexistent groceries, maybe I'll stop replaying the way he looked at me.

Chapter Four

Nate

"Let me make sure I have this right. You accidentally booked a topless maid on an app. And she's hot. What's the issue? What are you complaining about again?"

I roll my eyes—hard. Of course he's going to make this worse. That's what he does.

And Beck, my one and only true friend, grins.

Beck is like me—a shadow-born entity most humans only perceive in their nightmares. We met at Obscura a few decades ago, back when he was freelancing as a dreamscape architect—before he realized schmoozing with the fear execs paid better than actually harvesting it. These days, the execs spend their time wining and dining human ad firms who buy Obscura's product by the gigabyte, and Beck tags along for the free cocktails. He calls himself a consultant, but really, he just haunts their social calendars and gets paid an impressive salary for doing nothing.

The only reason I put up with him is that he's slightly less exhausting than being alone.

We're at The Rift Lounge, a bar somewhere near the water, close enough for the briny, salty scent of the sea to waft in at leisure. Beck lounges on a barstool in a battered leather jacket and ripped jeans like he owns the place, a cocky glint in his mismatched eyes—one gray, one gold.

Beck's human glamour is all flash: golden mullet, the kind of face that makes humans curious for all the wrong reasons. I think he modeled it after some rockstar he had a crush on in the '80s.

Mine's forgettable by design—something I saw once in a magazine and thought, *that'll do.*

The bar is a dreadfully trendy place. The music is so loud I *feel* it more than hear it, the drinks upscale and pricey. It's packed with creatures unwinding after another long workweek—and the occasional human, either here by accident, or here on purpose and looking for one thrill of a one-night stand.

As a rule, I hate these sorts of places. But I couldn't stand my apartment anymore, and Beck wouldn't stop bugging me, so here we are.

The bartender appears in a faint blur. He's a young vampire guy in a burgundy silk t-shirt that's open nearly to his waist in a deep-V. His hair is curly and cut closely-cropped to his head, his skin a warm brown. He shouts in Spanish to the other bartender at the end of the bar before turning to us.

"What'll it be, shadow-gents?"

With a wink, Beck slides his credit card across the bar. Strobe lights from the dance floor catch on his hair and wash it momentarily pink. "Just an Ash and Embers for me. And keep 'em coming. Tab stays open for us both."

The bartender takes his card with a nod and turns to me, half-grinning, one fang poking out of his mouth.

"An Eclipsed Heart to start with, please. Double," I say.

He raises an eyebrow. "You sure you wanna double it?"

"I wouldn't be here if I wanted to feel anything."

"Suit yourself."

He bustles away to prepare the drinks and Beck returns his focus to me.

"You didn't answer my question."

"Beck, I didn't come here so you could roast me. I came to relax and unwind."

"You never relax. Or unwind." At my withering look, he relents. "Fine. My bad. Go on."

"The damn dog finds something new in my apartment to destroy every day. I can't keep up. Hellhounds don't poop, at least not in this realm, so that's a bonus. Just piss to clean. But I had to hire a maid, she ended up being topless, and now—"

Beck shudders with badly-stifled laughter. Exasperated, I fall silent.

Our drinks arrive, and I take the opportunity for a distraction. Mine is deep, oily purple-black, swirling faintly with veins of silver beneath the light. When I knock back the first half, it's floral at first, then bitter enough to bite. It tastes like loss.

Unbidden, an image of the maid, Mia, crashes through my mind. Which is *exactly* what I came here to avoid.

Short and soft and maddeningly vibrant, with colorful locs falling loose around her shoulders in shades of rust and cinnamon and ash. A tiny silver hoop in her nose, little food tattoos scattered down one arm like charms—a bowl of ramen, a tray of tacos, a hotdog wearing a ballcap. Warm skin, honey-toned and radiant under my apartment's fluorescent lights. Hazel eyes that felt like an invitation to a joke she couldn't quite explain.

She looked like she belonged somewhere wild and feral and free.

Not trapped in my sterile world.

Not tangled up with someone like me.

I slide my eyes sideways to Beck's drink, a swirling copper-red cocktail that steams faintly in its glass. It smells like burned sugar, charred wood, and cinnamon that's much too strong to be cozy. He sips and promptly belches smoke.

"Never get tired of that," he says with a grimace, eyes watering. "So. Question. What is it about this maid that has you so discombobulated? I mean, she's just there to clean, right?"

I take another sip while I consider. "She was there when I came home. I went in for an extra daytime shift to try and suck up to Krell, but I left early again because I couldn't deal. I didn't have my human glamour on when I got home. Not at first."

At work, in dreams, humans always react the same way—panic, terror, adrenaline spikes. Minimums exceeded, fear collected. But she just...looked at me. Like I wasn't a monster. Like I wasn't even a mystery.

What I don't mention to Beck, because it's not relevant, is the *darkness* I sensed in her. It was brief, just a flicker—so fast I almost missed it. Being a creature that feeds on human dreams, it leaves me often quite sensitive to their emotions, and sometimes I'll get a flash of feeling here and there in the waking world, like picking up a whiff of perfume from a passerby.

And although Mia presented herself as cheerful and lighthearted, there was something buried beneath that called out to me. Something like carefully-managed despair.

Something I recognized—because it's how I feel, too.

Beck considers this. "So you're not actually upset because she's hot, or because she saw your expensive imported dog. You're upset because she looked at you and didn't flinch."

Maybe he's right. Maybe that's what it is. At work, fear is predictable. Quantifiable. You can chart it on a spreadsheet. But she didn't fit the pattern.

"She's a human. She'll be terrified soon enough."

Beck fixes me with a long look. "You're intrigued. Admit it. She wasn't even scared of you, was she?"

"I wasn't—she didn't even really have long enough to look—I dunno—"

"What's the big deal, then? She coming back?"

"Maybe? I booked a trial package of six cleaning services. It was on sale. Not sure if it's the same cleaner every time."

Beck snorts. "Practical and masochistic. Classic you." He lifts his glass and smirks. "Look, I'm just saying—if you don't want the hot maid, I will take her. Respectfully. Probably."

"Fuck off," I mutter, rolling my eyes again. It doesn't make the sinking in my gut go away. "It's just cleaning."

But he's right. My thoughts churn too fast, tangling into each other until I can barely breathe. There's a reason I keep my life so stripped down—no complications, no mess. Anything else drags me under. I'm tempted to drain my drink all at once, so I push it away, shaking my head.

Beck watches me a little too carefully. "You really think it'll stay that way? You swore you'd never touch a human again after—"

"It has to."

A memory rises, the one I've been trying to bury. My throat tightens.

A pretty human girl with soft hands and deep red hair backing away from me in terror.

A voice, my father's, colder than the depths of winter: "They should be grateful we even notice them. You did nothing wrong, Nathaniel. They're disposable."

A body in my arms. Unmoving. Cold. An accident, but still my fault.

And maybe that's why Obscura is worse than a prison sentence. With every nightmare I touch, every ounce of fear I harvest, I hear my father's voice telling me humans should be grateful. Telling me I overreacted to my lover's death.

I shove it all down, hard. Slam the door on it.

"Nathaniel," says Beck quietly, for once all bravado gone. "That was years ago. Hundreds, actually, at least the way you tell it. Your control is so much better now than it was then. You know how to walk dreams without hurting people. You can't assume the same will happen."

For once, Beck is the rational one. And maybe he's right. He means to soothe. But reason doesn't stop the gnawing dread in my gut. I've seen what happens when I lose control.

Once was enough.

"Humans don't survive entangling themselves with things like me," I say instead. "And I won't make another ghost. I refuse."

And I've stuck to it since. I don't date. I don't invite complications into my life. Four times a year, I haunt bars such as these, find temporary companions that become outlets for my mating urges, and while away my heat cycle with pretty strangers in my bed. That's as close as I come to intimacy.

So this hot maid can never be more than that. I won't allow it, no matter how much she intrigues me.

Beck doesn't argue. He just leans back on his barstool, sipping his drink, eyes thoughtful. I'm sure he disagrees, but maybe by now he's picked up on my mood. Knows there's no use in trying to convince me.

We lapse into silence. A pop remix comes over the speakers and the dance floor erupts in a roar of delight. Above the bar, one of the green neon signs flickers, half-burning out. It reads: *Stay Hungry. Stay Wild.*

The light sputters again, and all I can see is: *Stay Hungry.*

I reach for my drink and drain it. The burn lingers, faint and unsatisfying. Booze never does more than blur the edges for me, but sometimes even that feels like relief.

I rise from the stool. "I should get home," I say.

Before I forget what happens when I let myself want.

Chapter Five

Mia

Mercurial// "Your fate is waiting. The stars are watching. Be brave enough to take what's written for you."

Two long days and many cleaning shifts later, Tulgan and I finally make it to Moon Doggies for lunch.

I'm pretty sure he's been silently judging me for bailing on the late lunch plan before, but he's just too polite to say it out loud. And I've been too busy throwing myself at work. Trying to forget the party.

Trying to forget a certain gloomy client who was hotter than he had any right to be.

We swing by the drive-thru and then claim a low-key corner of the parking lot to eat. He cranks up the AC—it's hot as hell, and the humidity is just as high—and we lapse into a comfortable silence broken only by the crinkling of fast food bags.

Tulgan's European technopop bumps softly from the speakers at low volume.

"Sorry it took us so long to finally go here," I tell him after I've wolfed down half of my hot dog. It's delicious, exactly what I've been craving. The bun is fresh and steamed and squishes beneath my fingers, and the French fries are salted to perfection. I have no idea how much longer my thirty-one-year-old digestive system will allow me to eat like this without consequence, but I intend to enjoy it while I can. "I just kind of...spiraled for a bit."

"A few days, you mean?" he says around a mouthful of cheese fries. He snorts at the look I toss him. "Kidding. But I did notice. It was after that job in the Spires. Central Square, I think. Didn't want to ask at the time, but...did something happen?"

I nod. "The dude made one hell of a first impression. I was trying to keep myself busy with other clients...and not think about that one."

"Good or bad first impression?"

"Good," I admit, hesitantly.

"Oh," Tulgan says. He tosses his now-empty container of fries back into the bag and retrieves his fourth hot dog. "So you're attracted to him, is what you're saying."

"I didn't say that—"

"You didn't have to."

Heat creeps up my neck, and I busy myself with the foil wrapped around my hot dog, pretending I don't notice him watching.

I should've known I couldn't hide this from Tulgan. We haven't known each other long, but we spend a lot of time together, and we often get to talking. It's no wonder he's able to so easily pick up on shifts in my mood and behavior.

"Yes. Fine. He was cute. Weird. It pissed me off."

Tulgan smirks. "That's usually how it starts."

"But it wasn't just that." I pick at my hot dog wrapper. "There was something about him that got under my skin, and I don't want anyone under my skin again. So I've been trying to book myself solid with other clients."

He raises a brow. "Healthy coping strategy."

"...And I also kind of, sort of, might want to go to this Halloween party my old friend group is hosting in a few weeks."

"Ohhh. Now we're getting somewhere."

"My ex will be there," I add flatly. "Which means I need an impressive date. And for some reason, my brain keeps circling back to the weird guy at Central Square—probably the last client I should even think about asking."

Tulgan considers this, tilting his head to the side. "So you're browsing for dates among your rich clients? Even though one of them dumped a milkshake on you not even a week ago?"

"Yes." I'm not ashamed of it. Desperate times call for desperate measures. After everything with Mercurial, I need to prove—to myself, and to them—that I'm not some washed-up cautionary tale. "I'm calling the milkshake toss an anomaly. No one else has been that rude. I figure all I'll have to do is find someone who's not a total asshole, chat them up a bit, bat my eyelashes, and they'll agree."

"You're probably right. I will say, though, some creatures have a—uh. How do I put this? A human fetish? So just...be careful."

"I will."

"And if you can't find anyone in time, don't get desperate. I'll go with you. I can be arm candy for a night for a good cause."

I groan. "Don't make me sound like a charity case, please. But I do appreciate the offer."

Tulgan is a single father to two orclings who swore off dating after his wife died. He's also not at all interested in humans, so his offer makes me feel strangely teary and cared for in a way I wasn't expecting.

Besides Reika, I've only ever experienced one model of friendship, and it was with the Mercurial girls. They weren't exactly the *we've got your back* type.

As I finish my food, I scroll through the MaidForYou app to look over the afternoon's clients. Business as usual, it seems.

Two surface-cleans and one frustrating deep clean later, I'm back in the car. One more client, and then I'm done for the day. In the front seat, Tulgan accepts the app's GPS guidance, then goes strangely silent.

"What?" Without waiting for an answer, I lean forward to squint at the address on his phone.

12 Central Square.

Back to Nate—the shadow man's—apartment.

"Fuck!"

I have a feeling Tulgan is stifling a grin. I don't make eye contact in the mirror. I say nothing.

He deposits me at Nate's apartment a few minutes later.

"Be an adult," I tell myself in the elevator. "You can absolutely handle cleaning for someone who gives you the tummy flutters."

When I let myself in, Molly the hellhound dashes over to greet me. All three of her heads are whining and slobbering, her tail wagging like crazy.

"Hi, puppy!" I squeal, and offer her all the pets she can handle. When she's had enough, she sprawls out on the kitchen floor and watches me fetch the cleaning supplies from beneath the sink.

I close the cabinet. And I hear water running—the shower, from down the hall.

I freeze. He's *home*? No way is he home. Why—

Whatever. It's really none of my business. Most of my other clients are home when I clean, and they follow me around from room to room, watching me. That doesn't bother me. This shouldn't be any different.

I pop in one earbud so I'll be able to keep track of him, and get to work.

Today, again, there isn't much to clean. I wipe down everything I can in the kitchen and living room and sweep some coarse black dog hair off the floor. Then I return to the sink to scrub at the remains of what looks like peanut butter inside a Kong toy. As I reach for the dish soap, my wet hands fumble it, and the bottle falls into the sink with a comically-loud *thud*.

Moments later, a figure appears in the hallway. I ignore him and feign intense focus on scrubbing the stupid toy.

Then he strides into the kitchen and my fake focus shatters.

I can't help it. My gaze sweeps him from head to toe, from his bare feet to the high-end black joggers to the fitted dark gray t-shirt. His hair is wet and messy, falling into his eyes in black chunks. And there's a bewildered look on his face.

"You're...back?" he says.

I narrow my eyes at him. "Yes. You booked me again."

"I booked a trial package. I didn't realize they'd send the same person each time."

Ouch. "Well, sorry to disappoint."

"Not like that. That's not—not what I meant—" he splutters.

I raise a brow, waiting.

Nate rakes a hand through his damp hair, only managing to make it messier. "Maybe there's...something wrong in the app."

I huff. "Wouldn't be the first time." Shutting off the water, I reach for a paper towel and dry my hands. "Want me to take a look?"

He hesitates for a beat, then strides closer, tugging his phone from the pocket of his expensive loungewear and unlocking it. As he holds it out, the scent of his soap or cologne hits me—clean and smoky, with a hint of vetiver. It's tantalizing. And as tempted as I am to just stand here sniffing him like a sexy candle, I have a job to do.

Focus, Mia.

I snatch the phone maybe a little too fast and open the MaidForYou app. "Okay, let's see..." I mutter, swiping through. "Bookings, preferences, default settings—" I pause, reading. "Oh. Um."

"What?" Nate leans in to see.

I angle the screen toward him, trying not to hyperventilate at how close he's standing. "You flagged me as a preferred provider."

"I did *what*?"

Maybe he's one of those creatures who's so old they struggle with new human technology. It happens.

"Congratulations," I offer, deadpan. "You've officially subscribed to the Mia Cleaning Plan. Twice a week, indefinitely."

He groans, dragging his hand down his face. "I swear I didn't mean to."

"Sure you didn't," I tease, handing his phone back.

I'm trying to keep things light. He seems heavy, like he's carrying something invisible and immense. He's clearly uncomfortable having anyone in his apartment. His jaw tightens. He shifts slightly, gaze flicking away—not quite flinching, but close.

Weird. When I first met him, he wasn't rude. Awkward, yeah—but not cold. Now he's tense, like I'm a problem he doesn't know how to solve. Did I do something wrong? Maybe I made it worse by joking. Maybe creatures like him don't like being teased. Maybe I should've just nodded, taken the phone, and kept my mouth shut.

I hate how easily my brain jumps to blaming myself, like I'm one untended trash can away from getting fired or worse. I have the toxic work environment of Mercurial to thank for that. One mistake, and everything fell apart, no matter how hard I tried to hold it together.

I clear my throat, forcing a smile. "If you want, I can help you cancel it. Should be easy enough to undo."

He looks at me like I've just offered him a loaded weapon. "No. It's fine. I mean—you're good at what you do."

It's so grudging, so awkward, that I blink.

"Thanks...I think."

Molly thumps her tail on the floor. Nate rakes a hand through his wet hair again, making it stick up in chaotic little spikes.

"I'm just not used to..." He trails off, grimacing. "Company."

That's the understatement of the year. But it does explain his awkwardness.

"That's fine. I'm just here to clean. I'm not here to...make friends or anything."

It comes out harsher than I intended. Something flickers across his face, too fast for me to name. The faintest downturn of his mouth. A blink that lasts a second longer than necessary.

Disappointment?

"Right," he says quietly. "Just work."

"Exactly." I force the word out. But it lands wrong, flat. It doesn't feel like the win it should.

I should shut up. I should leave him alone and get back to, well, *doing my job*. But he hasn't fled yet. And I'm realizing I don't actually want him to.

I resume cleaning out Molly's Kong toy. "Most clients stick around while I clean, you know," I tell him. "That's totally fine. Doesn't bother me."

He studies me carefully. "I'd imagine," he says slowly, like he has to force it out, "that most of them aren't just watching you clean."

I blink at him. There's a slight flush high on his cheeks, and he looks away too fast, rubbing the back of his neck.

"I didn't mean—" he mutters. "I'm not—I didn't specifically want a *topless maid*—"

I bite back a smile. "Relax. You're fine. Very professional."

The words seem to confuse him more.

With the Kong clean, I dry my hands once more and turn to him, tilting my head. "So what do *you* do for work?" I consider how far to push it. The brief glimpse of his shadow form I saw the other day doesn't tell me much. Is he nocturnal? Something in-between? "Mid-afternoon seems early to leave an office job."

He freezes for half a second, as if weighing how much to tell me.

"Work has been...slow," he says finally. There's a long pause. I think he's lying, but I'm not sure about what. "Temporary schedule adjustment."

"Oh, okay." I put the Kong in the dish drain. "And the job itself?"

Another long pause. His mouth pulls into a faint, almost embarrassed line.

"Let's just say it's not very human-friendly."

Interesting. I want to know more, of course. He must make good money to live here. There's something about his work he's hesitant to tell me, though. And I don't understand. I consider myself a reasonably open-minded girl. What could be so horrible?

I consider pressing, just a little. I could probably get it out of him, if I wanted. But before I can say anything, my phone buzzes with a notification. Instinctively, I snatch it from my pockets and glance at the screen—and my stomach sinks.

It's a notification from Mercurial. Talk about a jumpscare. I thought I'd deleted that fucking app.

The message might be nonsense—exactly the kind of hip girlboss technobabble we engineered it to regurgitate—but it's a punch to the gut all the same. A reminder of everything I promised myself I'd stop doing—chasing after things that were bad for me, thinking I could fix the unfixable. The app, much like Selene and my so-called friends, turned into dead weight. I thought it would carry me forward. Instead, it broke me.

I tuck the phone back into my pocket, my throat tight, very aware of Nate's eyes on me.

This—letting myself want something I know won't end well—isn't real. It isn't safe. I'm a topless maid cleaning his apartment, and he's a stranger paying for a service.

It's just work.

Offering Nate a tight, professional smile, I turn back toward the bucket of cleaning supplies. "Well, your vague secret's safe with me."

For a moment, he almost says something. I can see it—the words hovering on his tongue. But then he just nods and steps back, giving me space.

I turn away too, wiping the same spotless counter just to keep my hands busy.

Mercurial wasn't just a job. It was a life I built around people I thought would catch me if I fell. Selene. Imani. The others. When it all collapsed, there was no net. Only the crash—hard and humiliating. And the realization that when everything broke, I was the one left sweeping up the shards alone.

I survived it once, barely.

I'm not stupid enough to risk anything similar again.

Chapter Six

Nate

I should have skipped tonight's shift.

I know it the second I step into the stall, before the familiar metallic hum of Obscura's dream servers swallows me whole.

But guilt gnaws at me—Krell's watching my numbers. And I can't stop chasing the hope that maybe someday, one nightmare might feel like art again instead of just data. Maybe my time in the chamber will inspire me with an idea the board will actually like. I don't want the quotas, and I don't want the board's praise as much as I want to prove to myself that I can still make something that feels alive.

That hope keeps me coming back, even when I swear I won't do this again.

So I close my eyes and let the dream take me.

But as the setting materializes, it's obvious something's wrong. I was aiming for some terror-slick landscape that would make the scaring easy and the work go by faster. That's what the suits want—maximum fear created and siphoned in as little time as possible. In and out and on to the next.

And this is...someone's bedroom. Too soft. Too grounded. Too real.

"Fuck," I mutter, as my surroundings fully materialize.

I'm supposed to be terrorizing a human into existential dread, checking a box, and moving on with my meaningless night. Not standing in a dream rife with cat fur and the smell of microwave dinners. It all feels too solid, too lush.

The walls of the apartment ripple with deep blue waves, low and hypnotic. Light drips across the ceiling like water seen from underneath, shifting with the slow pulse of some distant current, all courtesy of some fancy projector on the floor.

The furniture is sparse: a pale driftwood coffee table, a worn leather two-seater sofa, and thick, sun-faded rugs sprawled across the tiled floor like islands in a shallow bay. A jungle of plants dangles from every surface—some real, some dream-distorted into shapes too strange for land. A cat's sleek orange shape flickers past in the shadows, too fast to catch. And the smell—brine from fish tanks and the lingering ghost of something human: lavender cleaner, maybe, and the metallic tang of old worry.

I drift forward. The air is too heavy. Too lived-in.

I should leave. This isn't right. But I *need* those numbers, and even if the dreamscape is all wrong, the fear still counts for something.

Slowly, I keep drifting through the space. Heavy sleep breathing calls to me from the half-open bedroom door. I push it open and step carefully inside.

There's a figure entangled in aqua-colored sheets and blankets on the queen bed, their warm, golden brown skin contrasting with the bluish hues. The limbs are compact, the body one long sinuous curve broken only by deep burgundy sleep shorts and a sports bra of the same color. My eyes trail up the sleeping form to the face.

And I jolt, shaking the fabric of the dream around me.

I know this dreamer. It's *Mia*.

Out of all people, why the fuck am I in *her* dream?

Instinct jolts through me, hot and shameful. I shouldn't be here. I should turn around, tear the dreamscape to pieces, force a reset—anything but this. For a moment, I even *start* to. My shadows recoil, twisting towards the exit. I could call a premature stop and claim an error, or equipment failure, and just try again with a new dreamscape and a new dreamer. But Obscura logs forced disconnects. If I bail now, someone will flag it—and I'm already on thin ice.

The stall pairs us to dreamers through Obscura's servers—random on paper, but weighted by compatibility scores and algorithms I'll never see. Some twist snagged us together here tonight, and whether it came from her or me doesn't matter.

I should leave. But I don't. I'm too curious.

I step closer to the bed. She looks so peaceful in sleep. Not tired, or on edge. Her colorful locs are tucked away into a purple bonnet secured around her head with silk ties. I keep looking, taking my fill, noticing all the things a quick real life glance would miss.

Normally, I'd twist the dream, drag her into something horrific, force-feed the terror Obscura wants until the charts spiked high enough to satisfy. But Mia's emotion is already here, soft but saturated, bleeding into the air like mist. I don't have to build anything—her subconscious is doing it for me.

It's not terror. It's something softer. Exhaustion, frayed nerves, the bruised ache of wanting something she doesn't believe she deserves. Even if she looks peaceful, her mind is anything but. She's lost in a nightmare of her own. It just looks different than what I usually feed on.

But it pulls at me all the same.

I step closer, one reluctant step at a time. Until my shins touch the edge of the bed. The lavender smell is still there, clinging to her even in the dream. I thought it was a remnant of cleaning supplies. Maybe it's just *her*. Underneath it is something warmer. A salt-sweet human scent that hits me low and hard, against all my better instincts.

Curiosity about that darkness in her crackles in my chest like static. It's not just wrong—I barely know her, and have no right to the story of her past—it's reckless.

And I want to know anyway.

I could leave.

I *should* leave.

Instead, I reach out—only an inch, not touching, never touching—and let the siphon open between us.

Just a breath. Just a taste. Just a sip. It's still cleaner than what Obscura would have asked—dragging her into a full-blown nightmare, terrorizing her until the fear spiked and the numbers looked good.

She won't even notice. Dreamers never do. Their experience of the dream won't always match up with what we concoct.

The energy hits me immediately, heavy and bright and rich as blood. Nothing like the fear-slick sludge Obscura demands. This is something more raw. And it's not just fear, either. It's messier, more intimate.

I don't see her memories—not directly—but I feel the residue they left behind: the feeling of everything slipping through my fingers as I try to hold it tight. Desperation, helplessness, despair. Regret. A slow and sad sort of resignation. Enough to piece together shapes without faces, echoes without names.

Then nothing.

What *happened* to her?

This wasn't what I came here for. I took more than I should have, something raw that no dreamer ever means to give. But now I don't want to stop.

The curiosity and concern overwhelm me. The dreamscape is pulsing, a faint notification bell dinging at the edges of my consciousness—I've siphoned enough. I can leave. But I don't feel *done*.

I know what Obscura would want me to do: push her deeper, milk every drop of terror until the charts sang. That's the job. But what I want is worse.

I want *her*, not her fear.

I want to know what caused this darkness that calls to me so strongly.

My hands tighten into fists at my sides. I almost—*almost*—reach for her. If I touch her, maybe I can see more. Feel more. Maybe—

But that's not mine to take. That's not—

What would it cost her, really? A flicker of exhaustion, a shiver she'd never remember. She wouldn't even know I'd been here. But I'd know. And I don't know if I could live with the nightmare that makes me.

The urge is brutal. If I just lay my hand against her skin—

Just once—

I could feel what she's dreaming. I could find out what hurt her so badly. I could *fix* it.

But monsters don't fix things. Monsters only take.

The second notification bell chimes. I'm approaching my time limit. The reminder is enough to snap me back into reality. I've stayed too long, fed too much, and all this when I swore I wasn't even going to try.

I tear myself backward, severing the tether with a thought. As the tether severs, the dream buckles under the strain. For a horrifying breath, I wonder if I broke something—if I broke *her*. But the dream folds inwards gently, like a closing flower. Safe. Untouched.

Still, the guilt churns.

It didn't hurt her, not in any way she'll notice. But it feels like theft all the same. I'm gone before I can do anything worse.

Gone before I can betray the fragile trust she doesn't even know she gave me.

And still, the taste of her clings to me—bitter and bright. It sticks to my teeth, my skin, my soul.

I didn't just take fear. I took *something real*. Something I don't know if I can ever give back.

I find myself back in the dream stall, hands pressed to the walls, shaking.

I'm flush with power. Choking on it. My shadows writhe and roil, coiling up the walls of the stall like smoke seeping out of cracks I can't seal. I feel raw, oversensitized—everything too bright, too loud, too *much*.

How long has it been since I felt anything so potent?

I squeeze my hands into fists. Force the excess magic down where it can't be seen.

This was supposed to be easy.

This was supposed to mean *nothing*.

Outside, I hear the chamber tech's murmur of surprise, no doubt looking over the numbers I just brought in.

Snarling, knowing it's soundproof from the outside, I slam a hand against the wall. Let them marvel. Let them chart my "success" on their spreadsheets, proof I finally delivered what they wanted. They don't know the truth—that I crossed a line, that I took something I can't give back.

This isn't a win—it's my first real mistake.

And if I'm not careful, it won't be my last.

Chapter Seven

Mia

MERCURIAL//"Breathe. Sleep. Reset. Love like your past was just a bad dream."

That night, I have the strangest dream. And I don't realize I'm dreaming until I try to move—and can't.

Blue light sloshes across the ceiling from the vibe-y ocean landscape I chose on the projector. Salt and candle wax and crushed lavender cling to the heavy, damp air—all the familiar signs and smells of Reika's apartment.

But there's a man standing in the corner of the room. Tall and shadowed, faceless, somehow familiar. A name approaches the surface of my mind, then glides away in that flimsy, uneasy way of dreams.

He's just close enough to reach if I tried. But I can't move. I can only watch as he and his wide-brimmed hat—more shadow than flesh—glide towards the bed. His presence pulls at something deep in me.

I should be afraid. Instead, strange heat blooms low in my belly, along with a slow, agonizing need.

Touch me. See me. Stay.

I open my mouth to call him closer, but no sound comes out. I reach out a hand instead. I think if I could just touch him, just once, I wouldn't feel so alone.

But he stays out of reach. The harder I try, the farther away he feels. Dream logic never makes sense. My body is caught between fear and want, and I can't tell which one is stronger.

Then the world shifts, and I wake up gasping.

My heart hammers against my ribs. My chest aches like something's been carved out of it. The sheets are a tangled mess around my legs, and my skin feels hot and tight.

I swallow and almost choke. My mouth's desert-dry. Scrambling for the water bottle on the night table, I grab it and swig, feeling my pulse calm in increments. The cheap ceiling fan spins lazily overhead.

Everything is fine. Time to calm down. It was just a dream—just loneliness clawing its way through the cracks. A dream of shadows, saltwater, and a man in a hat who stood too far away and left me reaching for nothing. Most of my nightmares dissolve on waking. But this time, the feeling lingers, disorienting, as if something important was stolen while I wasn't looking.

Once I've had my fill, I set the water bottle down.

And I burst into tears.

The dream seems to have torn open this smothered ache in my chest, and now that the dam has burst, there's no patching it up.

Maybe the cracks in the facade have been there all along.

Memories flood through me, all of them awful things I usually ignore—

Normal Tuesdays at Mercurial that felt like firing squads, Selene picking apart a slide deck molecule by molecule, the rest of us nodding along like bobbleheads. Me wringing my hands beneath the conference table just to make it through without crying. Only Imani noticing, sliding me a Post-It that just said, Breathe.

Selene berating me in our apartment after work, following me from room to room, even as I sobbed and begged her for a moment alone. Selene telling me I wasn't careful enough with my financial report, that my mistake could cost us everything.

Selene freezing me out for days until the others started to follow suit, too afraid to challenge her. One mistake was all it took for her to decide I wasn't useful anymore.

Selene calling that fateful meeting: "We think it's best if you leave. It's your choice though, of course." And me fucking fleeing like the coward I am, because I didn't know what else to do.

My mom couldn't—wouldn't help me. Once I left the nest, I was on my own. I knew Selene was going to break up with me, kick me out of the apartment we shared.

So I took the only way out I could think of: the permanent one.

No, I don't want to relive that right now. Thinking about Selene is scratching the surface, and that's already painful enough. I can't go any deeper right now.

Suddenly cold, I drag the sheets up to my chin. Lay down. Curl up on my side. Tears stream sideways to dampen my pillow.

This isn't about the dream, not really. It's about me always reaching out like an idiot—thinking someone would stay. Would *help*.

They never do.

I bury my face in the pillow until the worst of it passes.

By the time it does, I've nearly dozed off again. I'm left hollow and empty, a scorched husk after a fire's burned through. There's a soft *pa-dump* near the edge of the bed, and I look to see Kiki strolling over. Normally, I shoo her away before I fall asleep, and wake up with her curled up somewhere nearby anyway. Tonight I let her stay. She nuzzles her head into my hand, purring, then circles once and settles down about a foot away, as if keeping a respectable distance.

I close my eyes.

Sleep doesn't come easy. But it comes, eventually—thick and heavy, dragging me back under. In the last half-second before it claims me again, I think: *No more reaching for things that don't want me back. No more hoping they'll stay.*

Then the darkness swallows me whole.

Chapter Eight

Mia

Mercurial//"Too much comfort can create attachment. Consider a mental reset with our guided detachment series."

The last thing I want to do today is walk into Nate's apartment and pretend I'm not a mess. But bills don't care about breakdowns.

When I let myself inside, I'm expecting the immediate and familiar scuttle of Molly's claws on the floor as she rushes over to greet me. Instead, I see her pop her three heads up over the top of the couch. She's sprawled across someone's lap.

Nate.

Nate is home again. Sprawled out on the couch in expensive sweatpants, with his hellhound puppy on his lap, watching TV.

"Oh," I let slip as the door clicks shut behind me.

"Hello," he calls, but doesn't move.

For a moment, I'm frozen, unsure how to proceed. I told him before it was fine for him to stick around and watch me clean. So why is it now that I'm on display that I feel like fleeing? I'm suddenly hot, my skin prickling as I strip down to my maid costume and find the bucket of cleaning supplies.

"I hope it's okay that I'm here," he says from the couch.

I offer a shaky thumbs-up. "Yup. No problem."

Inside, some part of me is screaming that this is actually a Very Big Problem indeed! I'm still emotionally on edge from last night's dream, and the fact that it starred a shadow man who looks suspiciously like Nate isn't helping.

Also: I have a crush on him.

I hate that I have a crush on him.

I shove it aside, put my earbuds in, and get to cleaning.

This was supposed to be simple. Clean a few apartments, avoid anyone with too many teeth, and try to forget the mess that is my life otherwise. My clients aren't supposed to rattle me like this, and in fact, I forget most of their faces as soon as I walk out the door.

None of them have lingered in my head the way Nate does. And it's not like he's even *doing* anything—he's just sitting there in *his* apartment, brooding, all shadowy-eyed and polite—and my brain is acting like it's found religion.

My gaze is drawn to him as if by magnetic force. *Nosferatu* plays on his flat-screen. Onscreen, the ancient vampire lurches into view—bony and slow, his shadow stretched impossibly long across crumbling castle walls.

Nate sits there like he's watching a documentary. Like he understands.

I shouldn't feel a pang of sympathy. But I do.

Molly is stretched long across his lap. His feet are up on the coffee table, legs crossed. Today he's wearing a fitted black t-shirt. I think of the brief glimpse of his shadowed form he let slip that first day. Why bother maintaining a human glamour in his own home? Does he prefer it? Or is it just that he knew I would be coming, and put it on for my sake?

At the thought of his shadow self, I pause, my hand stilling in the act of wiping the counter. The shadow man in my dream last night was unsettling and too-tall. And it had a hat...just like Nate's shadow form. The resemblance is too close to ignore.

Maybe I'm reading too much into this, letting Coral Key's odd nature get the best of me. A girl can have a bad dream featuring the hat man without also assuming it's one of her clients, right?

Dragging myself back to the present, I force my feet to move again. The sooner I get through this, the sooner I can leave and go back to pretending everything is fine.

I make a show of wiping down the counter, rinsing a rag in the sink, scrubbing at a spot that probably doesn't exist. But eventually, there's nothing left to do in the kitchen, and I have to cross into the living room, into his orbit.

Nosferatu hisses quietly from the speakers. Nate doesn't move, but I feel his attention flick toward me anyway—sharp, focused. A current I can't see but feel brushing along my skin.

Trying not to look at him, I crouch to pick up an empty snack wrapper off the floor—Hostess Sno Balls. Disgusting. But as I straighten up, the wrapper slips from my hand and flutters pathetically back down to the floor.

Of course. Thank you, nerves.

"Sorry," I mutter, snatching for it again. My fingers fumble. I miss it twice. It's a stupid, small thing—but my hands are shaking, just a little, and I hate that he might notice.

Nate shifts on the couch, drawing my attention. For the first time since I arrived, he really looks at me—eyebrows drawing together in a frown, deep blue eyes piercing mine.

"You look exhausted," he says, low and tentative. Not judgment—just fact.

I freeze, the wrapper crinkling in my clenched fist.

"I'm fine," I say, too fast. Too casually.

But his gaze lingers, and I know he doesn't believe me.

"I'm not... trying to make it weird," he says, rubbing the back of his neck. "But you don't have to pretend you're fine. I can make you a coffee."

The offer is so casual, so normal, it almost knocks the air out of me. I didn't realize how long it's been since someone noticed I wasn't okay—and cared enough to say it out loud.

Before I can respond, he pauses the movie and rises in one fluid motion. There's a smooth, blurred quality in the way he moves to the kitchen. Like he could try harder to seem more human, but doesn't.

Molly simply moves to another section of the couch and sprawls out once more.

I hover uselessly for a second, not sure what I'm supposed to do. Keep cleaning? Run away? Stay perfectly still, like a startled deer in the forest about to be offered an unexpected kindness?

With practiced efficiency, he grinds fresh coffee beans and loads the fancy espresso machine. I'm floored—I could've sworn he never used that thing. Soon the smell of hot coffee drifts through the apartment, and my eyes flutter closed despite myself. I could lie and say I'm immune. That I'm not that easily swayed. But today? Yeah. I could use a coffee.

I wipe my palms on my skirt and busy myself picking up the remaining wrappers and tossing them in the trash can.

By the time I turn back around, he's steamed milk, too, and presses a large mug into my hands.

Our fingers brush. It's nothing. Barely a touch.

And yet my pulse skips, stupidly, like it didn't get the memo that we're *not* doing this.

"Sit," he says. When I hesitate, he adds, "Or are you not allowed a break?"

Something inside me wavers—then gives out entirely. Stunned, I obey.

The couch dips under me as I sink into it, the coffee steam tickling my nostrils. And I lift the mug to my mouth for a sip, using the coffee as a shield.

It's safer that way.

"Shit, this is delicious." It's damn near coffee shop quality. "*God*, that's good."

The faintest hint of a smile flickers at the corner of his mouth as he sits across from me.

"Glad you like it."

He's still watching me. Hasn't yet resumed the movie. And I'm not sure what it is—the coffee, the offer of a break, or something else—but I feel something in me soften. He's a near-stranger. And there's no harm in a bit of conversation with a client.

"You're right, I am tired," I admit. "Didn't sleep well."

His eyes darken. Not pity—something heavier. The memory of the dream strikes me hot and fast like lightning.

Nate shifts slightly, the movement subtle, almost restless. "I'm sorry to hear that," he says finally.

A beat passes. If there's more he wants to say, he swallows it down and looks away instead.

I should shut up. Stop talking, and leave it at that. I'm not used to being offered kindness with no strings. Maybe it's the coffee, maybe it's the way he noticed my exhaustion instead of looking away—but the words feel safer with him than rattling around in my head. After another sip, more words tumble out, messy and too loud.

"I think I'm just...burned out. Underemployed, exhausted. And there's this dumb Halloween party coming up—my ex Selene and all my old friends will be there. They all think I'm a wreck, and I just...I want to prove I'm not."

As soon as I say it, I wince. The confession hangs there, raw and too much. Too personal. Too soon.

But when I glance at Nate, he's not recoiling. He's just watching me, steady and quiet.

"Sorry," I mutter, waving my coffee cup weakly. "You didn't ask for all that."

"No, it's—it's fine. I *did* offer you coffee and a break. What sort of asshole would I be if I expected us to just sit here in silence afterward?"

That makes me feel a tiny bit better, at least. So he's not just humoring me—whatever his motives are, this was a legitimate kindness, not something he felt obligated to offer.

I take another sip of coffee. The desire to keep talking to him hovers in the back of my throat. I'm just not sure what to say.

"Tell me about this party," he says suddenly, saving me the trouble.

"Oh! Um. I had a kind of...messy falling out with my ex. It wrecked the whole friend group. We all worked together, founded a startup together—it's called Mercurial. I left to get away from her, but I still got an invite to the annual Halloween bash, and I kind of want to go."

I glance down at my coffee. "It's stupid, I know. But that party was always the one night I felt like I belonged—like we were a team, like I *had* people. Losing that...losing them...it still stings."

Nate just listens, steady and quiet.

"Anyway. That crowd is all about status. If I walk in alone, they'll just nod and whisper and assume I haven't changed. That I'm still the same mess of a person they forced out." I force a laugh. "But if I walk in with someone impressive, looking like I've leveled up? They'll have to rewrite the story they tell about me."

His expression is unreadable, but he hasn't looked away once.

"I need that reset," I finish softly.

Nate absorbs all of this with that signature, unsettling calm. Then he picks up a Sno Ball from the box, tears it open, chews. And without looking at me, he says, "If all you need is a date to terrify your ex, I'm probably overqualified."

I blink. "Wait—are you serious?"

He shrugs like it's no big deal. Maybe it isn't. Maybe I'm reading too much into this.

I don't need a monster date specifically, but...I can't deny that Nate looks like he has his shit together. At least his human glamour screams poise and money. He seems untouchable.

He'd make Selene choke on her cocktail.

"Why would you do that?" I ask, trying not to sound suspicious.

He finally looks at me. "Because you look like you could use the win."

And I hate how much that affects me. "You're not wrong, but like, what's in it for you? You really want to show up to some human party with glitter and cocktails and petty emotional baggage?"

"I've been through worse," he says. "At least there'll be snacks."

I laugh, but it comes out too sharp. "You didn't answer my first question."

"I need an excuse to leave the house. You need a plus one. Seems fair."

Narrowing my eyes at him, I press on. "That's still not an answer." Nate doesn't flinch. But his jaw shifts—tightens. "You're not a prisoner. You can leave the house whenever you want. Alone. To anywhere. So why this?"

A pause.

"I'm behind on my numbers for work," he says eventually. Quiet, though not ashamed. "I haven't been harvesting as much as I should. I have until Halloween to get back up above quota, or I'm in trouble. And you..." He trails off, glancing at me like he doesn't want to finish the sentence. "Let's just say you make things easier."

"So it *is* about work?" Then the remainder of his statement finally hits me. "Wait, what do you mean, harvesting?"

He exhales, ocean eyes flicking toward the coffee table like he wishes he could disappear into it. Molly gives a plaintive whine at his side.

"It's...hard to explain without sounding pretty awful," he mutters. "I work with dreams. We harvest emotional energy from humans—fear, mostly. It's converted into power. Nightmares, specifically, are our product."

I freeze with my coffee halfway to my mouth. "You work in dreams?"

"I walk through them," he says, voice low and matter-of-fact. "Slip into a dreamer's subconscious while they sleep, amplify what's already there, siphon a little fear, log it. Sometimes I build a dreamscape. Sometimes there's enough raw material. Either way, the dreamer wakes up, shakes it off, forgets. I hit quota. The product sells to ad firms. Everyone's happy." A beat. Then, softer: "Except me. I'm supposed to push people harder because spikes look great on a chart. That's what I can't stomach. I don't want to leave humans worse than I found them. And when I pitch gentler concepts, they don't convert."

I stare at him. Force myself to sip my coffee. Try to process that.

Because if that's true, then maybe I wasn't just being delusional earlier when I thought it might have been him in my dream. Now, I'm almost certain it was. But I don't know how to navigate that conversation, and I'm not sure I want to.

If it was him—why my dream? Why me, specifically? Heat crawls up my neck. Part of me feels exposed; part of me wants to lean closer.

"So, what," I ask, struggling to put it all together. "You want to hang around me for—for the ambient bad vibes?"

His brow furrows. "I do sense a certain darkness in you, Mia, but it's not like that. Not quite."

"I mean, it's fair. You want bad dreams? Buddy, I'm a bottomless pit over here. A buffet, if you will. Take what you want."

I try to make it sound like a joke. It doesn't quite land. He senses darkness in me? Wow, I hate that. I thought I had all of my shit under wraps. But a part of me is secretly relieved I don't have to pretend around him.

"...Could it help, though?" The question slips out before I can stop it. "If you fed on the heavy stuff—would I feel lighter after? Even for a little?"

His expression shifts, shadowed. "Not the way you're hoping. At best, it's like pressure bleeding off a valve. You might get a night of relief. But push it too far, and it hollows you out. Leaves you numb. That's why I hold back."

A night of relief. Even that sounded like a miracle. If he can take loneliness and regret and leave me lighter, even for a little while...why would anyone insist on fear being the only option?

He meets my eyes, serious again. "I'm not there for...everything," he adds carefully. "I don't touch memories. I take the residue—the feeling left behind. Most of the time, that residue is fear. Sharp, spiking, easy to bottle. That's what Obscura wants. But with you, I don't sense fear exactly. It's heavier. Loneliness. Regret. Desire. That still fuels me, even if the board wouldn't call it useful. And with you, I don't have to manufacture the raw emotion. It's already... loud. I can stay near the surface and leave you unharmed. Relatively."

I know what it's like to be written off for not producing the right results. Maybe that's why what he said catches in my chest.

Maybe fear isn't the only thing worth taking.

Another pause, then he adds, "You don't react like most people do. To me. To any of this. You're not afraid of me. Even when you should be. Even when I was..." He trails off, like he's only now realizing how close he came to confirming he's been inside my head. He shakes it off, continues. "It makes things easier. Cleaner. You're not flinching away. When I feed from someone who's already terrified—someone already on edge—I feel like I'm making it worse. If I kept coming back to you, it wouldn't look the same. You might wake up tired. Drained. Maybe start wondering why your own emotions feel thinner, like they've been skimmed off the top. That's the risk."

I blink at him, unsure what to say. The more he talks, the more I notice the cadence—low, deliberate, like waves tugging at the shore.

He looks away again. "With you," he continues softly, "I don't think I'd feel like a monster. Like I'm breaking someone to hit a metric. At least not right away."

"So I'm just the right amount of emotionally damaged. You could feed from my dreams, at least for a bit, without hating yourself even more for doing it."

Nate responds with one short nod. "Yes."

"Tell me one thing, first, because you basically already admitted to it," I say, feeling suddenly bold. "Was that you in my dream last night?"

"...Yes," he says, after a moment's hesitation.

I breathe out slowly. "Okay. I thought so. Why were you there?"

"I'm not sure. I didn't request you specifically, and you didn't know what I do until now, so it's not like it was your fault. All I know is—" He stops, restarts, like he's not sure he wants to share this. "All I know is that something is drawing me to you, whether I like it or not."

I should probably be running. Or at least backing out slowly with my coffee and dignity intact. If this were a movie, I'd be screaming at myself on the TV. My hot and awkward client wants to feed off of my dreams, and not even the sexy ones? Girl, *get out of there!*

Instead, I take another sip.

"So," I say lightly, "what happens if I say yes?"

He looks startled. "To what?"

"To you. Feeding. From my dreams."

"You'd let me?"

I shrug. "I mean, you already did." He huffs out a humorless laugh. "If it helps you and doesn't hurt me, why not? Seems like we both have stuff to work through. Could be mutually cathartic."

Nate shakes his head. "It's not entirely harmless."

"Okay. Then tell me about the side effects. Will I wake up with nosebleeds and start levitating or something?"

"No. Nothing like that." His expression clouds. "You might wake up tired. Sometimes emotionally raw. But it doesn't last. Not usually. Not if I don't push too deep."

I study him carefully. "But it *did* last. The other night."

He doesn't deny it. Just says, softly, "That was my fault. I stayed too long."

"And if you do it again?"

"I won't," he says immediately. "I'll be careful. I'll stay near the surface. No deep dives. Nothing too...intimate."

"Right. Just mild psychic intrusion between acquaintances."

His mouth twitches. "Exactly."

I drain the last of my coffee, then lean back into the couch, staring at the ceiling. This is dumb. Dangerous. I shouldn't even be entertaining the idea.

And yet—

I picture Selene's face when she clocks Nate at my side, as my date to the Halloween party. The old team's brittle smiles. The whispers that would come later: *Looks like Mia landed on her feet.*

Petty? Yes. Satisfying? Also yes.

I glance over at him. "Okay," I say. "Sign me up."

I shouldn't feel relief. I shouldn't feel anything but dread. But there's something about the way he's looking at me—like I'm not a problem he has to solve, but a puzzle he wants to understand.

"You're serious?"

I nod. "I need a date, and you need to hit your feeding numbers." For a second, he just looks at me, stunned. Hesitating. So I add, "Nate, I'm a big girl. If I need a safe word or a break or something, I'll text you a skull emoji. Or three." Thrusting my hand forward, I ask, "Deal?"

His expression settles into something unreadable. Grave. Grateful. Hungry.

"Deal," he says.

His fingers are firm and warm when they close around mine. A jolt races up my arm. Not fear, not quite. Just the coffee, I tell myself.

"Cool," I say, managing a shaky grin. "Definitely the safest, least reckless decision I've ever made."

Chapter Nine

Nate

This is all a terrible idea.

I might be desperate to comply with Krell's directive—get my numbers up by Halloween or else—but even desperation must have limits. Without this job, I have nothing: no structure, no distractions, no excuse to keep the rest of my life at arm's length. The work keeps me hollow in a useful way.

And yet, I can't keep up. I could crank out another five-minute scare—dark corners, falling teeth, all the cheap tricks Obscura loves. But none of it lands the way it should anymore. My numbers stay flat. I stay flat.

Krell's deadline is a noose, tightening with every flatlined chart I deliver. If I fail, I'm not just demoted—I'm done. Legacy or no, they'll bury me in some back office and never let me out again, or worse, fire me entirely.

Feeding from Mia isn't just a risk; it's the only thing that's moved the needle in months—the only shot I have left. I should never have allowed myself to become desperate enough to prey on a vulnerable human like this.

My father's memory still buys me tolerance in the company, but it also paints a target on my back. Half the execs would love to see me fail, just to prove the Alston legacy isn't worth protecting.

I could've gone to Krell for help. I'd have hated myself for it, but the man is in charge for a reason—he would've given me extra chamber hours, pre-fabricated landscapes, anything to force my numbers back up. The numbers are the important part. My enjoyment isn't.

And yet.

The glimpse of complex emotion I got the other night, when I skimmed Mia's dream for the first time, has lodged itself in me like a fish hook to the gut. Fear is what the board wants—it's quick, predictable—but her dream wasn't just fear. It was loneliness. Regret. Longing. Messy emotions Obscura doesn't bother with because they're harder to package.

But they hit me harder than any spike of terror ever did.

And I have a sudden *need* to know what lies in the depths of her dreams.

Mia's dreams are different—layered, saturated. With her, I can pull more from one night than a week's worth of stock nightmares.

She isn't afraid, and that should make her useless.

Instead, it makes her invaluable.

I barely know Mia. I should've forgotten her already. But her dream clung to me. I've become so bored of fear that anything else tastes like power, and I can't get enough. If I keep going back, she'll start to feel it. She'll wake more tired. More hollow. And if I pull too hard, I could shove her into nightmares she doesn't deserve.

Still, I can't stay away.

That thought consumes my mind as I slip into the dream chamber when all the techs are on break. I start up my own session, unsupervised, and dump myself into the veil of human dreamland, the space between asleep and awake.

Silence.

A gray vastness stretches out before me. Without the techs to navigate, to pair me with a dreamer and run profit calculations—Obscura loves to boil human misery into neat data points: intensity, duration, market value—I'm on my own.

I'll have to find my own way. Moments later, a ripple unfurls through the gray. And millions of tiny, glowing red dots pop into existence. Dreamers, all available to me.

So how do I find Mia?

I shouldn't be able to.

Not without an ID tag or a direct tether. Not without the techs' interface to run the search. But the thing about repeat dreamers—the ones you've touched, even briefly—is that something always lingers. A thread. A scent.

A taste.

We're not supposed to repeat dreamers on purpose without clearance. Too much risk for both sides. But override codes are an open secret. And I've already broken the rules once, haven't I?

I close my eyes. Focus on lavender and salt, the bruised ache of guilt and wanting. The way her energy wrapped around mine like bruised silk.

There. A flicker in the dark.

One dot pulses, faint and hidden, like she's tucked herself away in some shadowed corner of the dream field. Almost like she doesn't want to be found, or is very deeply asleep.

But I'm already moving toward it.

And the moment I make contact, the gray falls away—replaced by soft blue shadows, the slosh of artificial ocean light, and the smell of something warm and human and heartbreakingly familiar.

Mia's apartment forms around me. The hum of the AC unit, the lingering smell of something burnt in the microwave—it all tells me I'm in the right place.

I stride forward toward the bedroom before I lose my nerve.

As I enter, Mia stirs. I draw my shadows tight, stretch tall, let my limbs go uncanny, liquid. Something off-putting from the corner of the eye. A nightmare shape.

Slowly, her brows slightly knit, Mia rises to one elbow. Her hazel eyes travel the room in a lazy, sleepy sweep. She skips over me at first—and then her gaze comes rushing back, eyes wide, sticking on my waiting figure in the corner.

"Nate?" she murmurs.

I say nothing. I ooze malice, waiting for her fear. If I can scare her, I can make it simple. I can keep my promise not to go too deep.

But her breathing steadies the longer she looks.

"You're trying too hard," she says. Her voice is warm, all soft edges from sleep. "It's kind of dramatic, actually."

I falter. Just slightly. Enough to feel the cracks spread through my carefully-constructed composure. My shadows twitch, uncertain. As my effort shifts from maintaining my form to the puzzle of *her*, one of my arms shortens with a sickening lurch, the shoulder breaking into smoke.

She's not afraid.

"You're supposed to be afraid," I mutter. That's the script, the quota-friendly version of me Obscura wants. But she isn't afraid—and I hate how much I prefer it that way. How much it intrigues me.

Mia shrugs and flips back down onto her bed with a soft *thump*. She curls up on her side, watching me. Like I'm a half-finished art piece she can't decide whether to mock or admire.

"Maybe you're just not very scary," she offers, her lips curling into a lazy smile.

I scoff. "That's ridiculous. I—"

She's teasing me.

I'm here to feed, to keep it simple, and instead she's teasing me in her own dream like I belong here. Like she sees something worth wanting.

And for a second, I want to be that thing.

I lunge closer, horror-movie quick, blinking across the space. And *there*. Her expression doesn't change. But there's a tiny little stutter in her heartbeat. She's not entirely immune, just harder to properly scare.

As if she knows what I'm trying to do, her smile deepens. Her eyes flutter shut.

"Go ahead and take what you need," she says sleepily. "We had a deal, remember?"

Her words settle in the space between us like a flare—bright, and a little reckless.

I hesitate, waiting for her to rescind. She doesn't. Her eyes close, her body softens. She's already drifting again, drawn deeper into sleep now that the tension has passed.

I wait for her mind to start spinning and weaving webs. Once I notice her eyes begin darting rapidly back and forth beneath her lids, I open the siphon.

Mia's dream energy is rich and layered. The quiet tug of regret. The slow churn of uncertainty. The weight of being seen and not knowing what it means. All of this spills into me like a complex drink on the tongue, warming me from the inside out. But it's not *enough*. Greedy, I pull harder, searching for more.

The dream pulses once, twice. The ocean projection flickers too-bright overhead. A breeze from nowhere rustles the dream fabric.

Mia shifts beneath the sheets, just slightly. Just enough for the fabric over her leg to fall away. And I've seen her bare leg before—soft and golden and real—so this should be nothing groundbreaking. But something about this glimpse, in this place, right now...

A bit of projector-seaweed drapes itself across her hipbone, drawing my attention to the luscious curve there. The muscles in my jaw lock.

Don't.

I look away, or try to. But the taste of the dream begins to shift beneath my tongue—fuller, now, tinged with something I'm not expecting. Not fear. Not sadness.

Longing.

Desire.

Not fear—this is heavier, hotter, and so much more dangerous. One breath of it leaves me fuller than a dozen night terrors. If I could bottle this, I'd never worry about quotas again.

Desire flares through me like a match to dry leaves, setting me alight. My shadows writhe, instinct rising. Hunger claws loose, and not the kind I'm allowed. The one I shouldn't and haven't let myself feel for a human. Not for a while, anyway. This hunger screams *touch, taste, take.*

My heat's coming early—predictable, brutal, impossible to ignore—and I'm too close to her.

Not now. Not here.

I keep that part of me buried and howling at a locked door. Four times a year, like clockwork, it drags my instincts to the surface and sets fire to whatever self-control I have left. I usually ride it out with meaningless one night stands.

And it's starting *soon.*

Fuck, how did I forget? How could I have been so stupid?

The shock dissolves my concentration, and the siphon tether buckles. Mia stirs in her sleep, murmuring something I can't make out. I've fed enough—that much I can tell—and the dream is pulsing around me with a low, rhythmic *thrum.* For a moment, I just stare at her sleeping form.

How is it that a human maid has unsettled me like this within only a few days of knowing her?

This is off-protocol. In an unsupervised session, there are no warnings, no safeguards. No techs to yank me out if I lose control. Just me. If I stay any longer, I could actually hurt her.

With effort, I tear free.

I land in the stall, breath ragged, shadows surging wild until they retreat, curling inward. My head aches, and my hands tremble. I'm charged with power, but it doesn't feel like triumph.

It feels like a warning.

Last time I left Mia's dream, I stumbled out of this stall drunk on magic, high on something I didn't want to name. On the edge of something giddy and golden. This time, there's no euphoria. No lingering thrill. Just the chill of regret settling over my skin like fine ash, and the taste of her still clinging to me—warm and want-laced, dangerous in a way I can't afford.

I can't do this. Not like this. Not with her.

It's only later, when the shadows have receded and my head's finally stopped spinning, that I remember what she mumbled right before I left—soft and half-asleep. Her voice loops through my skull, softer than the shadows. Unavoidable.

If I wasn't afraid... why didn't you leave?

Because it wasn't fear I was chasing. It was the pulse of something hotter, hungrier. Desire that hit harder than terror ever could. And I can't admit that—not to her, not to myself. Not yet.

Chapter Ten

Mia

MERCURIAL// *When the universe reintroduces chaos, it's a sign you're ready for your next evolution. Say thank you."*

Within a few days, we fall into a weird little routine.

I thought at first that I'd only be seeing Nate in my dreams and in his apartment. But something about the way he'd stumbled out of my dream last time—too fast, too shaken—must have scared him.

After that, he set a new rule: a real-world check-in before every session. He grounds himself, I consent, and he heads over to his dream chamber at work to do everything by the book. Without registering, there are no metrics, no quota, no saving his numbers.

I never bothered to push him on it. If I'm being honest, I *like* seeing him, even if the arrangement is utterly bonkers.

Nate swings by around ten in his human glamour—designer sweatpants and all. We make awkward small talk while I brush my teeth and do my nighttime skincare, and he does...whatever he does supernaturally to check in and make sure I'm alright before another feed. Then I go to bed so he can raid my subconscious for nightmare juice, and he goes to the office, and sometime after, he's routed into my dreams.

I'm sure Reika's neighbors are wondering who this new booty call of mine is.

It all makes sense, and I've gotten used to it.

Something about tonight feels different, though.

His knock at the door is softer than usual. When I let him in, he doesn't meet my eyes, mumbles something about having had a rough day. I shrug it off and head to the bathroom, making sure to leave the TV on. He won't admit it, but he's invested in whatever trashy reality TV I have on at night—right now, it's *Floribama Shore*.

As I tug on an oversized Hozier concert shirt to sleep in, my phone buzzes.

Reika Tsukino:

> Is your "friend" with the shifty aura here again? The apartment's being twitchy.

I roll my eyes, squirt some toothpaste onto my toothbrush, and type back with one hand.

Mia Williams:

> Yeah, it's fine. It's him. No danger. Tell the apartment it can stop sending you vague alarms.

I told Reika I was seeing someone, but beyond that, I don't elaborate. Mostly because I'm not sure I could *actually* explain it in a way that doesn't make me sound deranged. Invite the literal monster inside, go to sleep, let him feed off my vulnerability. Totally healthy! Nothing to see here!

It's become normal for me, a routine I look forward to. And true to his word, Nate hasn't pulled too hard from any one thing in my dreams, so I haven't woken up crying again.

It occurs to me after I spit into the sink that *I* can also just talk to the apartment myself, so I do.

"Hey," I say quietly aloud. "Chill, will you? Nate's fine. Everything's fine."

The cosmetic lights above the mirror flicker twice in something that feels like acknowledgement, and I'm satisfied.

Tugging my shirt down, I emerge from the bathroom to find Nate exactly where I left him—slouched on the couch, still watching TV.

"Don't act like you're above this," I say teasingly as I refill Kiki's kitty water fountain. "You know you live for drunk people screaming at each other."

That earns a faint huff of laughter. Barely. He doesn't look away from the screen.

"Sure," he says. But his voice is flat, distant.

With the water fountain full, I set it back down on the kitchen tile, suddenly hyper-aware of the subtle wrongness hanging in the air.

"You good?" I ask, tilting my head. "You usually commit a little harder to the brooding supernatural thing."

Nate's mouth curves at that—just for a second—but it fades almost immediately. "Yeah. Just...like I said, long day."

The way he says it is too casual. Forced casual.

I hesitate, watching him a second longer, but he sinks deeper into the cushions, clearly done with talking.

So I let it drop, choosing to trust that he can handle himself—for now—and climb into bed.

Still, as I settle in and turn off the lamp, a little knot of unease lingers beneath the comfort of routine—something is off, and my body knows it before my brain does.

Maybe Reika's apartment was right to be worried.

Nate might be good at pretending everything is fine. But I can't shake the feeling that his excuse is just scratching the surface. And before I can think about it any more, or wonder if it's a good idea to allow him unfettered access to my dreams right now, my nightly Benadryl kicks in, and I'm out.

Being fed upon emotionally in my dreams is something I don't think I'll ever get used to, but at least it's not as startling as it was at first. I sleep a normal sleep—until I wake up in the middle of the night. It feels like waking, but not quite. A lucid fog, where my limbs are heavy and the room is just slightly... wrong. Like I'm dreaming inside a snow globe that someone keeps shaking. Usually, we chat briefly, he feeds, and I go back to sleep, no problem.

Not tonight.

At first, I can't put my finger on it. The dream's casual hum feels too loud, off-kilter. The shadows are thicker. And Nate—Nate's already here in stretched-out shadow form, standing closer than usual. *Too* close. I could almost reach out and touch him if I wasn't afraid to. In his shadow form, he doesn't have a face, but I still sense his expression, and it's *wrong*. Less composed, less teasing. His faceless gaze drags over me, and for the first time since we started this, I don't just feel watched—I feel *wanted*.

Which is *not* how this is supposed to go.

"You're early," I try to joke, but my voice comes out thinner than I'd like.

He doesn't answer right away. Just looks at me like he's trying to hold himself together, and maybe not doing a great job. That knot of unease from earlier tightens, sharp and insistent now.

This doesn't feel like our routine. This feels like something is slipping.

The hairs on the back of my neck lift.

"Nate?"

"I'm fine," he chokes out. I can hear him breathing—the ragged, steady inhales and exhales of someone pointedly trying to compose themselves.

I didn't think he needed to breathe, at least not in this form.

I stare at him. The edges of his shadow figure are flickering, blurring, making me doubt if my eyes are working properly.

"Are you sure?"

He takes his time in responding. Quick, faster than a blink, he comes even closer, until he's kneeling at the side of the bed. I flinch. His presence feels heavier than usual. The weight of his attention nearly pins me to the spot. He reaches out towards me with a hand that has too many fingers. Then he seems to think better of it and quickly withdraws.

Disbelieving, relieved, he huffs out, "You're afraid."

Before I can answer—or even think—the air tightens, and something latches on.

It's not a touch, exactly. It's pressure. A hook somewhere deep inside my chest, tugging upward in slow, steady pulls. My breath catches as warmth floods out of me, draining like water spilling from a cracked vessel. Not painful. Not even cold. But wrong, somehow. Intimate in a way nothing should be.

My heartbeat goes sluggish. The dream flickers. The walls of my bedroom blur at the edges, colors bleeding like wet paint, as if the whole world is holding its breath alongside me. The ocean projector spins faster and faster until it's just a smear of light above.

I can't move. I don't think I want to. The pull is syrup-slow and drugging, coaxing me down, and I hate how easy it is to sink into it. That it feels like surrender.

And beneath all that, I can feel him. Drinking it all in. My regret, my fear, my—

Oh.

It hits before I realize it's coming, and this time, there's no mistaking it.

Not just loneliness. Not wistful aching.

Want.

Raw and molten, rising up from somewhere low and shamefully human.

Want, and the humiliating relief of being seen without judgment.

He calibrates to me. I can feel it.

Part of me remembers what his hand felt like when he brushed mine. Wonders what his mouth might taste like. The same part that's been *looking* at him—too long, too often, cataloging little things I shouldn't.

Tall. Strong. Sharp-eyed and self-contained, but dangerous in a way that makes my blood hum. He shouldn't be the one I want. But the part of me that wants doesn't care.

The desire isn't soft. It's *needy*. A sharp-edged, breathless pull toward skin on skin. His weight over mine. The whisper of control slipping away—mine, his, both of ours.

The second it spikes, everything fractures.

Nate jerks back—violently, like he's been burned, his shadow-form unspooling in frantic threads as he pulls himself back from me with visible effort. The dream stutters, shadows flaring too bright and then slamming dark again, glitching out like a damaged film. He makes a sound—guttural, harsh. Not hunger. Not pleasure.

Panic.

His shadowed form surges backward, breaking our proximity so fast it leaves me dizzy.

Then, without warning, the tether *snaps*.

I'm left breathless, chest hollow and buzzing, like he yanked the plug out of a wall mid-charge. Around me, the dream ripples violently—colors slamming back into place too fast, leaving everything off-kilter. My head spins. A brief and intense nausea rages through me, then recedes. And then I'm awake—awake for real. *Wide* awake, my heart racing.

I bolt upright in bed, disoriented.

What the fuck just happened?

The dream is gone—but Nate is not.

Not his shadow-form, not a flicker in my dream. His actual physical body is *here*—on the floor beside my bed, crouched, halfway curled in on himself like he's fighting something I can't see. His shoulders rise and fall in harsh, uneven breaths. The swaying blue light from the ocean projection casts sharp angles across his face, and he looks—

God, he looks *awful*.

Not like he just fed. Not calm or lazily content like usual. He looks like he's barely holding himself together.

Did whatever happened in there scramble him, too?

"Nate?" My voice is rough with sleep. I clear my throat, but it doesn't help much. "What the hell was that?"

He doesn't answer right away.

"Nate!"

Now I'm worried. I start to untangle my legs from the sheets, to go to him, but he tosses up a shaking hand in a clear boundary. I freeze. Then his head drops, a hand scrubbing through his hair as he stays crouched, almost hiding.

"That wasn't supposed to happen," he mutters eventually, voice hoarse. "I should've been dumped back to the chamber when the tether snapped. That's what always happens. But this time..." He trails off, his jaw tight. "This time it spit me out here instead."

I swallow against the dryness in my throat. My pulse hasn't slowed. Neither has the heat under my skin. Can he feel that? Does he know?

"Something's wrong, isn't it?" I say carefully. "I *felt* it. What's going on with you?"

That breaks him. Not completely—but enough. His head lifts, and when our eyes meet, his gaze is raw. Much too raw for someone who clearly likes to keep everything controlled and veiled.

"I didn't want to tell you." His throat works, like the words scrape on the way out. "I was going to keep it casual. Keep it safe." A bitter laugh escapes him. "That's... not going to happen now."

My mind is racing. Tell me what? Keep what safe? But I don't interrupt. I just wait, holding his gaze, silently demanding the truth.

Finally, he adds.

"My heat," he says flatly. "It's starting."

For a moment, the only sound is the hum of my AC unit. The words don't register at first—they sound so alien.

Heat? Like an animal? Like mating?

God, what did I get myself into?

"I don't understand. What does that even mean?" I ask, my voice not quite steady.

"Many supernatural creatures have a heat cycle. Seasonal. Instinctual. The biological purpose is for mating. But that's not always possible, nor is that always the purpose. Mine's quarterly. I tend to forget until it hits. And it complicates feeding. When it starts, my control vanishes." His jaw clenches. "Not just for fear. Not just for dreams. For *everything*."

I blink, still too stunned to process fully. My body and my head are still buzzing from whatever happened in the dream, and his words only make it worse.

"And you weren't going to tell me?" I snap, leaning forward. Sudden adrenaline cuts through the hazy, lingering dream fog of confusion and desire. "After you've been—what—sleepwalking through my head for days? After *that?*"

Nate grimaces. "I was trying to avoid this conversation. I thought I could handle it. But... you felt what happened. I can't."

His confession hangs there, stark and ugly and terrifyingly intimate.

And suddenly, nothing about this feels like a game anymore.

Trying to think, I cross my arms over my chest. The pressure grounds me. "And what exactly *did* happen? You're the expert here. You tell me."

Nate's expression darkens. Slowly, he maneuvers to sit cross-legged on my bedroom floor, but he looks away—toward the wall, toward the night beyond the window. Anywhere but at me.

"I slipped," he says after a beat. "That's the simplest way to put it."

"Slipped how?" I press, sharper now.

"I fed too deep. Closer to instinct than control. When I hit...that pocket of longing in you, it tangled."

Longing.

The word drops between us like a bomb. My face burns. "That wasn't for you," I say too quickly, too defensively.

His mouth twitches, but he doesn't argue. He doesn't need to. The tension humming in the room says enough. If he thinks I'm full of shit, he's not going to call me out on it.

"Doesn't matter," he says quietly. "The second I tasted it, my body didn't care who it was for. It just cared that it was there. That it was... ripe. And mine responded."

"To what?" I demand, my stomach knotting even tighter.

"To *you*, Mia."

The admission steals the air from the room.

I can't speak. I don't think he expects me to. For a second, we just sit there, the quiet between us sharp and unbearable.

I open my mouth, but nothing comes out. There's nothing I can say that doesn't feel like pouring gasoline on the fire.

Instead, I hug my arms tighter and glance away, pulse thrumming in my throat. "Okay. So now what?" I ask quietly. "You said you're going into heat. That you can't control it when it starts. What happens then? Am I in danger?"

I'm not sure which is worse—the threat of him losing control, or the truth that a part of me wants to.

His answer is immediate—and brutal.

"You should be," he says, low and grim. "But no. Not unless you wanted to be. I wouldn't... I couldn't force something like that. I'm not built that way. I'd burn alive before I took what wasn't offered."

I look back at him then, and for the first time tonight, I see not hunger or shadows or danger—but something rawer. Self-loathing.

"So you're telling me," I say slowly, piecing it together as I speak, "that the risk isn't me saying no." His jaw tightens. "The risk," I continue, "is that I might say yes?"

Silence falls again, heavy and knowing. It's the thing neither of us wanted to say out loud. And I know from his lack of response that I'm right.

I have so many more questions, none of them appropriate, and nothing I can figure out how to articulate right now. So I just stare at him, trying to ignore the thrum of heat in my core, the part of my mind spinning off into fantasy land, wondering what *exactly* might happen if I—

Nate pushes to his feet, visibly gathering himself. Shadows ripple faintly along the back and sides of his human form, but stay contained. Barely.

"This was a mistake," he mutters. "I shouldn't have come tonight. We should stop this before—"

"No."

The word leaves my mouth before I fully register it.

He freezes. Looks at me like I've just made everything worse. Maybe I have.

"You need your numbers for work. I'm not going to be the reason you get fired," I say, more steady this time. "I need you as my date for the Halloween party. And I'm not stupid. Cutting you off now would make it worse, wouldn't it? You'd get desperate. Or reckless. Or both. I don't want that on my conscience."

What I don't say is: *I've grown to depend on this. On you. I would miss you if we cut this off. Without this, I'd have nothing.*

A rough laugh tears out of him, humorless. "It's not the work I care about. It's what it says about me when I fail. My father built Obscura, and the board still whispers I only have a seat because of his name. If I get fired, they're right. He's right." His jaw clenches hard, like the words taste foul. "I can't give them that."

He hesitates—and that's all the confirmation I need.

"So," I say, swallowing my own nerves. "We keep going. We do this smart. We set boundaries. No touching. No...whatever that was tonight."

His expression twists, like he's not sure whether to argue or thank me. "You're serious?"

I nod, even though I feel anything but sure. "This is still platonic. Still work. You don't get to change the deal just because your body's being stupid." When he still just stares at me, I add, "I can handle it. I *want* to handle it. But I need you to meet me halfway, Nate. I need you to not lie about how bad this is anymore. You start struggling, you tell me, okay? Especially at the party. We're not going if you're just going to be trying to hump everything in sight like somebody's unneutered dog."

A long pause. The faintest twitch of a smile.

"I have a condition of my own," he adds. "If you'll allow it."

"Of course. What is it?"

"I'd like to check your pulse. Before and after each feed."

I raise an eyebrow. "What does that have to do with anything?"

Nate offers me another long pause that speaks volumes. He's worried about something, I just don't know what. Finally, he grinds out, "It tells me if I'm over-drawing, and it would ease my mind. About your wellbeing."

I shrug. "Sure, whatever. Fine."

He nods. "So there will be no touching beyond this quick pulse check. Agreed?"

"Agreed."

It doesn't feel like a win. Not really. More like locking the door after inviting the wolf inside—and pretending that'll be enough.

But we shake on it anyway. And if his hand lingers in mine just a second too long, I don't comment on it.

I tell myself this is practical—that I need a date, that I want to wipe the smug looks off Selene's and my old friends' faces. But it's not just that. Since the breakup, since the worst day of my life, I've been numb. Surviving, not living. And Nate... Nate rattles me. He's the first one who noticed I wasn't okay and didn't look away; the first to ask, to treat my feelings like something to handle gently, not weaponize. Even after tonight, after the broken tether and the panic, I'm more intrigued than afraid. That's what scares me most of all.

He pretends it's just about quotas, but I heard what he said—it isn't. For him, it's about not failing where his father once stood. For me, it's about proving I'm not as broken as

Selene made me believe. Different ghosts, same desperation. Maybe that's why neither of us told the other no.

Strictly platonic, is what we agreed.

But even later, after he leaves, alone in my bed in the dark, I can still feel his hunger licking at my skin.

And worse—I can still feel mine.

Chapter Eleven

Nate

Three nights. Too soon. Long enough for hunger to build, not long enough for danger to fade. I shouldn't be here—not after how close I came to losing control—but here I am anyway.

And her friend's Halloween party is soon. I won't be able to avoid Mia forever.

In this dream, she's sitting on a wide windowsill in a version of her apartment that doesn't exist—it's bigger, cleaner, the kind of fantasy space dreams often construct. Outside, an oddly-translucent moon hangs too low in the sky. She's wearing an oversize t-shirt, and her rust-colored locs are tied back in a bright red bandanna.

When she sees me, she doesn't flinch.

"Figured you might show," she says, voice soft but steady. "You looked so rattled when you left that other night."

Hesitant, I hover in the space near her. "I didn't mean to come here. I thought I'd land somewhere else." I pause, looking down at my hands, suddenly shy. The long, shadowed fingertips look like something out of a horror movie. I used to revel in this shape—now I just feel grotesque. Something made to haunt, never to touch. "Maybe I wanted this too much."

Mia shrugs. "Maybe I did, too."

Something shifts in me—sharp and dangerous. Hope, maybe, if I were stupid enough to believe in it. Her words shouldn't mean so much. They shouldn't slip under my skin like that. But they do.

The hush of dream wind fills the silence between us, dream waves crashing far away in a warning I don't know how to heed. Mia looks tired—but open. Present. She hasn't sealed herself off, even after all the terrifying things I've told her. And she doesn't look scared. Yet.

She nods toward the space beside her on the windowsill. "If you're gonna feed, keep it light. I don't want to wake up feeling like I ran an emotional marathon again."

I manage a faint smile and settle beside her, careful to keep a few inches between us. She offers me her wrist, and I take it, pressing my thumb gently to the proof of her beating heart. Her pulse is normal, steady.

Enough to make me feel a tiny bit better about all of this.

"Satisfied?" she asks after a moment.

I nod. But she doesn't take her arm back right away. Instead she's studying me, looking right where my eyes would be with my glamour on, her gaze warm and open and all kinds of intoxicating.

"Yes," I respond curtly, and push her arm back toward her. "Now, no touching. No boundary-blurring."

Her hand twitches in her lap. "Right. *Just* work."

But her voice doesn't carry much conviction.

Mine doesn't either, when I say, "Okay."

I let the tether unfurl between us.

When I feed this time, it's different. Slower, gentler. Less about hunger and more about *being*. I don't chase fear. I don't even chase that tantalizing burst of longing from before, the one that threatened to unravel my control entirely. I just... listen. And *feel*. Her sleep-thoughts shimmer just beneath the surface—fragments of memory, bursts of feeling, moments she probably couldn't even name if she were awake.

Warmth when I touched her hand. Curiosity when I watched her clean. Laughter. Frustration. That impossible mix of comfort and danger.

None of it's pointed. None of it's lust.

But all of it is *hers*.

I take only a thread of it—just enough to quiet the ache clawing at my ribs. Not enough to leave her dizzy. Not enough to leave a mark.

When I pull back, she exhales, her long lashes fluttering.

"That felt...different," she says.

"You said to keep it light," I add, as I unfurl my too-tall form from the windowsill, trying to keep my voice neutral. Professional. But even I can hear the strain in it.

Mia nods slowly, gaze tracking me as I rise. Then she tilts her head, studying me. "It was... nice," she says finally, and then snorts. "God, I sound like I'm reviewing a massage."

That gets a real laugh out of me.

She shifts on the windowsill, curling her knees up toward her chest, and rests her chin on them. "You didn't hurt me," she adds, more softly. "You could've, if you wanted to. But you didn't."

The knot in my chest tightens, then loosens. I want to say I wouldn't have. That I never want to. But the words get stuck behind instinct, lodged in my throat, as if saying them would make me lose her before I ever had her.

Because I have hurt someone before, and she didn't walk away from it.

Once was enough. I should tell her that. I should warn her how close this can cut. I'm a monster by design, a mechanism that feeds, and this is all an experiment—pretending I can want softly, pretend I can stop myself in time.

I can't explain any of that to her.

So I just nod.

We linger in silence for a moment longer, the dream quiet and still around us. Outside, the moon glows faintly red, as if bleeding behind cloudy glass.

Eventually, Mia glances over and murmurs, "You're still not going to tell me what your heat really involves, are you?"

I lift an eyebrow. "Would you want me to?"

She considers. "Not yet."

I bow my head in acknowledgment. *Not until I know I can survive it without tearing this fragile thing apart.*

"Then not yet," I echo. "Besides, you'd guess right."

Her breath hitches—barely audible, but I catch it.

I start to pull back, already feeling the edges of the dream dissolve. The tether between us softens. But before I go, I risk one more glance at her—so small and soft and steady in the pale red light. Watching me like I'm something she's not afraid of.

It undoes me.

"Thank you," I say.

She blinks. "For what?"

"For letting me be gentle."

Because sometimes, I forget how.

Fear is what Obscura wants. Fear is what I'm supposed to deliver. But Mia's the only one who makes me feel like there's more to take, more to be, than the box my father and the board shoved me into.

And then I'm gone—pulled back to the chamber like the tide from shore, already aching for the warmth I barely touched.

Chapter Twelve

Mia

MERCURIAL//"If it still hurts, you're not healing hard enough. Try rewriting your narrative before bed tonight."

By the time Halloween rolls around, I've officially lost the plot. Somewhere between *Sure, let the literal monster feed off my dreams* and *It's fine, totally platonic*, I tripped headfirst into actually missing Nate when he's not around. Which is exactly the kind of neon red flag I promised myself I'd stop ignoring when I blew up my life and slunk away to Reika's apartment in Coral Key.

But I keep replaying the way he noticed when I wasn't okay. The coffee he made without asking. The way he listened when I rambled about the party without making me feel pathetic. Ordinary kindness shouldn't stick. His does.

And yet here I am, wiping down a client's fridge while wondering if he's thinking about me, too. Spoiler alert: this is probably not what healthy looks like.

And I keep thinking about his hands—warm when our fingers brushed, steady on my pulse, all restraint like he wanted more but wouldn't take it.

I know better. I know *what* he is, and why this whole thing is supposed to stay clinical. And that's the problem, isn't it? Missing him doesn't just make me foolish. It makes me vulnerable.

And vulnerable girls fall the hardest.

I shake the thought out of my head and dig into the client's fridge. My hand lands on something spongy—a loaf of bread gone green with mold. Gagging, I pinch the bag and dump it in the trash.

Well. At least I'm not thinking about Nate anymore.

Rotten food always reminds me of Mercurial, though the bread there was never moldy, just stale—bagels leftover from Selene's sunrise investor "war room" breakfasts. Twelve-hour days on caffeine and cold carbs like it was a badge of honor. I used to set alarms just to remember to drink water. Compared to that, scrubbing mold is merciful. At least this work ends when the timer on the MaidForYou app does.

I'm scanning the fridge for more disgusting food when my phone buzzes, startling me so hard I bang my head against the shelf. Eyes watering, I reach for the phone. It hasn't stopped buzzing—which means a call and not a text.

Imani Brooks, the screen reads.

Fuck. I forgot to RSVP. And even if we haven't actually spoken in weeks, I know there's nothing Imani hates more than not getting a response.

I swipe to answer, already bracing. "Hey," I say, forcing brightness. "What's up?"

"What's up is I'm finalizing headcount for the catering order, and you never RSVP'd," Imani says, brisk and efficient as always, but with just enough warmth to soften the scolding. "Also, how've you been? Are you coming tonight or not? Because the caterer needs final numbers now, Mia."

I wince, rubbing the sore spot I just hit on the top of my head.

"I'm coming," I blurt, too fast. Can't give myself time to chicken out. "Of course I'm coming. I'm bringing someone, actually."

I purposely ignore her question about how I've been, because truthfully, I don't have an answer.

Imani's voice on the other end sharpens, perceptive. "Oh? Someone?"

"Uh huh." What am I supposed to say? *Yeah, the terrifying shadow monster I've been allowing to feed off of my dreams? Who also looks kind of hot in sweatpants?* "Just...a guy I've been seeing," I add, vaguely. "It's casual."

"Sure," says Imani kindly, but she doesn't sound convinced. Now that she's confirmed my attendance, I can feel her attention darting away to the next task like a Japanese bullet train. "Good. See you tonight. And remember, costumes required."

When the call ends, I stare down at my phone, feeling rattled.

I shove my phone into my pocket like that might help shove the feeling down with it. It doesn't.

I cut my usual shift short to give myself time to get ready, and say an early good-bye to Tulgan, who's headed to pick up his kids from orcling daycare and take them trick-or-treating.

By evening, I'm still carrying a weird knot of nerves. The awareness that this isn't casual, not really. Not anymore. It sits heavy beneath my ribs as I smooth my hands down the front of my costume, eying my reflection like I can will myself into feeling bolder.

Because I am insane, and Halloween is the one time I can wear something like this in public and get away with it, I chose a slutty mouse costume. Tiny deep gray dress, thigh-high stockings, a headband with cheap ears, and makeup that looks a little too effortful to pretend I don't care. I've piled my dreads into a messy knot on top of my head and secured them with a bow. With some careful finagling and the help of several bobby pins, I arrange my headband so the bow sits perfectly in the center of the ears.

It's a ridiculous costume. But my life as a whole has been fairly ridiculous lately, so I figure it's fitting.

A brief panicked thought crosses my mind—what if this is too much for Nate? Then I remember that he has literally watched me clean his apartment topless in a maid costume multiple times. It's fine. He's going to be fine.

This is still platonic. Still work. Still safe.

Except my stomach knots back up with nerves as soon as I'm standing outside his door.

I knock lightly. No answer at first. Then heavy footsteps, slower than usual. When the door swings open, human Nate goes still in the doorway, tension coiled so tight it's practically vibrating off him. His hair is a little messy. There's a faint flush along his cheekbones. His mouth opens, but for a second, nothing comes out.

Then his eyes rake over me—the bare stretch of my thighs, the curve of my hips beneath the flimsy fabric, the stupid fucking mouse ears—and I swear the air leaves the room.

"What," he says hoarsely, "exactly are you supposed to be?"

I point at the ears. "A slutty mouse, of course." He continues to stare. "I told you costumes were required," I add lightly, aiming for casual, but my voice comes out softer. Warmer. A little too close to breathy.

He drags his gaze back up to my face, his throat working as he swallows. Hard.

"Right. Uh. Well, mine is built-in." Nate steps aside and beckons me in. A faint metal rattling comes from the direction of his bathroom, followed by a low, whining wail. At my raised eyebrow, he explains, "I'm experimenting with crate training for Molly."

"Ah. Okay."

I don't think that's going to go well, but I'm not about to tell him that.

I step inside, and the door clicks shut softly behind me. The sound feels final somehow, the air between us going tighter, heavier, warmer.

Nate doesn't move right away. Just stands there, watching me like I'm something he's not sure he's allowed to touch. The flush on his cheekbones has deepened, and even though he's trying to keep himself together, the edges of his glamour flicker more prominently now—like whatever keeps him buttoned up is starting to fray.

The warmth in the room isn't just figurative anymore. It presses in close, baking against my skin, and I shift uncomfortably, tugging down the hem of my dress even though it doesn't help.

"Nate," I say quietly, cutting through the thick silence. I hesitate, then meet his eyes head-on. "Are you good? Like... really good? Because if you're not, we can call this off."

His jaw flexes, and for a second I expect deflection, the usual *I'm fine* line he's been feeding me all week. But instead, he breathes out slowly and lets himself be honest, just for a flicker of a second.

"No," he admits, voice low and tight. "I'm *not* good. But I can handle it."

I don't miss the subtle shift of his fingers curling at his sides, the sharp control etched in every line of his body. Holding back. Always holding back.

Still, he makes no move toward me. Just stays locked in place, banking whatever roils just under his skin like it costs him everything.

For some reason, that makes me feel safer than any reassurance could.

"Okay," I murmur, nodding. My throat is dry. "But if you start to lose your grip out there, you tell me. I mean it."

His mouth tips up—barely. It's not really a smile. More like a grim, appreciative acknowledgment.

"Deal," he says softly. Then, dragging his eyes away from me with visible effort, he gestures loosely toward the door. "Come on, Mouse. Let's go make bad choices in public."

I enjoy the way his voice curls around the word *Mouse* far too much.

I follow him to a different elevator—one he unlocks with a keycard—and it deposits us directly in the lower-level parking garage.

It's cooler down here, the air thick with concrete chill. Nate leads the way, his gait easy but careful, deliberately relaxed. I'm too keyed up to fully match his calm, so I trail close behind, fiddling with my purse strap.

We stop beside a car I wouldn't have looked twice at in daylight. It's sleek, dark gray, and absurdly low to the ground, a spill of polished steel, understated and predatory.

He glances over at me as he unlocks it. "Is this acceptable?"

"What if I said no?" I ask dryly. "Would you just offer another one of your, what, *twenty* cars?"

He huffs a sound that's almost a laugh as he opens the passenger-side door for me.

"Yes," he says. "Your party, your fabricated image. You can have whichever version of me you think will most impress."

Sliding into the passenger seat, I instantly feel swallowed up by soft leather and faint, clean cologne. It's intimate, somehow, despite the coolness of the car. Nate joins me a beat later, his presence larger now in the close quarters. His thigh brushes mine as he starts the engine. He inhales, sharp and fast, then seems to stop breathing entirely.

Neither of us comments on it.

Once we're on the road, he glances over. "So, your ex who'll be at this party—"

"Selene."

"—Selene. What do I need to know?"

The question makes me realize I've been grinding my teeth, and I force my jaw apart. I told myself bringing him was strategy: Selene only respects what she can't destroy. But she's not just an ex. She's a demolition artist in heels, and she knows how to exploit all the cracks in my foundation.

The thought of showing up with a man who looks like a special effect felt...useful, before. With the way his glamour keeps flickering, though, I'm not so sure I haven't just painted a target on something already fraying.

"Selene..." I drag the name out, then deadpan, "is an eldritch horror."

Nate huffs, low and amused. "Well, I'm worse, so I win. She won't stand a chance."

My laugh comes out brittle. "You don't get it. She's awful. At Mercurial, I made one mistake—and everyone let me take the fall. She could've helped, but instead she kicked me when I was down. She strips people down to splinters, that's her default. And I've always been her favorite target."

Steady and unbothered, he glances at me again. "Then she's predictable. And predictable things are easy to defeat."

A shiver works its way down my spine, equal parts comfort and warning. Only Nate could make reassurance sound like a threat.

The drive isn't long. In fact, it feels absurdly fast with the kind of silent smoothness only stupidly expensive cars like this can pull off. Before I know it, we've left Coral Key behind and are already weaving into the brightly lit streets of downtown Miami minutes later.

And then we pull up outside the Gilded Orchid.

God, I hate this place.

Which is the funny part—I used to love it. The spectacle, the awe, the illusion that polish meant safety. But Mercurial burned that out of me. Now the Gilded Orchid feels like a Great Gatsby set piece: all chandeliers and champagne to distract from the rot under the gloss.

Even from the curb, it's everything I can't stand: chrome trim, floor-to-ceiling windows, soft lighting that makes everyone inside look like a magazine cover. A valet swoops in; Nate tips him, and I step out, tugging at my dress like I'm bracing for impact.

Nate comes around the car to join me. He's not wearing his human glamour anymore. Somewhere between the garage and here, he's shifted. Not the wild, desperate shadow from my dreams—something sharper. Slick. Just unsettling enough to catch the eye. His edges flicker like candlelight on water, polished darkness made to impress.

And judging by the heads turning as we walk, it works.

A group near the door—half-drunk, their costumes clearly expensive—actually stops and stares.

"Oh my God, what are *you* supposed to be?" one woman calls, giggling.

Nate doesn't even slow down. "Your worst nightmare," he says casually.

They all laugh like it's charming and clever, and I roll my eyes. Humans really will eat anything up if it looks convincing enough.

Inside the Gilded Orchid, the opulence is dialed up to eleven. Gold mirrors, floating candles, costumes that look tailor-made. A devil in horns laughs too loud; a mermaid clutches her champagne flute like a life raft. Everyone here looks like they belong at a networking gala whose registration fee costs more than my rent.

All signature signs of an Imani Brooks party.

I spot her almost immediately at the far end of the room, dressed as Cleopatra—a gold lamé gown with a thigh-high slit, a sleek collar at her throat, and a glossy black bob wig. Gold eyeliner and lipstick cut the perfect contrast against her deep brown skin.

She's commanding a knot of well-dressed guests like she's hosting a TED Talk on how to be effortlessly perfect. Her eyes catch mine, and she flashes a sharp smile—then clocks Nate beside me and arches a perfectly-plucked brow.

Nate leans down slightly, his voice low in my ear. "You weren't kidding. This is brutal."

"Welcome to my old life," I murmur back. "Hold onto your soul. The drinks are expensive, but the existential dread is free."

He snorts softly, and for a second, the tension between us eases—just enough to feel dangerously good.

"Is that your ex?" he wonders carefully a moment later. "You're staring."

"No, that's my friend Imani," I respond, the reminder suddenly making me wary. I don't see Selene at all, which is unusual—she can smell weakness the way sharks smell blood, and this party full of insecure social climbers is ripe for exploitation. "I don't see my ex yet."

Nate's focus lingers on me for a beat longer than necessary, but wisely, he doesn't press. Instead, he seems to sweep the room with his gaze—taking in the glittering chandeliers, the curated decadence, the sea of costumes ranging from elegant to absurd.

He doesn't seem impressed.

"I hate it here already," he murmurs, but with a hint of warmth, like he's enjoying the private snark of saying so.

"Good," I say, tugging at the hem of my dress self-consciously. "Then you fit right in."

He huffs, but follows when I nudge us deeper into the crush of bodies. The Gilded Orchid is packed—elbow-to-elbow with strangers and almost-strangers, their laughter bouncing off the gold-tinted walls. Everything smells like money and effort. Fancy perfume, craft cocktails, desperation. A pianist in the corner plays a lively jazz rendition of "Monster Mash."

I catch snippets of conversations as we pass—something about equity partners, destination weddings, who's too drunk already. Familiar voices call out to me here and there—old coworkers I wasn't close with, friend-acquaintances I've been dodging for months. They pull me into brief, polite exchanges, but it's easy to keep them short. Most of them are too busy sizing Nate up, anyway.

Because Nate—well. This shadow form is subtle, restrained, but still very much a living ripple of liquid-dark energy in vaguely human shape. He looks like a high-end special effect imported straight from a movie, and Imani's guest list of rich normies are losing their shit.

I forget sometimes that most people can't see through the illusion. Reika cracked that open for me without meaning to. Once you've seen a barista with horizontally closing eyelids hand you a latte, or watched a pair of children sprout gills and a tail after cannonballing into the community pool, you can't unsee it.

Heads still turn as we move through the crowd, drawn to Nate's flickering edges like moths to a flame. They smile, whisper, nudge each other, convinced he's some special effect they can't quite figure out.

"Convenient, isn't it?" he mutters. "People see shadows and assume special effects." A brief pause. "I'm starting to think some humans deserve what they get."

"You say that," I murmur, nudging his arm, "but we're your dinner, right?"

His head tilts slightly. Shadows curl faintly at his edges, restless. "Normally. Crowds are easy, empty calories, if you will. I could gorge myself without trying. But not tonight."

That gives me pause. "Why not? This would be... easy, wouldn't it?" I glance around at the swirling crowd. Laughing, flirting, half-drunk and insecure. "Low-stakes snack bar."

His attention fixes on me. Something about the intensity of it makes my breath catch.

"That's the problem," he says softly. "It would be too easy. I'm already fraying, Mia. And the only thing I want is standing next to me."

My breath snags. The meaning lands a beat late, like thunder after lightning: he's starving himself on purpose. Not because he has to. Because he won't risk breaking—because what he's actually hungry for is *me.*

Because taking anything more right now might push him past a point he's scared to cross.

Goosebumps prickle up my arms even as heat curls low in my gut, my body caught between flight and something far stupider. Every nerve says danger, but the pull beneath it is worse: I want him to keep looking at me like that.

He could feed on anyone in this room—but he's not.

He's staying hungry.

For me.

We find our way to the edge of the dance floor, tucked slightly back near the cocktail tables. Nate stays close to my side, as if on guard—which makes my insides do stupid, fluttery things.

Still, I can feel the shift happening beneath the pleasant buzz of attention and drinks. He's too quiet. His form, though controlled, keeps...shifting. Flickering faintly with tension. When a man in a leather gladiator costume stops to flirt—blatantly eying me while asking if I want a drink—Nate's shadows flex dangerously.

The guy notices, laughs nervously, and quickly retreats.

I arch a brow. "You can't growl at everyone who talks to me."

His form gives one violent flicker. "I didn't growl," he says indignantly.

"You did *something*."

"I didn't like him."

I don't know whether to be annoyed or flattered, so I change the subject instead. I lean in slightly, letting my shoulder brush his arm—casual, but deliberate. I'm surprised to find that he feels just as solid in this form as in his human one, even if he *looks* like a slip of incorporeal darkness.

Too late, I remember our no-touching rule. If Nate cares, he says nothing.

"You're still holding it together, right?" I ask quietly, meaning more than just his general mood. Not just about the party. About the *heat*. The hungry, dark thing he said was simmering just beneath his skin.

Nate doesn't answer right away. Is he weighing exactly how much longer he can keep himself in check?

"I'm fine," he says at last, low and tight. Not convincing.

I swallow, but force myself to nod. "Okay. Just... keep me updated, alright?"

Nate makes a noise somewhere between amused and dangerous. But he nods, and for a few more blessed minutes, everything slides back into place. The party keeps humming around us. Nervous, I sip my drink too quickly and have to remind myself to slow down. He watches the crowd, his shadows subtly curling and shifting as he works to stay contained.

It's fine. Everything's fine.

At least until my eyes catch on a familiar figure cutting through the throng like she owns the place.

For a beat, my brain refuses to process it. I stare, ice sliding down my spine in slow motion.

Matte black bodysuit, skintight and effortlessly lethal. A glint of silver at her throat—a diamond collar. Sculpted black ears perched atop dark, glossy hair twisted into a careless knot. Of course—Catwoman. Minimalist, cutting, and predatory. The perfect costume for a woman who always did love playing with her prey.

And it's so very Selene.

She hasn't seen me yet, but she's close—and moving with purpose, much too close to us.

My stomach drops. "Oh, fuck," I breathe.

Not because I didn't expect her—I *wanted* her to see us. But not like this. Not when Nate feels one breath away from unraveling. Selene doesn't just ruin nights. She ruins things. And this—whatever this is with Nate—suddenly feels too fragile to survive her.

Nate stiffens beside me, following my gaze.

Shadows curl tighter, sharp and instinctive, as if his body recognizes danger before his mind does. "What?"

But before I can answer, Selene's eyes find mine across the crowd. She's spotted me. Her smile sharpens—hungry.

And she's coming straight for us.

Chapter Thirteen

Mia

MERCURIAL//"Your aura's finally stabilized! Perfect time to open your heart and test your triggers. Trust the spiral."

"Mia," Selene coos on arrival.

Her voice is high and clear, tinkling like a fancy stone waterfall. Her tawny-brown skin glows under the golden lights.

I force a smile. "Selene."

This is the moment I thought I wanted—her seeing me with someone untouchable at my side. I pictured the win.

So why does it already feel smaller than it did in my head?

Next to me, Nate's shadows flicker again. Selene's hungry smile slides sideways into a knowing smirk. She rests her weight on one hip, Catwoman bodysuit gleaming, a dainty-stemmed glass balanced in her manicured fingers. Espresso martini, if I had to guess.

Her eyes flick upward towards Nate's facial area. If she's at all impressed or unnerved by his "costume," she doesn't show it. "And you are?"

"Nathaniel Alston," he says, and I realize it's the first time I've heard his full name. It sounds formidable, weighty and ancient, and I find that I quite like the sound of it rolling off his tongue. "Mia's date."

Selene blinks. "Alston," she repeats, as if chewing on the name. "As in, the Alstons who founded Obscura Group?"

I roll my eyes. Of course she knows the name. Leave it to Selene to poke and prod at the smallest of details, digging for any scrap of social capital she might be able to use. Selene doesn't care what Obscura actually does—half of this area name-drops it without knowing the details. For her, it's just another rung on the social ladder.

Glancing at Nate, he seems unfazed.

"Yes," he says gruffly. "The very same."

Selene's gaze narrows, amused. "That's not a costume. Something about you isn't right. But it's very... convincing. Who did you hire for the visual effect?"

"Selene, that's *his* business—" I cut in, trying to chop off her investigation at the knees.

Nate only shrugs, shadows smoothing like smoke in a draft. "Obscura does a little R&D in immersive effects. Consider this a demo." He lowers his voice, courteous more than secretive. "Do me a favor and don't spread the word. This one hasn't gone public yet."

"Right," Selene agrees slowly. Her eyes dart between the two of us. After a moment, she angles her body between us. "Interesting. Listen. Do you mind if I steal Mia for a moment? It's been a minute, and we have a lot to catch up on."

Nate hesitates. I give him a quick nod and hand him my now-empty glass. "Get us another round of drinks?"

"Sure. Take your time."

He plays along, but the slow glide of his retreat has me wondering if he really wanted to leave. And I can't help tracking his movements throughout the room. It's a cruel sort of relief when Selene takes me by the elbow and guides me to the club's outdoor terrace area, cluttered with tropical plants, costumed partygoers lounging on patio furniture, and a roaring fire pit nobody asked for at the end of a Florida October.

We dodge a cluster of younger guys all dressed as Teenage Mutant Ninja Turtles and eventually settle into plush cushioned seats in a quieter pocket of the terrace. The music from the heart of the party is just a faint echo here, now a piano version of "I Put a Spell on You." The party itself feels terribly far away. And Selene is close—too close—the way she always used to be when she wanted to get under my skin. Her fingers trail down my bare arm before letting go.

I cross my arms over my chest to put distance between us and glare at her. "What do you want?"

"I missed you, you know," she says lightly, her voice warm as honey and just as sticky. "At first."

Scoffing, I roll my eyes. "Is that why you dragged me out here? To say you missed me, but not really?"

Back in college, we fell for each other's ambition—late nights in the student business incubator, chasing big ideas and bigger futures. I used to think Selene's intensity meant passion. Care. That being chosen by her meant I mattered. It was intoxicating. I didn't realize until too late that what she wanted was something to chew up and spit out.

And when I slipped up at Mercurial, suddenly all her dazzling intensity turned sharp. Every critique cut, every silence froze me out, until I was nothing but a liability.

One mistake was all it took. She couldn't stomach being tied to someone who might drag her down, not when her whole identity was built on climbing higher, faster, shinier than everyone else. So she cut me loose. Not because I was unlovable, but because I was inconvenient.

Her smile turns sly. "You're still so reactive. That's what made me fall for you. And what made you exhausting." She lets the word hang there. I try my best not to react to it, but it slices through me like a blade all the same. "But you found yourself a new hobby, didn't you?"

A *hobby*. Like Nate is some sort of object.

"He has nothing to do with this," I say tightly.

But Selene only leans closer, resting her elbows atop her slim thighs. Her bodysuit squeaks with the movement. "Tell me—still in finance?" she asks lightly, eyes flicking down my dress and back up. "Or did Mercurial make you... reconsider the corporate track? I'm assuming you're not a CFO anymore."

"I've been cleaning," I spit out. "Gig work. Taking a breather."

"So you're still cleaning up other people's messes? At least this time it's literal. Better than blowing up the company's accounts, I suppose."

The jab lands hard, because that's the story everyone believed: that one mistake made me incompetent. Of course the young CFO was a disaster from the start. And Selene? She made sure no one forgot it.

I can't help it. I flinch, and she doesn't miss it.

"I didn't blow up the accounts, Selene. That's a gross exaggeration. I miscalculated one forecast and had to revise it. That's it. Hardly the end of Mercurial, but you sure reacted like it was."

"Oh, come on," she continues, ignoring my statement. "You always loved when I poked at you. Made you *feel* something. You hate being bored." Her eyes gleam. "So. Your new arm candy. Is that real, or is he just your attempt to walk in here with some sort of armor?"

Fuck. She's not even seeing him—she's seeing *me*. I hate how easily she's always been able to read me, and still can.

I force out, "I'm not talking about him. So I'll ask you again—what do you want?"

"I'm glad you came," she says softly, almost too softly. "I wasn't sure you would. You've been so... off the grid."

That's an understatement. We both know what happened while I was *off the grid*. Everyone does. The fact that she won't just say it outright pisses me off more.

"I needed space," I say carefully.

Her lips twist. "Of course. Space. To find yourself. Or lose yourself. Same difference."

She takes another sip of her espresso martini, lets the silence stretch—then lets the real hit come, casual as can be.

"You never could just... coast, could you? You always need a project. It was Mercurial all day, all night, until you cracked. Then me. And now him?"

She makes it sound like a choice. Like this was all me unraveling for sport. But the truth is, I was already drowning at Mercurial—and after one mistake, they held my head beneath the surface, left me to take that hit on my own. Selene could've pulled me out. She didn't.

I stiffen. The pointed attack has all my thoughts rushing together, gummed up like a crowd at a narrow exit.

Selene watches me quietly, and when I don't answer, she presses in closer, voice dipping low. "I guess I should've seen it coming. You going back to guys was always going to happen eventually, wasn't it? All those months I spent wondering if I was too boring to keep your attention." She gives a pointed glance toward the party. Toward Nate. "I guess now I know the answer."

That hits lower than I want to admit.

It's not even about Nate. It's about us. About all the nights she accused me of looking elsewhere, and the constant, paranoid, hungry need she had for me to prove that no one else mattered. The questions she weaponized when things started to unravel.

And now she's standing here, framing me like it was all my fault and my fault alone—first my screwup at work, then the rapid unraveling of our relationship.

I'm starting to feel sick. My expensive cocktail churns in my stomach. But I can't move—self-loathing has frozen me in place.

"You left everything behind and vanished when it got hard," she continues smoothly. "You let me become the villain. And now here you are, picking up the first stray you come across, hoping this one won't turn on you."

She didn't become the villain. She twisted every word, turned every look into a test I could never pass. Turned everyone against me. Made everything so uncomfortable I had no choice but to leave. And Nate isn't a stray. He's—I don't know what he is to me, exactly, but he's not that.

"That's not fair," I snap, voice rougher than I mean it to be. The heat of humiliation prickles down my spine.

"Isn't it?" Selene's voice gentles then, the cruelest shift of all. A scalpel wrapped in silk. She looks at me like she's sorry for me, like she's still the one who knows me best. "You're still chasing it, Mia. That need to prove you matter to someone. At Mercurial. With me. Now him." Her eyes glint, catching the light like the edge of a razor blade. "You wouldn't recognize real care if it was right in front of you. You sure didn't when you had me."

The pity is the worst of all.

And it drags the memory with it—how fast she turned on me after Mercurial. One mistake, and suddenly every word was a blade. Criticism cutting to the bone, followed by days of silence, cold shoulders, doors closed in our apartment until I broke first. The walls closed in so tight I nearly found a way out I wouldn't come back from. One step closer and I wouldn't be here at all. The thought flickers sharp and fast, leaving my palms damp. I shove it down before she can see it on my face.

But maybe she already knows. Maybe she always knew exactly how close she'd pushed me, and still kept pressing anyway. And here she is again, smiling like it was nothing.

And all of a sudden, I know this was a mistake.

I thought showing up with Nate would prove I was fine. That I'd moved on. But standing here, surrounded by my old life, I don't feel strong.

I feel small.

Raw.

I don't even know why I'm here.

I don't want Selene's approval, or Imani's, or anyone's. I don't care what they think. I don't even want to be around them.

Why did I come? Why drag both Nate and myself through this torture?

My ears are ringing. My palms are slick with sweat, and I can't tell if I'm about to cry or throw up.

The swell of self-hatred pinning me to the spot crests, only now, instead of rendering me immobile, it gives me the momentum to move. I push to my feet before she can finish hollowing me out completely.

"I should get back."

This was supposed to be proof I was fine. That I could walk back into this room and not bleed for it.

She smiles faintly, watching me. Like a cat who already caught the mouse and is letting it scurry away out of boredom.

"Good luck with this one," she says airily, before turning back toward the party. "I'm sure it'll end differently this time."

I wait until she's out of sight. Then slip back into the party like a ghost.

Everything feels thin now. The chandeliers burn too bright, the laughter a muffled echo, like I'm underwater, watching the night from the bottom of the ocean.

My feet move on autopilot, weaving through the crowd, avoiding faces. My costume clings uncomfortably to my skin. I tug at it once, twice, too aware now of how cheap and silly it looks.

I catch sight of Nate across the room, standing near a cocktail table, shadows calm and edges smooth as he listens politely to someone I don't know. He looks normal. Unbothered. Like he belongs here, even though he said he hated the vibe.

And somehow, that's the thing that breaks me.

Because I came here to feel powerful again. To show that I'm doing fine. Better, even. But all I feel now is small. Off-balance. Like I'm slipping again, the same way I did before—one mistake away from losing everything.

My chest tightens, my breath stutters. I need air. I need a drink. I need something to pull myself together before anyone notices I'm unraveling.

I turn sharply, pushing deeper into the crowd.

Away from Nate.

Away from the person I thought I still had a chance to be—the woman with a career, with a beautiful partner on her arm, with something that looked like a future.

Away from the person I was stupid enough to think I could be again.

Chapter Fourteen

Nate

The party was unbearable before. Without Mia, it's excruciating. And she's been gone too long.

She said she was fine. Said she'd be right back. I have to trust that she can handle her ex, who despite the Catwoman costume, made me think of an oiled viper.

But every minute that ticks by without her returning feels like torture.

I'm trapped near the bar, listening to a man in a too-tight Spider-Man bodysuit explain how he's *really into the dark aesthetic, bro,* and pretending to laugh at his anecdotes when appropriate.

Then I see her. Mia's compact frame in the mouse costume slips back in through the side doors, blending into the crowd, and immediately, I know something's wrong. She trails through the crowd for several minutes, wandering aimlessly. Then, she finds me, joining me and Spider-Man at the bar with an obviously forced smile. She won't meet my eyes.

"Hey," she says.

Her shoulders are still, her smile brittle—and my shadows twitch like they can sense the ache beneath her skin. She doesn't look at me as I hand over her drink, instead accepting it with a low, muttered thanks. I drift closer, trying to catch her eye, but it doesn't work. Her fingers shake faintly when she grasps the glass.

Spiderman keeps on rambling. I don't hear a word.

Maybe it's because I've been in her dreams, fed off of them, tasted the worst of her emotions on my tongue. Her affect hums against mine now; even without looking, I can feel where it hurts. Or maybe it's because I'm starting to care for her too much, and cataloging every innocent detail of her existence is becoming second nature.

Whatever happened outside with her ex cut her deep.

Something ugly and possessive curls hot beneath my shadows, uncoiling with danger-ous intent. Heat makes instinct loud—territory, threat, protect. Whoever did this—put that fragile edge in her posture, her smile—I want to pull their limbs apart piece by piece.

But this is just a Halloween party.

Only fake monsters allowed.

So instead, ignoring Spiderman, I ask, low and careful, "Mia, do you want to leave?"

Now she looks up at me, her hazel eyes wide in surprise. She hesitates, and I think that's what breaks me most—that she's weighing if she's allowed to leave, or if staying might be safer, more polite, less weak.

The pianist must go on break, because a moment later a barrage of thunderous, Halloween-themed house music starts pumping through the speakers. I lean in more, shadows brushing her ear, to be heard over the music.

"You don't have to stay here if you don't want to. You don't owe anyone in this place anything."

Her breath snags, then steadies. She nods, small and fast.

"Okay," she whispers. "Let's go."

The moment the word is out, she looks relieved. As if my permission was all she needed.

I don't give her time to change her mind. I take her drink and set it aside, and with a light hand on her back, steer her toward the exit. Nobody stops us. Nobody notices us leaving except Imani, who glances over from across the room and lifts her chin faintly in question.

I ignore it. Mia comes first.

By the time we hit the sidewalk, she's clinging to composure by a thread. The sun has set, and the overabundance of lights downtown combined with the humidity render everything in a blurry, warm orange glow. Tears streak down Mia's cheeks, but she doesn't seem to notice. As the valet fetches the car, she stands silently at my side, flinching once as someone in a grotesque gorilla mask shouts and whizzes by on a skateboard.

When the car arrives, I open the door without ceremony and usher her in. The second the doors shut, a weighted silence falls. I crank up the air conditioning for her benefit. It's close to midnight, most Halloween revelers just getting started, and the glittering heartbeat of Miami feels like it's gone into overdrive. My hands are tight on the wheel as I steer us away from the costumed crowds, trying not to let every protective, frantic instinct bleed through.

It takes longer than it should to navigate out of the city center and back toward Coral Key, toward home, and every red light feels like an eternity, like the city itself won't let me get her somewhere safe.

Mia stares out the window, arms folded tightly across her chest. She hasn't said a word.

Finally, once we're on the highway, coasting along the ocean's meandering sprawl back toward Coral Key, I risk breaking the silence.

"What happened back there?"

For a second, I don't think she'll answer.

Then she exhales shakily and says, "Selene."

She says the name like she's biting down on broken glass. Even now, just the sound of it makes my shadows bristle.

I say nothing. Just keep driving, waiting. She talks, eventually—because I think the silence feels worse.

"She's always been good at...getting under my skin. Reminding me of everything I'm not. Or everything I'm afraid I am." Mia's voice cracks on the last part, soft and miserable. She glances away like she regrets admitting it. "I thought I'd be okay. I thought I could handle seeing her again, that showing off would make me feel better. But she knows how to hit where it hurts. And now I just feel worse."

I process that. My hands flex slightly on the wheel. I realize I'm wound tight, so I drop one hand to rest on the gear shifter, willing myself to relax. I might want to rage about Selene, tell Mia every awful thing I thought about that woman, but that's not going to help her right now.

"I'm guessing she didn't approve of me as your date," I say lightly, though I'm not sure why I bother softening it.

Mia huffs a bitter laugh. "Oh, she approved, alright. She thinks I like you because you're broken. Because that's what I do—take on projects. Try to fix things that are too far gone, and burn myself out like a dying star in the process."

Her gaze flicks to the window, voice dropping. "And she's not wrong that I fix things. I always have. At Mercurial, I was patching broken projections, smoothing messy books. Now it's scuffed floors and overflowing trash. Different messes, same compulsion—make it presentable, make it work."

Then she looks back at me, softer. "But with you...it isn't a project. You made me sit down and drink a coffee when I was shaking. You didn't pretend not to notice. You asked before you touched. You keep trying to be gentle even when it costs you. I can't tell you what that means to me."

She says it too easily. Too lightly, as if she hasn't realized the weight of the words herself.

But I do. I feel it like a sudden crack in my foundation, spearing me right through the middle.

Selene framed it like pathology. Underneath it, I hear the dangerous part: Mia chose me. Not as a fix. As a *person*.

She likes me. Maybe not in the way I've pictured, in the dark and dangerous corners of my mind. Maybe not for the right reasons.

But still.

Still.

I hadn't let myself believe that was possible. Not really. Not until this moment. My first instinct is denial. I tell myself she's just saying it to make a point. That it's projection. A defense.

But a quieter voice slips beneath all the rationalizations. *You matter to her.*

Not just as an arrangement. Not just as a convenient fix to her loneliness, or mine. After all, the party's over. If she wanted to, she could have left me right outside the club—found another ride home. But she's still *here*. She looks at me and sees, maybe, something worth fixing. Worth keeping.

I still don't know how she ended up in Coral Key. Most people here... they have roots. Magic. Secrets. Mia has none of that, as far as I can tell. Just grit. And something sad and stubborn that the town seems to have accepted. Like it let her in because it saw what she was trying to hide.

Her getting in the car with me again shouldn't mean anything. It shouldn't matter. But it does. It carves something open in me, because I don't know what to do with that possibility. I've lived centuries expecting fear and hunger and need—but not *want*. Not from someone like her.

And I know I should push the thought down. Crush it. It's dangerous.

Instead, I hold onto it like it's the first warm thing I've been given in a very, very long time.

I'm not sure where the words come from, or how I know they're what she needs to hear. But they spill from me all the same.

"Selene doesn't get to decide who you are. She's not in your life, you're not in a relationship, and her words are meaningless." Mia glances over at me, wary, but listening.

"If the brief interaction I had with her is any indication, this is exactly the reaction she wanted from you."

Mia drops her gaze to her hands. "You're right," she says finally. "But it doesn't make what she said hurt any less."

Then her hand closes over mine atop the shifter, her skin warm and soft. I freeze—breath locking, shadows curling inward like they're afraid to startle the moment.

"Thank you," she says softly.

I nod, but I can't quite look at her. My throat feels too tight. Her touch blazes through me, an inferno that nearly ruins me completely. I dump all of my focus into not crashing the car. Because suddenly there's an ache thudding beneath my skin in rhythmic, unrelenting waves. It roils higher with every mile closer to Coral Key, to home. The heat that's been stalking me for days is cresting now, mean and eager, and worse still—

I don't want to push it down anymore. Not while she's sitting there in that ridiculous mouse costume, biting her lip, her eyes glassy with leftover tears. Not when she's touching me. Not when she keeps giving me hope.

I take the exit for Coral Key out of habit, then force myself to ask, "Home or my place?" When she doesn't answer, I keep heading for the garage.

She tucks her hand back into her lap eventually, and my head clears. But only momentarily. By the time we pull into the underground garage, my hand on the wheel is basically a claw, I'm gripping it so hard. Mia doesn't seem to notice—she's gone quiet again, small in the passenger seat, withdrawn like she's running low on whatever courage got her through tonight.

I kill the engine, but neither of us moves right away. The heavy silence returns, thick enough to choke.

"You don't have to come up," I say roughly, breaking it. The offer feels stupid even as it leaves me. "I can take you home."

I don't want her to go. I want her close. Too close.

Mia glances over, makeup faintly smudged beneath her eyes. She studies me for a beat—then shakes her head, quiet but sure. "I don't want to be alone."

Fuck.

Again, I just nod. I get out before I can say something stupid, circling the car to meet her. We move toward the elevator without speaking. It's late enough that the garage is dead silent, only the soft hum of lights overhead and the faint tap of her heels breaking the stillness. When I swipe my keycard and the elevator doors slide open, Mia steps in first.

I hesitate, just for a second.

Because I'm not confident my self control can survive the trip—the enclosed space, the proximity, the scent of her skin already clinging to me from the car ride over. The way I am roaring within right now, desperate and cornered and aching to devour whatever tiny scrap of softness she's willing to give.

But she turns, blinking at me from inside the elevator, and says softly, "You coming?"

I have no defense against that.

I step in. The doors close.

And the tension that's been pulling tighter all night snaps like a wire stretched too far.

As the elevator begins to rise, Mia shifts closer automatically, reaching out to steady herself on the rail—and the second her arm brushes mine, I lose every inch of good sense I have left.

I move without thinking. I crowd her against the mirrored wall, caging her in between my arms, my hands gripping the rail behind her. I'm close enough that she has to tilt her head back to meet my eyes, and when she does—

Her throat bobs on a swallow.

Her lips part slightly, as if she might speak, but no words come out.

"I—" Fuck, where are my words? I can't think. All I can focus on is the luscious golden brown of her exposed skin, the long column of her throat, the curve of her bare shoulders.

"I forgot," she says. Her pupils are blown wide now, hungry and fragile all at once. "No touching. Sorry."

My voice comes out hoarse, my control hanging by a single frayed thread. "Don't apologize. But you should probably push me away."

I wait for her to obey. She doesn't. Instead, she keeps looking at me, her chest rising and falling, her breath uneven.

"And if I don't?"

I could break, right then. But instead, I give her a final chance. A last, desperate out. I lean in, my shadows curling tight around us, hungry and barely leashed.

"Mia," I warn. "Tell me to stop."

Her mouth twitches with the slightest hint of a smile. Then: she shakes her head at me, just slightly.

"Why?"

I don't understand this—this recklessness.

"Because you listened when no one else did," she whispers. "Because I want this."

Her fingers fist in the front of my shirt and yank me down with surprising force, dragging me into her like she's daring me to lose control.

And I can't resist anymore.

I devour her mouth like I've been starving for centuries.

The taste of her short-circuits everything—sweet, electric, human.

I'm *ruined*.

The kiss isn't gentle. It's starving, devouring. A messy collision of teeth and lips and breath. Her nails dig into my shoulders, a sting I'd let her carve deeper, and I groan into her mouth when she bites down lightly on my lower lip before tugging me back in.

I shape my shadows into lips and use them to claim Mia's. She makes a faint, desperate sound when I deepen it—when my shadows surge and close in around her like they're claiming territory. They snake up and down the backs of her legs like climbing vines, tugging her closer.

She doesn't pull away. She opens to it, to me. Her lips part and let me in, matching me kiss for kiss as if she's just as starved. My hands find her waist, sliding up the curve of her hips to her sides. I want to be careful, I *mean* to be careful, but her skin is too warm and soft beneath the thin material of that ridiculous dress. I grip tighter than I should. Pull her closer. Until she's flush against me and there's no space left to think.

Mia breaks the kiss just long enough to gasp in air, but doesn't go far. She presses her forehead to mine, breath heaving, lips kiss-swollen and pink.

"This is insane," she pants.

"Tell me to stop," I manage, though my voice is ragged and my hands aren't exactly cooperating. They've slid down to cup her ass now, dragging her flush against the ache straining inside my jeans. In this shape, I'm solid where I choose to be. Heat gives the body weight.

The friction turns my vision hazy.

"No," she says stubbornly. And instead of backing away, she slides a leg up, twining it around my upper thigh, and when she rocks against me with sharp, deliberate pressure, my entire body jolts.

A low, guttural sound tears from my throat.

I seize her by the thighs and tug her off the ground entirely, my shadows pulling her legs around my lower back. The move knocks a startled gasp out of her, which I swallow with my mouth as I press her harder against the mirrored wall, the glass groaning faintly with the impact.

She meets me eagerly, hips rolling in a slow, devastating rhythm that turns my brain to static.

It's not graceful.

It's not pretty.

It's frantic and hot and clumsy and *too much*.

Her dress rides up higher with every grind, my fingers clutching at bare skin, my shadows coiling tight around her calves and knees like they never want to let her go. She claws at my shirt, my hair, at anything she can hold.

She moans softly into my mouth when she shifts, chasing friction.

I'm going to lose control.

I know it in my bones. I can already feel my leash on the shadows slipping as they writhe against the mirrored elevator walls, hungry and reckless, desperate to get in between her legs. They surge higher—one brushes too close, ghosting the inside of her thigh; the way her breath hitches nearly destroys me. I yank it back before I can give in completely, my body screaming in protest.

I can't. Not yet.

And then—

DING.

The elevator jolts to a halt. The doors slide open. Fluorescent hallway light spills in. For one suspended beat, neither of us moves.

Then reality crashes back down with brutal clarity.

I tear myself away, gasping like I've been punched in the stomach, moving back a full step even though my body protests. Mia staggers against the elevator wall, swaying slightly. She looks dazed, her costume rumpled from where my hands crushed the fabric. A strap has slipped down her shoulder, baring more golden skin, and the sight almost drags me right back in.

I want to drag her back in and finish what we started so badly my hands actually shake. But I don't.

"This is..." I rasp, shaking my head, stepping into the hallway. "You should go home. I'm not safe right now. My heat's too close. My shadows want too much."

If I feed or take more now, I slip. Want turns into hunger, and hunger doesn't leave room for choice.

I mean it. Every word. The heat simmering in me now is dark and all-consuming, and if she steps back into my space, I don't think I'll be able to stop again. I don't trust myself. I could hurt her.

"Your shadows? Or you?" she asks.

Mia looks at me—really looks—and then steps forward again anyway, filling the space between us, and tips her chin up stubbornly.

The elevator doors slide smoothly shut behind her, leaving us in the hallway.

When I don't respond, she adds, "I don't want to go home."

I stare at her. She means it. She's choosing this. Choosing *me*.

And I don't know how to make sense of that.

My throat works, but I can't swallow the instinctive protest. I drag a hand through my hair, shadows snapping faintly at my edges as I force myself to hold steady.

"You don't get it," I say hoarsely. "If you come inside with me right now, I'm not going to be able to keep pretending. Not tonight. I'm—" I break off, pulse hammering. "I'm running out of control."

Mia just watches me, her lips parted slightly, breath shallow. But there's no fear in her eyes. Just something soft and steady and devastating.

"I know," she says quietly. "I trust you anyway."

That destroys me more than the kiss ever could. Trust isn't something I've been given in a very long time, and I want to hoard it like it's the only real thing I've ever been offered.

I hesitate—just for a second longer—before unlocking my door and holding it open.

"Once you step inside..." I warn softly, shadows curling like smoke in my wake.

Mia's gaze holds mine as she crosses the threshold. "I know," she whispers. "No more pretending."

She tugs me inside after her, and my shadows press the door closed behind us both.

Chapter Fifteen

Mia

MERCURIAL//"Is it anxiety or is it desire? Trick question, girlypop—it's transformation. Let it wreck you a little."

The second the door shuts behind us, the silence feels different. Not the fragile quiet from earlier—the car, the elevator. This is heavier. Thicker.

Nate steps away from me immediately. He moves like a man on the verge of snapping—pacing the length of the living room with restless, predatory energy. His shadows uncouple from him and ladder up the walls, pooling in corners like they'd rather hide from him. Or me.

"You should go," he says, his voice raw and frayed at the edges. He won't look at me. "I'm not safe right now."

The sound makes my skin prickle—it's not air pushed through lungs, but something shaped out of shadow itself. Close enough to human to fool anyone else, but I can hear the dissonance—a second voice almost in sync.

I don't move.

I cross my arms and anchor myself, feet planted, like that might keep the moment from sliding away.

"Are you going to hurt me?"

"Not if I can stop it," he says—and the honesty in it is the warning.

"Then I'm not leaving."

He freezes mid-step. Slowly, he turns. I've never seen a pair of eyes when he's in his shadow form, but there they are—or the idea of them—two glossy voids. The intensity in them feels like it belongs to someone else entirely. Someone dangerous.

But that danger is exactly what I'm reaching for.

The weight of his stare drags across every inch of bare skin the stupid mouse costume leaves exposed. My heart thuds so violently I half expect it to shake the walls. He won't need any stupid pulse checks now. But I don't drop my gaze.

"You don't understand what you're offering," he says hoarsely. "What I want right now, Mia… it's not gentle. It's not nice. It's selfish and ugly and—" He cuts himself off, jaw tightening. "It's better if you walk away."

"No," I say softly. I take a step toward him. Then another. "You helped me tonight. You were there when I needed it. Let me help you back. You're in heat, and you need to feed, don't you? You can take what you need from me. *However* you need. Only if you want."

He shakes his head sharply, like the idea physically hurts him. "It doesn't work that way. Heat wants contact. Feeding wants fear. They're not the same." His jaw flexes. "But one makes the other harder to refuse."

"Maybe it does," I counter quietly, closing the distance between us. Close enough now that I can see an uneven flickering at the bottom of his throat—his pulse, racing as fast as mine. "Back there, in the elevator, you kept giving me an out. And you're doing it even now. You care, even when you act like you don't. You think you're this terrible, destructive thing, but you've never been anything but careful with me."

His breathing falters. I press on, steadier now, speaking the truth I suspect might reach him.

"You're not broken to me, Nate." I touch his chest lightly—right over where his heart would be. "And I'm not scared of you."

It feels reckless, maybe even stupid, but I want him to know I mean it. That I trust him. Trust him more than I should.

The space where his eyes should be glints. I can't explain how I can read his eyeless, faceless expression, but I *can*. Something raw and vulnerable flickers there in that shadowed space.

"You should be," he says. Not a threat. A confession.

But I don't run. I don't shrink. I step forward, closing the last sliver of space until I'm flush against him.

"I'm *not*," I whisper. "So stop acting like you're doing me a favor by keeping your distance."

He exhales sharply.

Then the last thread of his restraint shatters.

His hands are on me in the next heartbeat—hot, desperate, grasping. He shoves me against the wall, mouth crashing down on mine. Something wild and caged inside him breaks loose. He kisses me like holding back has been an agony. His lips are rough and feverish as his hands roam—down my back, over my hips—dragging me tighter until there isn't a molecule of air between us.

And I don't hesitate. I meet him halfway. Lips parted, body arching into his. I don't want careful. I want him exactly like this—dangerous, hungry, losing control for me and only me.

Kissing him like this is different. There's no stubble, no familiar give of skin—just heat, pressure, sensation, like kissing the edge of a storm. The shadows shape themselves into lips under his will, solid where they touch, molten everywhere else.

I gasp softly when his shadows surge again, threading and tugging, slipping under the hem of my costume like curious fingers. They're warmer than I expect—warmer than in the elevator, almost gentle despite the way they band around my thighs and hips, cinching me to him.

Nate groans when I roll my hips instinctively against his, chasing the friction. His head drops to my shoulder, breath hot and uneven against my skin.

"Fuck," he rasps. His voice is cracked open—vulnerable and desperate and human in a way that makes my chest ache. "You don't know what you're doing to me."

"Yes, I do," I whisper, threading my fingers into his hair and tugging just hard enough to make him look at me. "And I want it. All of it."

Another gleam stirs in that shadowed face—need, yes, but also hope. Then he lifts me, carrying me through the dim apartment like I weigh nothing. His shadows slip ahead, nudging the bedroom door, licking along the walls as if they know where we're going.

When he drops me gently onto the bed, I go easily, breath catching in my throat as he looms over me—watching, devouring, hesitating. His form stretches, becoming taller, thicker, more monstrous. His shadows curl and pulse around us, storm clouds about to break. For a terrible, breathless second, I think he's about to vanish—slip back into the dark like he has before, leave me reaching for nothing.

Heart thundering, I stare up at him, desire curling low in my stomach. But I'm not afraid. I thread my fingers into his shadows, tugging him down.

"I'm not stopping," I whisper. "So don't you dare. I trust you. I want this. I want *you*."

Whatever control Nate has left crumbles with those words.

He kisses me harder—less frantic, no less hungry. He pushes my costume up; I help peel it off, leaving me bare.

The second I am, something shifts. Long tendrils move reverently, skimming my skin—almost shy. He doesn't lunge. He pauses—savoring—then drags his mouth down my throat, over my collarbone, lower. I arch, nails scraping his back.

"Nate," I gasp, needing more.

He groans against my skin. His hand slips between my legs, and when his fingers slide through the slickness already there, he curses softly—like the confirmation of how much I want him breaks something fragile and final inside him.

"You're perfect," he murmurs, kissing me again, slower now. "You feel... fuck, Mia. You feel so good."

A few of his long fingers slip inside of me, and I buck my hips against his hand, letting the pleasure curl tighter until my thighs tremble and my breath shortens into desperate little gasps. His shadows shift with me, coaxing and cradling and adding to the overwhelming sensation until I'm close—*too* close.

"Nate," I cry against his shoulder. "I—"

A low chuckle rumbles through him. "You're taking my fingers so well," he whispers. "What about...?"

His shadows shift with restless intent, splitting and reforming like smoke caught in slow-motion rewind. They're warmer now, alive in a way that sends a pulse of instinctive recognition through my body—like they know me.

His fingers disappear, and I start to whine in protest. Then a tendril of shadow teases at my entrance. Hesitating.

"Would this be—"

"Fuck, *yes*, please!"

One thick tendril slides inside me. Not slick or rigid—silken and alive, pulsing with heat. It shifts with precise curiosity, pressing against every tender spot, stuffing me pleasantly full and shifting angles in a way that feels *intelligent*. Not fumbling. Not random.

Learning me.

Some trembling part of me knows they could tear me apart if he stopped caring. But he doesn't stop caring. He shapes them to pleasure instead of pain. And that choice ruins me more than fear ever could.

Another shadow slides higher, up around my hip, teasing and circling my clit with feather-light brushes, alternating between soft pulses and slow, delicious pressure—like a hand flexing in time with my heartbeat. The shadows *thrum* against me as I clench and gasp, syncing themselves to the rhythm of my pleasure.

It's not fear they want. It's... *this*. Want. Willingness. Joy.

My eyes roll back; my mouth opens on a wordless moan. It feels holy and forbidden all at once. I've stepped out of my old body, out of shame, into something entirely new.

The building, coiling pleasure in me winds tight.

In a low voice, right in my ear, Nate murmurs, "I could watch my shadows stuff you all day long."

And I break, keening, in high, uncontrollable moans that leave me breathless. The shadows don't stop once I come—if anything, they only become more eager, coaxing the pleasure higher and higher until I'm dizzy with it. When they finally withdraw, I'm shaking.

Nate sprawls beside me, watching my legs tremble with pleased intent. I grab for him, and he falls into me with devouring kisses. I want him *now*, swollen and slick from his shadows inside me. I hook a leg over his, trying to put him where I want him. One many-fingered hand slides possessively around my throat as he pulls back just enough to meet my eyes.

"Let me have you," he says softly, voice wrecked and reverent at once. "Please."

The plea shatters whatever composure I have left.

"Yes," I breathe. "Nate, yes."

That's all he needs.

His shadows gather, thickening and hardening under his will, shaping themselves into something unmistakably male. Dark, slick heat presses against me, and then he drives into me in one long, slow thrust, stretching me full until I gasp his name.

It's so much I cry out, clutching as shadows lace along our legs, cinch our hips, hold us together while he moves—slow at first, savoring every inch, before giving in to the relentless rhythm his body demands. Every thrust is deep and consuming, every roll of his hips dragging me higher and higher toward oblivion.

As his hips roll against mine, his shadows pulse again—this time curling up and around my face, tender and intimate. They swirl just beneath my jaw, almost stroking the spot where I felt Nate feed from me in my dream.

But I'm not afraid.

And when I moan and arch, when I give him everything freely—something changes. The shadows drink it in. They take pleasure instead of terror, greedily drawing every broken sound and whimper straight from my lips and skin.

They don't tear anything out of me. They take only what I give—and give something back, something warm and shivering that leaves me breathless.

Nate groans roughly above me, head tipping back.

"God, Mia," he rasps.

Like my desire feeds him more than fear ever did.

And through it all, he doesn't stop touching me. His hands are everywhere—palming my waist, threading our fingers when I reach up blindly to anchor myself. His mouth is soft and desperate against mine between moans, whispering broken words like *beautiful*, *mine*, and *thank you*.

When I come, it's with a sob, clinging to him as the wave breaks everything I thought I knew.

He follows—rhythm stuttering, body locking. I feel the moment he lets go; his shadows pulse inside me in deep, molten beats, echoing the rhythm they already learned. Wrapped around my thighs and waist, they hold me flush as if they can't let go. He groans against my throat, breaking on my name.

His breath hitches, sharp and strange. I don't know what he's feeling. But whatever it is, it makes him hold me tighter.

When it's over, he doesn't pull away.

He collapses beside me, dragging me half onto his chest.

For a long time, neither of us speaks. We just breathe—tangled together, hearts still racing, my skin damp with sweat. But beneath the warmth, he's still taut; shadows flicker at the edges like restless animals not yet tamed. It's intimacy and danger tangled together, and I'm not sure which is stronger.

Then, quietly, as sleep starts to pull me under, I murmur against his throat:

"You didn't take fear."

Nate goes very still. His arms tighten just slightly, almost like he's holding onto me—or the moment—a little too hard. I'm too tired to ask what that means. Too warm, too full of everything, to worry.

I remember the dream, the way I collapsed afterward, hollowed out and shaking. But now... I don't feel empty. I don't feel used. I feel warm. Steady. Like he gave something back instead of taking.

Whatever this is...For tonight, I choose to believe it's real.

I'm barely aware, through the haze of sleep, when Nate shifts. His hand traces my spine; his lips brush my shoulder. A kiss—gentle. But beneath it, he's still wound tight. Still needing.

The shadows haven't left, either—they're faint at the edges of my vision, flickering, patient, hungry.

Before sleep takes me fully, certainty lands sharp and sweet: This isn't over. Not even close.

Chapter Sixteen

Nate

It doesn't stop.

She never asks me to stop.

She never *wants* me to stop.

I lose track of how many times I take her.

Halloween night blurs into the next day, then the next evening, and that evening into something darker still. All I know is the way she keeps reaching for me—pliant, flushed, murmuring my name like prayer and permission combined.

Even after we collapse into my bed, tangled in the sheets, even after sleep takes her for a few stolen hours, and I rest, the hunger returns. Each time more urgent, more frayed at the edges. She keeps letting me take, keeps opening for more, and I keep giving in.

She trusts me completely.

Even when I take her bare. I can't give her a child—not like that. But she doesn't even ask. She just lets me in.

My shadows love her.

They thrill at her shudders, her pleas, the way she opens. They drink her in like nectar, winding tighter every time I bury myself deeper.

By the second day, I'm drunk on her. Halloween weekend still, so for now she's mine.

My shadows are lazier now, more languid when they wrap around her, but no less greedy. She meets me willingly every time I pull her close. She laughs against my mouth, whispers filthy, breathless things when I pin her to the mattress. When I carry her to the shower, still half-asleep and pliant, she kisses me like she wants to drown in this.

It's not until her breath hitches in that ragged, hollow way—her legs giving out beneath her in the steam-heavy shower—that reality slams back in, hard and cold.

Her legs buckle. Not from pleasure this time. Just gone. Spent. Her head lolls as I catch her, my otherworldly reflexes kicking in before she hits the floor. The collapse knocks the breath right out of me.

"Mia?" I ask carefully.

"Hm?"

"Are you okay?"

"Mm-hmm," she mumbles. But she's limp in my arms. She can't even keep her eyes open. She's shaking. Fragile. Human.

And I'm the monster who forgot that.

This is how it starts. Trust, pliancy, softness. She lets me take because she thinks I know when to stop. She trusts me not to take too much. If she knew what happened last time, she never would.

I should tell her.

I can't.

I've kept her too long in this. Kept us too long inside this heat and hunger and oblivion. I'm the one who has to stop. She won't, not when she's like this.

I press my lips to her temple, steadying her trembling body in my arms. The water beats down, cold now, but I barely notice. All I can think is: I have to stop.

Before I take too much. Before I make her forget she can say no.

How long has it been? I've lost all sense of time. The hazy heat-fog begins to clear; normal thoughts slink back in, lazy and late.

I shut off the shower and wrap us both in towels. Mia is asleep before I even put her to bed. And even as my rational mind is waking up, it wars with my body's physical exhaustion. I don't sleep often—my kind doesn't need regular rest like humans—but when I do, it's deep and absolute, and I feel the irresistible force of it looming on the horizon.

Quickly, I toss down some fresh puppy pads for Molly and refill her food and water bowls. Darkness crawls at the edges of my vision as I stumble back to bed and collapse next to Mia.

I don't dream.

Ironic, right?

Maybe it's because I spend so much time inside other people's nightmares. For me, sleep is one long blink.

When I open my eyes again, sunlight streams through the windows. I forgot to close the blinds. A glance at my phone on its charger reveals it's November 2nd, two days after Halloween.

A nauseating mix of concern and panic rises in me as I whip my head over to Mia.

She's curled on her side, facing me, sprawled naked with a bath towel half-covering her and a mess of sheets beneath her.

And she's not moving.

The world stops. I move closer, disbelieving, and—

There. She's breathing, just very slow and even. Deeply asleep. That's what terrifies me most. Humans don't know when they've given too much—until they don't wake up at all.

My hand hovers, then presses lightly to her throat. Her pulse. Slow, steady. Still there. Relief floods me so sharply it makes me dizzy. But the fact that I even had to check—

What if I'd killed her? For a moment, I thought I had.

It's not like it hasn't happened before.

The sight of her so still calls the memory back before I can stop it.

Soft skin against mine. Limp. Still warm, but no longer there.

Her lips parted like she was still whispering my name. Eyes closed. Not peaceful — vacant.

I'd kissed her forehead and murmured for her to wake up. I'd said it again and again until the words broke.

She never did.

Mia's gentle snore sends me crashing back to the present. Relief skitters through me, leaving me shaky and lightheaded. Seeing her curled up peacefully, unaware of the danger I pose—unmoors me.

I sit frozen, staring at her chest as it rises and falls.

She's fine.

She's alive.

But if she wasn't?

She doesn't know how rotten I truly am. How could she? She trusted me. She gave herself over completely, let me take and take because she thought I'd stop before it became too much. And I almost didn't.

That girl had trusted me too. She'd laughed in my arms, told me she loved the way my shadows curled around her in the dark. She never asked me to stop. Even when I started dream feeding on instinct—when the hunger tangled with heat and I went back for more—she never said no.

She just faded.

They said her heart gave out. Or her brain. Or maybe nothing at all—maybe it just *happened*.

But I know the truth. I took too much.

She was a waitress I met at a business lunch, bold enough to flirt when I was trying to disappear into the crowd. She kept pursuing until I let her in. I told myself her fascination was love, and for a while I wanted to believe it. I even pictured a kind of future with her—not children, not the family I'll never have with a human, but something quieter. A *life*.

But I destroyed any possibility of that.

The guilt coils like a live wire in my gut.

I double over, bracing on my knees, dragging my fingers through my hair like I can scrape the memory out.

Now Mia's curled beside me the same way. Limp. Spent. Her body humming with my leftover magic, her mind somewhere far away.

And I don't know if I'll be able to stop next time, either.

I force myself to move, one step at a time. With my heat over, it's easier to pull my human glamour to the forefront and keep it there. Sometimes I actually prefer it—it makes me feel almost human. I pull on clothes, find Mia's, lay them out. Her purse is on the floor in front of my wardrobe, long since discarded. Her phone has spilled out of its open maw. A glance at it reveals several texts, mostly from someone named Reika, each increasingly sharp in tone. A couple from Imani, clipped but polite. None of them dire yet.

I consider sending reassuring messages on her behalf, but stop short.

I keep my actions automatic, robotic, to avoid thinking of what I have to do. I order food, thinking of Mia's tattoos as I do—ramen, spring rolls, and pork dumplings. By the time it arrives and I hear her stirring nearly an hour later, I leave it on the kitchen counter in view of the bedroom. And I flee into the bathroom like the coward I am, so I don't have to be there when she wakes up.

I need her to eat first. Replenish her energy. She won't want to stick around once she hears what I have to say.

I turn on the shower and let the water run for effect. Then I crack the door, watching as she wakes. She blinks, sits up, wincing, rubbing her eyes.

"Nate?" she calls. Her voice is hoarse and doesn't resolve even after she clears her throat. I feel a burst of dark pleasure at that—she was certainly quite vocal when I was inside her—but it quickly fades. She glances at the cracked bathroom door. "In the shower, I guess..."

Soft, affectionate. Unaware that I'm watching.

She rises gingerly, spots the takeout, retrieves it and her phone, and settles back into the bed, Molly following closely behind. It seems effortless for her to make herself comfortable—balancing food on her knees, scrolling, Molly laid on the floor at her feet like this happens every morning.

Like this is her space. Like she's *mine*.

The thought guts me.

She could be mine. If I let her, she already would be. And I can see it—a version of this that doesn't end with broken things. She'd keep leaving her purse on the floor, and I'd keep hanging it on a hook in the closet for her. She'd delight Molly with endless games of tug-of-war. She'd fall asleep wrapped up in my shadows and wake up each morning just like this: rumpled, unafraid.

She could be mine.

And I could ruin her just as easily.

That truth is a sharp blade through my cute little fantasy. Wanting her isn't enough. Isn't safe.

By the time she's wolfed down her ramen and made a dent in the dumplings, lounging naked and relaxed against my pillows and giggling at TikToks, I've already made my decision.

I can't let this happen again. I can't pretend this might work.

I stick my head in the shower for effect, then roughly towel-dry my hair and leave the towel on my shoulders.

I pull on my mask like armor.

"Hey," Mia says softly when I step out of the bathroom.

The warmth and openness in her gaze only makes this all worse. She looks at me like she's waiting for me to join her, to wrap her up in my arms and spend the day in bed again—not fucking, just recovering, relaxing. And I *want* to. Fuck, do I want to.

But it can't happen.

I keep my voice steady and my expression cold.

"How are you feeling?" I ask. "Any injuries?"

A slight furrow knits her brows. "No, I just feel like I have one hell of a hangover. I mean, physically, I'm pretty sore, but I can handle it." She studies me. "Were you worried you...hurt me?"

Oh, she has no idea.

I nod. "I was far too rough with you. I'm sorry."

Several expressions cross her face in the span of a few seconds. Her mouth pulls to the side, like she's not sure if I'm joking.

"I mean... yeah, you were intense. But I liked it. You *know* I liked it." Her voice dips—shy, teasing, trying to bridge the gap.

"I shouldn't have let it get that far. You needed rest."

Mia sets her phone down, all playfulness fading from her voice. "Nate, I'm not mad. Or scared, or whatever you're thinking. I trusted you. And still do."

Pretending to dry my hair again, I drop my eyes. "You shouldn't."

Silence. Then, softly, "Okay...what's going on right now?" When I don't answer, she pushes again, gentler but threaded with unease. "You're acting like I did something wrong. Did I? Did I cross a line, or—"

"No, you didn't do anything." I force myself to look at her. Straight on. Unflinching. It's easier to make it hurt that way. "This was my mistake. Not yours."

She recoils, just a bit. Blinks like she's trying to make sense of a foreign language.

"What mistake?" Her voice is thin now, uncertain. "Nate, it wasn't just sex. It wasn't just about the party, or your numbers. At least not for me. You know that, right?"

God. She means it. She really means it.

She's sitting there—messy-haired, hoarse-voiced, still tender and aching from the night before—asking me to tell her it mattered. That it was real. That *she* was real to me.

And she is. She *is*.

She's the one who stayed when she should've run. The one who let me put a coffee in her hands. The one who didn't look away when my shadows bared their teeth. The one who let me feed without fear. She saw me—me—and kept choosing to stick around.

But if I say that, she'll stay. And if I let her stay, I'll ruin her.

So I do the only thing I can. I kill it.

She hesitates, searching my face, and then adds in a small, strained whisper, "Is... is that all it was for you?" Her throat works. "Because if it was just sex—just the heat—then tell me. Because I thought it was more."

I should say something. Anything. But I say nothing.

I watch it hit her. Watch the light dim behind her eyes as she draws her own conclusion. Her face doesn't crumple—not right away. It stiffens, like she's holding the pieces together by force.

That's what I need her to do.

That's what kills me most.

Mia stares, then lets out a small, disbelieving laugh. It's brittle. Shaky.

"Wow. Okay." Her voice is tight now, wounded, even as she tries to hide it. "Guess I read it wrong."

I twist the knife. "You should go."

She freezes for half a second. Then nods, sharp and quick, like she's cutting herself free. "Yeah. Okay."

She dresses quietly, every movement careful, distant. She doesn't look at me again until she's at the door. When she does, her expression is closed off—more confused and aching than angry. But she says nothing, and then she's gone. And when the door clicks shut behind her, the silence hits like a punch to the chest.

The last one had gone still in my arms. This one walks away. Both feel like death.

The apartment feels like a tomb without her.

Molly lets out a soft, confused whine and looks to me like she's waiting for Mia to come back. When the door doesn't open again, she slinks down onto the rug, lowers her heads, all six eyes on me. Accusing. I sit there and take it.

I already killed someone who cared for me once. I won't let it happen again.

The last one had looked at me with the same bewildered hurt before she slipped away, and I swore I'd never repeat that mistake. So I did the only thing I can: put the blade in myself first, sharp and deliberate, and watched Mia bleed for it instead.

Mia trusted me like the last one did, and I am killing that trust before it kills her.

Even if it means letting her leave thinking she never mattered at all.

Chapter Seventeen

Mia

Mercurial// *"Growth means outgrowing people. Especially the ones you begged to stay. Realign, not rewind."*

I'm fine. Totally fine.

I say it out loud—to the ceiling fan, to Reika's plants, to the damn apartment itself—and pull the comforter over my head.

My phone won't stop buzzing. Reika, Imani, Tulgan. I've glimpsed messages from all of them, stared at the screen until the words blurred. Even after I flip it face down, it won't stop bothering me.

I'm fine. But I don't want to be known right now.

The apartment is silent save for the steady hum of the AC unit. It still smells like the gas station hot dogs I ate in bed last night. All things that should be safe, familiar. But the comfort doesn't land today, and the longer I lay in bed, ignoring my phone, the more everything feels like it's caving in.

And after what happened last time, caving in is not an option I'm willing to entertain.

With a rush of determination, I whip the comforter off and grab my phone. I skip the notifications—straight to the cleaning app.

I scroll through the rest of the week. There's an option to pick up extra shifts, which I usually ignore in favor of work-life balance. With a few swipes, I take them all: ten hours one day, six the next. If I keep moving, I won't have time to think. Won't have time to replay the cold dismissal in Nate's voice as he looked at me naked in his bed and told me to leave.

But I do anyway. I keep seeing his face—how the intensity drained into distance. That's the part I can't scrub away. Just the look. Like I didn't matter.

Like I never had.

I shove the thought aside.

Unfortunately, I'm supposed to clean his place this morning. And I just...can't. I won't avoid him entirely—he is a regular client, after all—but I need to clear my head first. I cancel the shift in the app and don't offer a reason. If he cares, he'll reschedule. If he doesn't, I guess I have my answer.

I leave the rest of today's schedule intact. Easier to scrub a stranger's grime than step back into a space where I thought I was wanted.

With the shift canceled and a few hours to kill, I try something I haven't done in a while: take care of myself. Not in the eat-hot-dogs-in-bed way, either. Real care—steam, soft towels, the expensive serums I keep insisting are worth it.

I crank the shower hot, let it fog the mirror, bead the ceiling. I scrub until my skin feels almost new, then wrap up in the fluffiest towel available and slather on the overpriced face mask Reika left before she skipped town.

I light a candle. The scent is called Ocean's Whisper. Mostly, it smells like loneliness and lies.

And still—none of it helps.

The warmth doesn't sink in. The face mask feels like a disguise, not a comfort. And the silence grows heavier the longer I sit in it.

Just as I'm about to rinse off and get dressed, my phone buzzes again.

NATHANIEL ALSTON:

> *Saw you canceled. Hope you're okay.*

That's it. Six little words.

And somehow they're worse than silence.

I stare at the message so long the screen goes dark. I don't know what I want—an apology? A conversation? Some kind of explanation that makes last night make sense?

But all I can manage is:

MIA WILLIAMS:

Fine. Just a cold.

Let him think that. Let him think I'm still soft and human and minor enough to be explained away by the sniffles.

I don't think he'll call me out on the obvious lie. I hit send, switch to Do Not Disturb. By the time I get dressed and head out the door, I feel like I've aged ten years.

Outside, the sunlight is too bright. Coral Key's usual salt-thick breeze normally feels good on my skin. Today it makes me itch to retreat indoors.

Tulgan is waiting at the curb, the most loyal security driver I could ask for.

When I slip into the backseat, he twists around to fix me with a stern look.

"So you are alive."

"I'm fine," I tell him automatically, and shut the door.

Tulgan's thick, bushy brows draw together in a frown. "You've been offline for four days."

"I've been tired."

He gives me a look, but doesn't press. Just puts the car in drive and lets the silence linger. We know each other well enough by now that it's not an awkward silence. But it still feels heavier than usual.

"I only knew you weren't dead," he says after a beat, "because the app told me you picked up a dozen shifts this week."

I shrug, eyes on the window. "Trying to stay busy."

He sighs, but lets it go.

The first apartment is a mess—cloudy mirrors, filthy floors, grime around faucets, overflowing trash. I go through the motions. Scrub, rinse, wipe. Repeat.

The next one isn't better: a sink of dishes that reek like rotting meat. I don't gag. I scrub until my knuckles ache.

The clients barely look at me. Which is ridiculous—they should be looking, that's the whole point of paying for me. But today I can't even clock it. Can't even be offended. All I want is to scrub their mess, clock out, and vanish.

Doors open, doors close. The MaidForYou app fires off a cheery animation after each tip.

My hands feel raw by the time I get to the last place. It's a bright studio apartment on the edge of town, close enough to the ocean that the air tastes like brine. There's a suspicious amount of seaweed in the fridge—maybe the owner is some sort of ocean-dweller.

I'm halfway through cleaning the bathroom—which is unusually crusted with salt deposits—when I lose focus. My mind drifts back to the way Nate looked at me.

And my grip slips.

There's a jagged lip of tile along the edge of the shower floor; the outside of my palm catches on the edge. A flash of red spills onto my rag. I jerk back and stare at the slice. Blood wells up slowly, thick and dark.

I...don't feel it. Not at first.

There's just a kind of ringing in my ears, and a creeping numbness that has nothing to do with pain. My body's here, but I'm not. I rinse the cut under cold water until the blood slows. The sting barely registers. Not deep, just... clean. Neat. Like a wound you'd draw with a red pen.

For a split second, the blankness feels familiar, just like the way my mind went quiet that night I tried to end it for good. Telling myself it would be easier not to feel at all. I shut the thought down fast. I promised I wouldn't go back there.

I wrap the cut with paper towels, then cover it with a bandage from my emergency kit—more muscle memory than care. By the time I finish, I don't notice the sting anymore. I shove the hand into my jacket pocket and flee to the steady safety of Tulgan's car.

The drive home is a blur. I slide out with a mumbled thanks and let myself into the apartment.

I don't even notice Tulgan followed me inside until I've dropped my bag on the floor and turned to close the door—and he's already halfway across the apartment.

"What—"

"You didn't lock it behind you," he says calmly, scanning the space. His massive frame looks too big in here—like a giant orc action figure in jeans and a t-shirt stuffed inside a tiny dollhouse. "That's not like you."

My mouth hangs open. I don't actually know how to respond to that. Tulgan takes a slow inventory of the apartment, strolling around with his arms crossed. At one point, he even unfolds a wad of tinfoil from my trashcan to give it a sniff.

It takes a minute to dawn on me—he thinks I'm on drugs. The ridiculousness snaps me back to reality.

"What are you, the DEA?" I deadpan. He shoots me a look that says: *not funny*. "I'm not on drugs, Tulgan. Relax."

He turns to face me fully. "Then what's going on? I'm just covering the possibilities," he says. "You didn't respond to messages for four days, when I know you're terminally online. You picked up twenty-seven hours of shifts in one week, even though just last week you were telling me how exhausted you were. This isn't normal for you. Of course I thought you were on drugs."

I don't answer, because he's right. I just don't have a good explanation. I sink onto the edge of the coffee table, shoulders hunched, the dull throb in my palm the only thing grounding me.

Tulgan steps closer, slow and careful, like I'm some cornered animal.

"I haven't clocked out yet," he says. "Officially, I'm still your security driver and responsible for your wellbeing. And I'm not leaving until you tell me what's going on."

I let out a humorless laugh. "You're pulling the security clause?"

"I'm pulling the friend clause." A pause. "Backed up by the security clause."

I press the heel of my good hand to my eyes. Try to breathe, even though it feels like the most monumental effort. My chest feels too tight, ribs are clasped shut around something dangerous.

And I'm not sure what it is that finally breaks me—Tulgan's gentle, patient silence, or maybe my own selfish, needy desire to be seen. But I open my mouth, and the whole miserable story comes pouring out.

The words are small, like they belong to someone else.

"I had a...thing. With one of my clients. It didn't go well."

I give him the basics—Nate, a nightmare creature; a flirt, a curiosity, something I wasn't ready to name. We danced around it for weeks until Halloween, when everything happened. I leave out the bargain—his dream-feeding in exchange for being my date to the party. It's too vulnerable, too intimate, and looking back, it feels like the dumbest decision in the world.

Tulgan says nothing. Just waits.

"We slept together," I say, voice thin. "It was... amazing. And then it wasn't."

I pull my hand away from my face, meet his eyes.

I keep my voice flat, like I'm just reporting data. But even I can hear the fracture in it. "He told me to leave. Like none of it mattered. Like I didn't matter."

That's what scares me the most. Not that Nate stopped wanting me—that I let myself believe I mattered enough to keep.

Tulgan's expression shifts—sorrow, and something like fury simmering under it.

"You don't have to say anything," I add quickly. "I'm not looking for comfort or advice. I just needed to say it out loud once. And I'm fine, I promise. I'm a tiny bit fucked up. I'll bounce back."

Tulgan exhales slowly. Maybe he was afraid it was worse—that I wasn't coming back.

"Okay," he says finally. The word is soft, but it lands heavy. "I don't like it. And I really, really don't like that shadow motherfucker."

I manage a tired half-smile. "Yeah. Join the club."

"But," he adds, "I'm glad you told me. And I'm glad you're talking. Even if it's mostly bullshit bravado."

My eyebrows lift. "Wow. Thanks."

He shrugs. "You said it. Not me."

Another silence stretches between us—this one a little looser, less loaded.

Tulgan glances once more. "All right. You've convinced me you're not dying or on drugs. Still think you should text someone back who isn't me, though. I'm imagining mine weren't the only messages you ignored."

"Yeah, yeah." I wave him off, but the guilt's already creeping in.

He pauses in the doorway, hand on the knob. "You know I'd stay if you needed me, right?"

"I know."

"And you'd tell me if you weren't fine?"

I manage a smirk. "Eventually."

He sighs. "Figures." Then, with one last look: "Take care of your hand. Don't ask—I saw you fiddling with the bandage in the car. If it gets infected, I'll come back and yell at you."

"I believe you."

And then he's gone.

My phone buzzes *again* almost the second the door clicks shut.

REIKA TSUKINO

> Hey, the apartment is telling me you're either not doing great or giving some serious weird vibes, or both. Want to talk?

I stare at the screen for a few seconds too long, then groan. So the apartment tattled and told her I was stomping around in a nasty mood this morning? Figures.

I guess there's no true privacy when your sublet is partially sentient.

MIA WILLIAMS

> Fine, I promise. Just needed a reset day.

I hit send before I can overthink it. It's a lie, but it's hardly my worst. I'm not ready for Reika's soft ferocity. Not when I just finished stitching myself together

Another quick shower helps me shake off the day. When I step out, I have the strangest sense of the apartment sighing, then *apologizing* to me, in the vaguest, most abstract sense.

It's trying to *help*.

The lights dim without me asking. Not enough to be scary—just enough to soften the corners, make me feel like someone's listening. The air shifts from frigid to a slow, warmer breeze laced with the faintest lavender. Reika's charmed essential oil blend to lower stress, I spotted it in the cabinet earlier.

Even the floorboards hush beneath my steps. The fridge quiets. The whole space holds its breath. When I shuffle back into the main space, I notice there's a plate on the counter that wasn't there before. A bowl of cheesy gnocchi—one of my emergency frozen meals—sits waiting for me, perfectly heated.

"Holy shit," I murmur. The apartment's never done *that* before. I guess it can sense just how bad I'm struggling.

I bring the gnocchi back to bed. Kiki hops up onto the bed and curls near my feet, her warm side pressed lightly against my ankle. She doesn't bother me. Just settles with a low purr, flicking her tail once, then going still.

It's not overwhelming. The apartment isn't demanding. It just... *tries*. Like it knows I'm unraveling and wants to make it better, even if it doesn't quite know how. And it makes me want to cry. Not because it's too much—but because it's so *kind*.

Kind is worse.

I never grew up with that kind of softness. My mom believed in schedules and discipline. When I broke, she called it weakness. After, she made me promise not to embarrass her again. Comfort wasn't in her vocabulary. Survival was.

So I don't know what to do with this—the lights dimming, the air warming, the space itself trying to take care of me. It feels foreign. Unsettling. Like the town decided to give me the mother I never had.

"I appreciate the effort," I tell it once I'm done eating. "But please don't. I'm fine."

The lights stay low. The warmth doesn't vanish.

But the room pulls back—just a little.

I take my Benadryl, curl under the blankets, and try to pretend the kindness never happened—and that I didn't want it at all.

Chapter Eighteen

Nate

I miss her.

I hate myself for it.

And I definitely, absolutely, should not be using company technology to visit her after hours again.

Dreamwalking is supposed to stay transactional. No attachments. No bias. Repeat visits break that: emotional entanglement, recognition, degradation.

I should've said all of this out loud when we made our bargain. I didn't. I told myself I was protecting her from the fine print; really, I was protecting the part of me that wanted an excuse to see her again.

We're not supposed to get noticed. If a dreamer starts seeing *you* instead of the fear—then you've already failed. Repeaters trigger auto-flags: recognition spikes, fear yields drop, and fixation wrecks metrics.

But Mia is different. Has been, from the start.

I met her before I ever touched her dreams. I knew her name, her laugh, the shape of her voice in a room. We've been off-script since the beginning. I see no reason to step back into line now. Not when every hour without her feels like rot spreading under my skin.

As I reach for the door to the nightmare chamber, a surge of worry stills my hand. I glance over my shoulder as if someone might peel from the shadows to reprimand me. I shouldn't be here.

But I need to see Mia again. I can't go to her door. I made myself the villain on purpose; showing up would only reopen the wound and break the one boundary that keeps her safe from me.

I grab the handle, open the door, and step in.

The nightmare chamber is dark, cavernous, silent. Just before four A.M., all assigned shifts done, the overnight techs on break.

And there's no one around to witness my misdeeds.

If anyone asks, I could call this post-exposure monitoring. But that would require a log, which I have no intention of doing.

My footsteps echo on the tile. Dream stalls stand in a long, eerie line of stainless steel before me, stretching on into the darkness. One dim fluorescent burns over the main station. I don't need it. But it reminds me I'm on borrowed time. Sooner or later, a tech will return from break.

I need to make this quick.

Punching in the right buttons, I dump myself into a stall. Obscura's dream tech spools up with a soft hum, and the gray space of human dreamland unfurls before me. Mia's presence shines like a beacon.

With little effort, I navigate toward it—the gray falls away—and slip into her dream.

I shouldn't be doing this. But I am. Again.

The dream representation of her apartment is the same—low lighting, sea salt and lavender, the hum of a window AC. Her bedroom door is partially ajar. Each time I visited before, when she knew I was coming, her slumber held a thread of hesitation; as I crossed the threshold, the whole dreamscape would thrum, shift into sharper alignment, tuning itself to my presence.

There's none of that now. Her dream is flat, stagnant. Recognition used to lift toward me. Tonight the whole room tilts away. It feels like the door's shut now—where before, she left it cracked, waiting.

Inside her room, I fold my nightmare form into a corner, lingering. She's sprawled out on her side, the covers down around her waist. I watch her chest rise and fall. The orange cat blinks at me, unimpressed, and sleeps.

I wait for Mia to stir as usual. I don't know what I'll say—maybe I just need to hear her voice, even if it's angry. I kicked her out of my apartment, out of my bed, after the intensity of our weekend together. It was the right choice. I regret it anyway.

If all she'll give me are cruel words hurled back the same way I did to her, I'll take it.

Minutes pass.

Then an hour. She doesn't wake. She's exhausted, sleeping deep.

Or so good at pretending I can't tell the difference.

Disappointment spills through me, cold and slow. I slip from the corner and pull myself out of the dream entirely, sick with it.

The gray collapses. Waking slams into my chest like a hand through my ribcage. Limbs heavy. Throat aching. I don't want to be back here.

Maybe I waited too late into the night, and if I'd come earlier, she might've woken. Maybe she was so deeply asleep because my rejection wore her out. Maybe—

"Alston."

My thoughts crash to a halt. Outside the stall stands Director Krell, shimmering in his pinstriped suit, and a tech I don't recognize, face pinched in apology.

I close the stall door behind me and go very still. Krell's face is impassive as ever. What does he know? How long has he been standing here holding the tech hostage, waiting for me to emerge?

"Shit," the tech blurts. "I didn't realize you were logged in. I would've flagged it—sorry—"

Krell lifts one gnarled gray hand; the tech falls silent. "Not to worry," he says, soft—comforting to the tech, threatening to me. "I'm sure Nathaniel has an excellent justification for his unauthorized, after-hours access."

Fuck me.

Excuses flit through my mind—none strong enough to withstand Krell.

Best to come clean and hope for leniency.

My silence has dragged on for too long.

Krell raises an eyebrow. "Nothing to say in your own defense?"

I shake my head. "No, sir. There's no excuse."

He tilts his head, faintly puzzled, then motions to the tech. "Pull his last—let's say—ten uses of the chamber."

The tech scrambles. For a long moment, I consider and discard fleeing. Finally, they hand Krell the tablet. The sleek black tech looks ridiculous in his inhuman fingers.

Krell hums appreciatively as he ponders the evidence. "Four flagged entries, all unauthorized, into a personal civilian dreamspace," he says, swiping through the data. "Likely more if we dig deeper. All in the last few weeks, same ID. Yields are...atypical." His rheumy gray eyes, so light as to be almost translucent, flit up to meet mine. "Not fear-spikes. Starting to look like a pattern. Have you got yourself a pet, Alston?"

I bristle. My form ripples—shadows ruffling like an angry bird tossing its feathers. Too late to hide it.

But Krell only laughs. It's brief—a dry, raspy chuckle that makes his usually stoic face dance with mirth—but the tension that follows is sharp enough to remind me this isn't a joke.

"Relax. Hardly the first time someone took a liking to a dreamer. That's why we have protocols, right?"

"Yes, sir," I grind out.

Krell drops his gaze to the tablet. The system anonymizes dreamers as numerical IDs. Obscura doesn't want the names; it wants fear—measured, trained, sold.

Repeat visits dull fear. Recognition contaminates the data. With Mia, the recognition is already there, which makes it worse. It means I'm not just breaking protocol, I'm contaminating the system with something it was never built to measure: attachment.

So there's no real danger in the idea of him identifying Mia, or knowing her name. He can't do anything to her. Her most valuable asset is her nightmares. The only danger here is me—and the fact that I don't seem willing to stop.

"If you wanted this one monitored," Krell says calmly, "you should've filed a watch order."

A watch order assigns a second pair of eyes: every contact logged, no solo entries. I didn't request one because I didn't want a chaperone between me and Mia, for the twisted deal we struck.

"I know, sir."

Krell sighs and pinches the bridge of his nose. It's impossible to tell how upset he is at any given moment, or how much trouble I'm in. I grit my teeth and wait.

"Four unauthorized entries, Alston. Protocol is protocol. I'll have to document this. A formal reprimand."

"What does that mean, sir?"

I know what it means. It's the step before ethics review. One more flag and they'll pull me off human work for a quarter.

But I need to hear him say it. Need to feel the weight of what I've done as a reminder to stop.

"It means keep your nose clean. Your numbers skyrocketed by Halloween, just like I asked—better than I've seen from you in years. That's the only reason I'm not dragging you into an ethics review right now. So technically, you're safe. For now. But let's just say the board's eyes are sharp this quarter. I'd hate for them to start seeing patterns." With a heavy sigh, he taps a few buttons on the tablet before handing it back to the tech. "I'm issuing you a temporary suspension of company dream feed access. Seventy-two hours, and your access stays dark until ethics clears my note. Slip up again and I escalate to the board, got it?"

Three days is mercy—and a leash. Enough time for me to prove I can behave. Or find another way.

"Yes, sir," I agree, nodding like a bobblehead. "Of course."

Relief trickles through me, cold and sharp. He could've done worse. And even this isn't the setback he thinks it is.

I don't need the chamber to find her. After multiple feeds, resonance lingers—an inaudible note my body remembers. If she's sleeping and I'm close, I can ride that note.

I can see her without her ever knowing.

Krell's reprimand is symbolic. I don't need the paycheck. But I can't stomach being ousted from the company my father built. Obscura is legacy. Pride. If I walk away, it's shame—not freedom—that follows me. So I stay. I work.

I pretend it matters.

If Krell thinks seventy-two hours keeps me out of trouble, he's forgotten what my kind does best: find the dark anyway.

Krell dismisses me and slinks off to his early morning haunt. I leave before the morning crew shuffles in.

I'm halfway home before I realize I have no idea what I'm going to do with myself.

Seventy-two hours: no chamber, no feeds. Nothing to keep me from spiraling into the dark nothing that always nips my heels.

But all I can think about is how I'd rather spend those hours in Mia's orbit—hearing her laugh, watching her talk to Molly, even just sitting across the room in silence as she cleans my already-clean apartment.

And I *can't*. Because I ruined it, even if for good reason. Because I pushed her away.

The ache that simmers in my chest has nothing to do with hunger or magic. It's raw. More human. A gnawing grief I don't know how to name.

I don't remember deciding to go to Beck's. I just look up, and I'm there—outside his building, regret thick on my tongue.

Maybe I need advice. Maybe I just need someone who knew me before I went off the deep end with a human I should've left alone in the first place.

I take the elevator to the third floor and knock once. The door opens before I can second-guess it, revealing Beck in an elaborate black silk dressing gown, lit cigarette in hand, golden mullet damp and curling around his ears.

Beck blinks twice, then pulls a face. "This is not quite the sunrise booty call I was expecting."

"Sorry to disappoint," I say, my voice hoarse. "Can I come in?"

He studies me, then steps aside. "Yeah. Sure. You look like hell."

Inside, Beck's apartment is lived-in but intentional—creative clutter arranged with care. Warm wood floors peek out between scattered guitar cables and stacks of old film magazines. A soft golden light glows from mismatched floor lamps, and the air smells faintly of cigarette smoke and coffee. The walls are lined with floating shelves holding camera lenses, vinyl records, and a few cracked mugs filled with pencils. A battered couch with a colorful knit throw faces a wall of speakers and vintage tech. It's cozy, a little chaotic, and unmistakably his.

"Heads up, by the way," he says, shutting the door. "I'm getting shipped out to the astral labs in California for an oversight review for a few weeks. Try not to do anything too stupid while I'm gone."

"No promises," I mutter, and drop onto the couch as if my bones have all vanished.

Beck drops into a chair opposite. "I'm assuming there's a reason you're wandering the city in your shadow form right as all the humans are on their way to work? You trying to give everyone a heart attack?"

Startled, I raise a hand in front of my face. Sure enough, all I see are shadows. I didn't even realize.

"Fuck," I mutter, and scrub a hand down my face. When I lift it again, it's pale white, all human skin.

Beck exhales a plume of smoke toward the ceiling. "Rough night, huh?"

"Something like that," I say.

"Let me guess." He ticks off on his fingers. "You did something emotionally reckless. You're pretending you didn't. Now you want me to tell you you're not a complete idiot."

"That obvious?"

Beck shrugs. "You only show up like this when you're spiraling or heartbroken. Sometimes both."

I huff a bitter laugh and start picking at a hole in the knit throw blanket. "I got suspended. Seventy-two hours. Dream chamber access revoked. Reprimand filed."

That gets his attention. "Damn." His brows lift. "What'd you do, spit in Krell's morning Earl Grey?"

I hesitate, watching him lean forward, balancing his cigarette on the rim of a chipped ashtray.

Beck sees it, of course. He's always seen too much. "Was it her? The cute maid you were bitching about before?"

"I wasn't *bitching*—" His look shuts me up. I sigh. "I checked in on her. After hours. Again."

"Again?" he questions.

He doesn't have the full context—we haven't talked since we went for drinks after I met Mia. So I tell him in fits and starts, enduring his smug grin. When I finish, he lets out a low whistle.

"Nathaniel, that's—"

"I know," I cut in. "I know the rules. I know it was stupid."

We sit in silence for a moment, the kind that's ripe with things left unsaid. Finally, I mutter, "I don't even know why I'm here."

"You're here," Beck says simply, "because you don't know where else to go. And because you knew I wouldn't ask you to explain it all right away."

I don't respond. He doesn't press.

Instead, Beck stands and moves to the kitchen. A few seconds later, the whirr of an appliance kicks on. "You want coffee or tea? Or either with booze?"

"Whatever's stronger."

He snorts. "Coffee with liquor it is."

I let my head fall back against the couch, stare at the ceiling like it might offer answers. It doesn't.

In the kitchen, Beck moves with easy familiarity—cups clinking, liquor sloshing. It should comfort me. It *almost* does.

But it's not enough to soothe the self-inflicted hole in my chest.

I hunted terror for centuries and never minded being unseen. Now the one person I *want* to see me chooses sleep.

I grew used to visiting her dreams and feeling her consciousness rise to meet me, eager and waiting. I didn't imagine what it would feel like for her to shut me out. She didn't wake. Didn't look at me. I don't know what scares me more—that she never sensed me...or that she did, and stayed asleep anyway.

Beck returns with two mismatched mugs and hands me one. I accept it wordlessly, the warmth bleeding into my palms. It smells like coffee with a splash of gasoline poured in as a treat.

"You did what you thought was right," he says, settling into his chair once more.

I nod, slow. "Yeah. I just don't know if it was worth it."

Beck doesn't answer. Just raises his mug in a lazy toast.

"To consequences," he says.

I lift mine, too. "To consequences."

Our mugs clink.

I sip at the bitter warmth. And I pretend it fills the space she left behind.

Chapter Nineteen

Mia

Mercurial//"If you feel distant from your purpose, check your hydration, your rising sign, and your ability to say no."

"Are you sure you want to do this?"

I meet Tulgan's concerned gaze in the rearview mirror. We're idling at the curb outside Nate's apartment in the Spires.

"I have to," I reply. "I already canceled on him once. The app doesn't like you to cancel on repeat clients. It's not good for your review score."

Tulgan rolls his eyes. "Don't tell them I said this, but *fuck* the app, Mia. Fuck your review score. Is this good for *you*? Do you really see any positive in forcing yourself to see this guy again?"

He has a point. Nate made it clear that I was nothing more to him than the maid who cleaned his apartment, an easy way to fill his work quota to keep from getting into trouble, and a convenient outlet for his heat. We're not dating. We're not friends. I could stop accepting his shifts and focus on my other clients.

But I don't want to. His tips are great, sure, but it's more than that. After wallowing for a few days, something in me firmed up and snapped back into place.

Nate is just a man—a shadowed nightmare of one at times, but still just a man.

And I refuse to let any man break me the way Mercurial broke me.

Glancing down, I clench my injured hand around the bandage. If I move it the right way, the cut on my palm still stings, and the pain helps ground me against the cowardice welling up in my core.

"You're right, there is no positive," I agree. "But it's a pride thing, Tulgan. I need to walk in there with my head up, not let him win."

An exasperated sigh is Tulgan's only response.

I head inside.

As soon as I let myself in via the app, Molly's scuttle of paws greets me, and moments later she rushes at me, all three heads whining and snorting in excitement. It's a major mood-booster, for sure. At least Nate's *dog* likes me.

"Hi, Molly!" I crouch, pat and rub each head, endure the face-licks.

When she's greeted me sufficiently, she sits back on her haunches, and I straighten up, smiling despite myself. At first, I think Nate isn't here at all. The TV is on in the living room, tuned to *The Real Housewives of Atlanta,* but I think that's just for Molly's sake. Then I hear the faint rumble of his voice from down the hall.

I step quietly in that direction and strain my ears. His bedroom door is cracked; a peek reveals him seated on the floor, back to the bed, laptop open on a video call.

He speaks again, his voice low and tired. "...look, I shouldn't have gone in again. I know that. But it didn't feel right just leaving her like that." A pause. "Can we just get back to the expense report, please?"

Her?

Wait. *Me?*

My stomach drops. Is he in trouble because of *me?*

I'm not prepared to handle that right now. Regretting my own curiosity, I back away quietly, fetch my cleaning supplies, and get to work. Earbuds in, feelings off.

If Nate wants to talk, he will. Otherwise I'll do my job—find things to clean in his stupidly immaculate apartment.

I clean snack wrappers off the coffee table and dog hair off the remote, and re-fluff the couch pillows. He still hasn't fixed the hole in the back where Molly tried to eat through.

In the kitchen, I wipe everything down, clean the fridge, which is damn near bare as usual—just a few Monster energy drinks, a container of Thai takeout noodles of indeterminate age, and a half-full carton of kiwis.

When I straighten up and close the door, Nate's standing right behind it.

My heart leaps into my throat and I shout. I go to tap my earbud to stop the music—currently, Hoobastank's "The Reason"—but instead I smack the stupid thing right out of my ear, and it goes skittering across the floor.

"Sorry," he mumbles, bending to retrieve it. As usual, he's wearing black sweatpants, though the pristine white hoodie on his top half is a new development. His voice is quiet, and it hits like a pulled thread unraveling everything I just stitched back together. "Didn't mean to scare you."

I force levity into my voice. "No worries!"

God, I don't even want to look at him. I want to punch him in the face. Instead I hold out a hand for the earbud, and he moves to return it to me, then—

"What happened to your hand?" he asks, scrutinizing the bandage. Something pulls taut in his tone that makes me hesitate.

"Oh. I, um—"

Before I can actually answer, he closes his hand around my injured one and pulls it closer—pulling *me* closer with it. I almost crash into his chest, and my pulse takes off into a gallop. Nate's face contorts into a deep frown. His concern is harder to face than his cruelty was.

"Who did this to you?"

"No one! Me. I did it to myself." He looks like he might unwrap it, so I gently pull back, and he lets me go. "On accident. Sliced it open on a bit of sharp tile during a cleaning shift."

"Deep cuts on palms can get filthy fast," he says, voice going clinical. "High infection risk. Have you had any redness? Fever? Streaking?"

What is it with everyone's obsession over my hand like I'm about to drop dead?

"It's *fine,*" I snap.

Nate blinks, swallows. He seems to finally realize how close he pulled me—then drops the earbud into my other hand and steps back.

"I'm sure you've got it handled," he says with a short nod.

My head is spinning. My damn heartbeat feels like it's doing cartwheels. The words are on the tip of my tongue—*why do you even care?* But I choke them back. And I take another step back, putting even more space between us.

For a moment, the only sound is the faint murmur of his television. I'm pretty much already done, but he doesn't need to know that. And I don't know why I suddenly don't want to leave, when less than an hour ago I didn't even want to step foot inside.

"Anyway." I clear my throat. "I'm just about done. Just need to sweep."

Nate studies me for a long moment.

There's something strange about the way he's looking at me. His gaze is sad. Guarded. A little too intense. Like he's got a mouth full of things to say that he just can't bring himself to let loose. It's uncomfortable, and I don't know what to make of it, how to reconcile *this* Nate with the cold and cruel one who kicked me out the other day.

An inhale. "Mia—"

Whatever it is, I'm suddenly sure I don't want to hear it.

"Are you in trouble?" I interrupt. "Wasn't trying to eavesdrop, but I heard your work call."

The glimpse of openness on his face shutters, but slowly. A heavy door falling shut in slow motion.

He gives another sharp nod. "Somewhat. I—I've been suspended from dream chamber usage. Temporarily. It's a disciplinary measure for unauthorized usage. Since there's little else for me to do, I've just been catching up on administrative tasks from home."

Unauthorized usage. I think back to what he said earlier. *It didn't feel right just leaving her like that.* He told me before he wasn't supposed to revisit the same dreamer. Have we been skirting his workplace's rules this entire time?

"But you haven't been in my dreams recently," I ramble, thinking aloud. "Not for days. Not since—" I cut myself off with a sudden flinch. Nate winces. So he *is* at least aware of how much he hurt me. "How could you be in trouble for something that happened days ago?"

Nate's silence stretches on for too long, and that's when it hits me. All of those nights he visited me as part of our strange little bargain *did* help him meet his quota. But that doesn't seem like what got him in trouble. No, I think actually, he got suspended for something that happened more recently, which means—

"I tried to visit your dream two nights ago," he admits in a small, quiet voice.

A hot, confusing flare hits—anger first. I didn't want him in my dreams, not after what he said to me. But he went anyway. And yet underneath it, the traitor part of me warms. He came back. He wanted to.

I'm both furious and flattered at once.

"You didn't wake up," he adds. "Too deeply asleep. So I left." A pause. "I shouldn't have gone in the first place."

I force my voice to stay casual. "No, you shouldn't have."

It doesn't make any sense. He had every reason to leave me alone after Halloween. Instead, he kept poking around at my dreams.

"What the hell are we doing, Nate?" I snap. The words pour from me like vomit, unruly and uncontrollable. "You told me this was just about meeting a quota, and I believed you. You looked me in the eye and said you didn't want to exploit me—and then you *did*. When it was convenient. When it made your job easier. And then when all was said and done, you tossed me out like garbage."

He flinches. A real, visible flinch, my words striking something vital.

"I didn't mean—" he starts, but I cut him off with a laugh that comes out sharp and brittle.

"No? You didn't mean to lie? Or you didn't mean to *mean* it? Because those are different things, Nate. And I'm honestly not sure which is worse."

His expression crumples. The hollow behind his eyes deepens.

"I lied," he says finally, voice raw. "It wasn't just about quota. And I shouldn't have been in your dreams again if you didn't want me there."

The words hit harder than I expect, making me recoil in confusion. In *want*. In foolish, foolish hope. My breath hitches, and I hate that part of me still wants this to mean something.

"There is something real between us," he adds, quieter now. "I don't know what to call it. But it's real. And that's the problem."

I blink. "How is that a *problem*?"

"Because I'm not supposed to *feel* anything for you, Mia." His voice rises, sharp with frustration. But underneath it, I hear the tremor. "Because attachment makes me stay too long, and staying too long is where people get hurt! My job depends on detachment. On turning emotion into a transaction. You're supposed to be a client, a dreamer—your feelings, your fears, even your fucking *longing*—those are supposed to be the product. But I'm not detached. I'm not neutral. I'm *wrecked*. And every time I look at you, I feel like I'm losing control of the only thing keeping me upright."

He exhales, ragged, like the words cost him.

And I just stand there, stunned.

My brain fumbles for something to latch onto—anger, maybe, or closure. But all I feel is the echo of what he said. *Wrecked*. He's wrecked. Over *me*.

I should say something. I should scream at him or shove him or laugh in his face. But instead, I'm frozen in this bizarre limbo between tenderness and disbelief.

"You..." My throat tightens. "You never said anything."

"I couldn't." His voice is low now. "Because if I did, I'd want to mean it." A pause. "And because it's much safer for you to believe I don't want you around."

I blink. The words settle over me like ash—weightless at first, then heavy enough to smother. I don't know what I expected. An apology? A reason? Some convenient villain for me to pin all this confusion on?

But not this. Not *him*, cracking open like that. Not the honesty that feels like it took too long to arrive.

And now that it's here, I don't know what to do with it.

"You really think this is just about feelings?" I ask, quieter now. "Like the problem is just that you *have them*?"

His gaze flickers—maybe to the bandage on my hand, maybe to my mouth.

My voice trembles, but I force the words out anyway. "You didn't just push me away, Nate. You made me feel disposable. Like I was nothing. And I've spent the last few days trying to scrub that feeling out of my skin. Now you're telling me I *meant* something, but it can't matter because your job is built on pretending people *don't* matter?" I shake my head. "That's not fair. Not to me. And not to you either."

I swore after Mercurial I'd never let anyone make me feel disposable again. And yet here I am, fighting for scraps of honesty from someone who keeps shutting me out.

His breath catches, and for a second, I think he might say something. But he just stands there, hands clenched at his sides, jaw taut.

I wish I could hate him. It'd be easier.

But all I can feel is this aching, exhausted kind of sadness. Like we're both stuck in something bigger than us, and neither of us knows how to stop the slow-motion collision that's already in progress.

So I do the only thing I can think to do.

I whisper, "Tell me the truth. If none of this mattered—if your job didn't exist, didn't depend on pretending—I mean really, *honestly*—would you want this? Would you want *me*?"

It's...hopelessly vulnerable. I hate myself for asking.

Nate doesn't answer right away.

Then he says, barely above a whisper, "Of course I would."

My heart jolts. The truth in those four words is enough to knock the breath from my lungs. My mouth parts on instinct, ready to ask what that means, to reach for something that finally feels solid—only for him to add, almost immediately:

"But it doesn't matter. We—We can't. I won't do that to you."

"Do *what?*"

He flinches. Not dramatically. But I feel it like a slap.

"You don't know what I've done, Mia," he says at last, voice hoarse. "What happens when I don't stop. I can't risk that again. Keeping my distance from you is the only thing I can still pretend is the right call."

God, I am so sick of this. This constant back and forth, vulnerability alternating with gates slamming shut. I feel like I'm a piece of taffy stuck on the pull machine.

"Nate, that's not an answer. What aren't you telling me?"

He doesn't reply. He looks haunted, almost, by a nightmare of his own. Something I can't see and he can't—or *won't* share. He just pins me with a look—piercing and endlessly sad.

When he finally speaks, his voice is sanded down, brittle with restraint. "I won't lie to you again, Mia. There is something real here. But that doesn't mean we get to have it." His gaze drops. My whole body wants to argue. But my courage is stuck behind the lump in my throat. "You think I hurt you before? That was nothing."

I wait. Hope. Ache. But nothing else comes.

So he won't lie...but he also won't tell me what's actually, *really* holding him back.

"So that's it?" I ask. "Back to maid and client?" My laugh comes out brittle. "Guess I should've known better than to think I was anything else to you."

First Mercurial. Then Selene. Now Nate. I keep mistaking attention for something I can trust.

His spine straightens, inch by inch, like reassembling armor, and he nods once. "I'm sorry. I—I don't want you to get hurt."

"Maybe I should make it official and drop you from my client list, save us both the performance."

"No," he says quickly. "If you cancel me as a client, it doesn't just hurt me. It tanks your reviews, your income. You don't deserve that on top of everything else. So we'll keep things professional. Cleaner and client. Nothing more."

The words land like the tumblers inside of a lock, sealing something shut. Sealing *me* out.

Right. This is the part where they decide you're too much. Too complicated. Too dangerous to care about.

I scoff. "Wow. That's rich. You kick me out of your bed and now suddenly you're worried about my review score? Don't pretend this is about my livelihood, Nate. I'm not stupid—you just don't want to let go. And instead of admitting that, you're dressing it up as concern."

I don't wait for a reply. I gather my things, tossing supplies back into their cabinet beneath the sink. My movements are stiff, mechanical. It's the only way I know how to keep myself from shaking.

He doesn't stop me. Of *course* he doesn't.

Fucking coward.

By the time I reach the door, my throat's tight, eyes hot, and my heart feels like it's folding in on itself. But I don't cry. Not here. Not in front of him.

This is what happens when I think I'm more than just *useful*.

He says he's protecting me. Selene said she was protecting herself. Different excuses, same result: I get discarded. I'm only worth something until I'm inconvenient, until I bruise.

And isn't that exactly how Nate's stupid job works, too? Fear is all Obscura measures. All they want. Anything else—care, trust, resilience—is disposable. Maybe that's what I'm most sick of. Being told the best parts of me don't count for anything.

"Fine," I say, hand on the knob. "Cleaner and client. Nothing more." I twist the handle. "See you at my next shift, boss."

And then I leave without looking back.

Chapter Twenty

Mia

MERCURIAL//"Not everyone is ready for the unfiltered version of your success. Unsubscribe from guilt, babe."

For a few days, I just float.

I turn my brain off, sinking far enough inside myself that nothing can reach me. If I just go deep enough, maybe I'll avoid the damage. Avoid everything I'm feeling. Metaphorically, I stick myself at the bottom of the ocean.

And down here, nothing can touch me.

I go through the motions, projecting the illusion of keeping my shit together.

I don't cry. I don't think about Nate.

Somehow, exactly like he asked, we slide back into a cold facsimile of cleaner and client.

When I show up for shifts, he's not home, or makes himself scarce. I clean as quickly as I can without cutting corners and all but flee the space. Part of me wants to drop him as a client, but I haven't. Instead, I focus hard on my *other* clients—politely chatting them up, making myself endearing and indispensable, playing whatever social game I have to to convince them to keep selecting me via the app.

For the better part of a week, I carry on like this—smiling, cleaning, making small talk, and pretending I'm not dead inside. There's one moment at Nate's where he comes home, seems like he wants to speak—then doesn't. I don't press, and the moment passes.

I do such a great job convincing myself everything is okay, that I'm fine, that even *I* almost believe it. Until something reminds me I'm not.

So when the call from Imani comes, it damn near tosses the earth out from under me.

It's just after 7pm, and Tulgan has just dropped me off at home. My phone rings as I step inside. I roll my eyes, assuming it's Reika, that the apartment tattled again. I'm not in the mood to chat—I want junk food, reality TV, a hot shower, and a fat dose of Benadryl to knock me right into sleep.

But when I glance at the screen, it's not Reika.

It's Imani.

Frowning, confused more than anything, I pick up.

"Hello?"

"Hey, Mia." Imani's clipped, businesslike tone sounds warmer, rounder. In the background, fine silverware clinks over a low murmur of conversation. "It's last minute, but I'd like to discuss something. Meet me at Donatello's? For old time's sake?"

As if on cue, my stomach growls. Fucking traitor. I *love* Donatello's. And honestly, as suspicious as I am of Imani's out of the blue call, as soon as the image of the swanky, dimly-lit Italian restaurant and their endless garlic knots swims into my mind, I'm sold. I haven't eaten yet. It's not far away.

I hesitate for only a moment, then decide, *fuck it*. Garlic knots win.

"Sure," I tell her. "I'll be there in fifteen."

After a quick change of clothes, I head out. From Reika's place, Donatello's is only a few minutes' walk. When I used to come here with the Mercurial crew, it felt so far away, and Selene would inevitably make an awful joke about slumming it. Now I live minutes away, and feel more comfortable here than I do in the glimmering opulence of the Spires on the other side of town.

Funny how things have changed.

At the restaurant, the hostess shows me to an intimate booth in the far back corner. Imani's deep maroon lips widen into an easy grin as I approach.

"You made it," she gushes, and rises to grip my upper arms in a quick hug.

"Yep. Can't turn down Donatello's," I respond, and she laughs.

Imani, as usual, looks runway-ready—sleeveless silk blouse the color of a ballet slipper, and grey pinstriped pants cropped just above her slender brown ankles. And this is *casual* for her. I feel like a sloppy bum in my dark wash jean shorts and cat meme t-shirt.

She slides a menu my way. "Order whatever you want. My treat."

I blink at her. "What?"

"Don't look at me like that. I'm serious!"

It takes all of my self control not to make a face. Despite Imani's immense generational wealth, she was only generous with the business, stingy everywhere else. She'd pull five-figure sums of last-minute seed funding from her own coffers, but at the same time refuse to take turns paying for group meals, and if she did pay, she'd insist we all Venmo her the exact amounts from our individual orders.

So her offering to pay is...new. Suspicious. But I made a promise to myself to hear her out.

Shrugging, I give in. "Okay. Sure."

Moments later, a bottle of red wine is delivered to the table, along with a basket of the famous garlic knots. My mouth waters. I am actually mere seconds from drooling onto the thick white fabric of the tablecloth. I give the waiter my entree order—chicken parmigiana. And then we dig in, Imani by placing a garlic knot delicately on her salad plate and cutting it into pieces like a steak, me by ripping the hunks of steaming dough apart with my bare hands like a drunken raccoon at a trash banquet.

"So," I ask, moments later with my mouth full of garlic knot, "Why exactly did you summon me here?"

She rolls her eyes, but it's playful, not hostile. "It was hardly a summons. A summons would've come from my email."

"Imani."

At my look, she sighs, sits back, smooths her napkin. She's stalling. My guard slams up.

"Okay, fine. I'll just spit it out." She blows out a slow breath. "I want you back, Mia. *We* want you back. If you're willing."

I freeze mid-chew. "Excuse me?"

Imani seizes another garlic knot and pours intense focus into cutting it into pieces. "I know the circumstances surrounding your departure weren't...great. But we always told you the door was open if you ever wanted to return, and this is me telling you not only is the door open, but there's an invitation. It doesn't even have to be finance. It could be whatever you want. I'll make it work—you write the job description."

Slowly, I resume chewing, thinking this through.

I made one mistake on a quarterly forecast—a decimal in the wrong place that Selene spun into a near-crisis in front of the board. Instead of correcting the record, she painted me as reckless, irresponsible, unstable. And Imani and the others? They stayed silent. Not because they believed her, but because it was easier to let me take the hit than to pick a fight with Selene when she had the investors eating out of her hand.

I wasn't fired, not technically. But the silence and cold-shouldering afterward was loud enough that quitting felt like the only choice.

So why has Imani come crawling back now? What changed?

I temper my tone and ask, "Why? I'm nothing special. You need another CFO? Just go pluck one right up from the many other perfectly-qualified folks out there."

Imani nods. As she brings tiny bites of garlic knot to her mouth, I catch it—the slightest of wobbles in her wrist. I file it away.

"You're right. We should have no trouble filling the role." Her eyes flick up to mine. "But none of the new people we've hired since you left have been a good culture fit."

"None of them? So, multiple?"

"Three."

Fuck. That's nearly one for each month I've been gone. What the hell have they been doing to those poor new hires? I haven't been following industry news since I left. I'm so out of the loop.

"That doesn't make any sense," I say bluntly, sipping wine. "Mercurial's on every top-ten list of companies to watch. You've burned through three new hires since I left and none have worked out? Sounds like the problem is you guys, not them."

The only sign of a crack in Imani's armor is a slight tightening of her lips. She places her fork and knife down, takes a long, tidy sip of wine.

"You're right," she admits. I almost fall out of my chair. "We *are* the problem. Since you left, Selene's toxicity has only gotten worse. All of us are keeping our distance from her. Nothing's good enough, even in the C-suite." Imani's chin wobbles, just briefly, so fast I'm not sure I even really see it. "I put together this whole campaign proposal for Scorpio Season—really cool stuff, transform and rebirth your finances or whatever—and she said it was 'a hot pile of duck shit'."

I choke back a laugh. The words are funny, but nothing else is—not Imani's struggle, or Selene's reign of terror, or the knowledge of how many other Mercurial employees are now likely suffering the way I did. But I don't know what she wants me to say.

"Immy," I start, and the sudden slip of the old nickname has her watery eyes glued to mine. "Look, I'm really sorry to hear that. Selene is a bitch—she was always a bitch, even when we were dating! And I hate that she's treating you all like this. But how does me coming back fix any of that?"

Sighing, Imani grabs another garlic knot—and eats it with her hands. "It won't. But it might *help*. She was always so threatened by you—personally, professionally. I know it's stupid, but I thought somehow you coming back might snap her back into reality, make her fall back in line."

"Why not just fire her? Ask her to leave? She's a CEO, not a military dictator."

"Too messy," Imani says, shaking her head. "She's like a cancer. Cut her out too quickly and the company might not survive." She shudders. "I'd just try to make things uncomfortable enough to force her out, but we're all already so miserable, I don't think she'd even notice."

A sudden fierce and defiant bitterness surges in me at that. *Force her out.*

"You mean, like you all did with me?"

To her credit, Imani doesn't look away. She holds my gaze, and in hers I see all the pain she's hiding, the uncertainty and discomfort of even bringing me here to ask me this. I see the desperation that left her with no choice.

And I want nothing to do with it.

"Yes," she says finally, softly. "Not my proudest moment, for sure. Any one of us absolutely could've stepped in, contradicted Selene, but we didn't. I was scared—of her, and of crossing her in front of investors. She had them charmed. If I pushed back, I'd risk our funding—and having my head on the chopping block next. I never wanted you to leave. It's not an excuse—but I need you to know that I'm sorry about the way things panned out."

For a second, I almost laugh. Sorry doesn't erase the silence, the nights I went home shaking with fury because no one said a word while Selene shredded me alive. But if I'm being fair...Imani wasn't always silent.

One meeting sticks with me. Selene was in rare form, ripping my quarterly forecast apart in front of the entire team, circling another misplaced decimal like it was proof I should be exiled from finance forever. My stomach was in my shoes, and I could already imagine the investors' disappointment on the horizon.

Then Imani spoke up. Just one line, delivered so breezy it sounded like an afterthought: "Pretty sure Mia's numbers line up with the data I pulled last week."

Selene ignored her, of course—steamrolled right over that comment—but Imani shot me a quick look under the table. A tiny smirk: *we both know she's full of shit.* It wasn't enough to save me, but for that split second, I felt like I wasn't standing totally alone in the crosshairs.

That smirk stayed with me. Proof that Imani cared, just a little—even if she wasn't ready to speak up any louder.

An apology from her was about the *last* thing I expected walking in here. It stuns me into silence. Our entrees arrive—steaming, pristine plates of seafood linguine and chicken parmigiana—and it provides a much-needed pause on my rapidly spiraling emotions.

Truthfully, I tell her, "I don't know how to respond to that."

"You don't have to. Just think about it. Eat. I need a few moments, too, or I'm going to lose my shit right here."

We eat, each taking the mental space we need. My chicken is perfect, the breading on the outside crusty and flavorful, the inside moist. It's heaven. I've been living off microwave food for so long I forgot what a real meal tasted like. And as I fill my stomach, some of my anxiety about coming here begins to settle. I sort back through Imani's words, looking for hidden meanings and agendas. And find none.

Imani and the other founders of Mercurial were awful to me, once Selene decided she wanted me out. Of course they would look to a familiar face to save them from a sinking ship. And I won't lie, her offer is tempting. A regular, stable salary with retirement and health benefits? Another fancy title? The option to get my own place again, furnish it how I like, instead of relying on Reika's kindness and paying her dirt-cheap sublet rent?

The possibility of never having to torture myself by cleaning Nate's apartment again, not if I don't want to?

It's...tantalizing. All those possibilities stretch out before me in a winding road, glittering the way the sun sometimes makes the ocean sparkle at the right angle.

I could have it all. Everything I had before, and more. I thought that's what I wanted.

It should be a victory. So why does it feel like a trap?

Because the truth is messy: I don't have a five-year plan. Finance used to be my everything because it was so plan-oriented—measurable, ordered. Now it hurts to think about. I want the security it promises, sure, but not the people or the bullshit that would come with it. Sometimes I imagine a version of a finance job where I set the rules, where I don't get eaten alive by power plays; sometimes I imagine something completely different—consulting, or a tiny bookkeeping business for local artists.

Most mornings I can't hold anything that big in my head.

So I hold onto smaller things instead: a cat I'm allergic to in an apartment that isn't mine. Greasy hot dogs with a friend who keeps me honest. And old songs that pull me back to a time before my days were just an unending slog of people needing things from me. Stability, not glory.

It's not a career plan, but it's a shape of a life I can picture when everything else feels foggy.

I finish my food. Imani has made a careful dent in hers, but I'm a goblin, and my plate's been annihilated. As I reach for another garlic knot, I glance around, soaking in the atmosphere.

The Mercurial crew and I had countless business lunches here. Garlic knots at one end of the table, Selene at the other, holding court like she owned the place while the rest of us nodded along. Once, after she left early to charm an investor, Imani leaned across the table and whispered that she wished Selene would choke on a breadstick. We laughed so hard the waiter asked us to quiet down. Funny how that camaraderie only ever surfaced when Selene wasn't around.

It's a fitting place for Imani to ask me to return. She knows it, too. When I return my attention to the table, she's watching me.

"What do you think?" she asks, far too casually.

The words are on the tip of my tongue. Practical. Automatic. Expected. But in the split second before I agree, it hits me, my inner voice screaming suddenly around a corner about impending danger—this emotional warfare is the same sort of thing Nate has put me through. Pulling me in only to shove me out again. Leaving me dangling, half-wanted and half-forgotten, like that's all I'm good for.

It's a slow erosion, and it's worn me down until I've forgotten what it even feels like to be whole.

I bared my soul to him, took a leap of faith, and it still wasn't enough. He's still too scared of *something* he won't tell me to take a stab at making this real. Just like Imani is too scared of burning everything down and trying to build something new from the ashes of what remained.

If I go back there, I'll just be subjecting myself to this treatment again. I'll be Selene's punching bag as much as I am the plug in the sinking ship.

If I keep making myself available to Nate, I'll just be torturing myself.

So really, I should just cut ties. With all of it.

I swallow, open my mouth again. Imani looks like she's bracing for impact, which tells me just how desperate she truly is. But it doesn't change my decision.

"I appreciate the offer, I really do," I tell her. "But I can't."

And Imani Brooks—the most uptight FinTech startup girlie I know—dissolves into quiet tears.

I stick around long enough to make sure she's all right, comfort her a little bit. Somehow, without me noticing, she polished off nearly the entire bottle of wine herself, so she's a little bit drunk. I let her lean on me all the way outside, and hold her up while her car service comes to collect her.

As her driver walks up and steers her gently into the backseat, Imani looks back at me with wide, watery eyes, blinking placidly like a deer. She gives me one short nod.

"Good for you," she says, before turning and vomiting into the backseat.

Her driver curses, slams the door, and drives away.

Aimlessly, I start walking.

I should be feeling better—bigger, stronger, all of that. Proud, and on top of the world that I turned down the offer that was formerly everything I ever wanted, right up until I realized what it would actually mean. But something else is needling me, and it keeps festering, poking at my consciousness, even as I wander onto the nearest public access path for the beach.

It feels wrong to send a quasi-breakup text while on the beach, but I can't avoid it. I'm done being the collateral damage in someone else's emotional war.

I won't survive that again.

I pull out my phone, navigate to my messages with Nate, and type out a goodbye.

MIA WILLIAMS:

> *I can't keep doing this to myself. I'm sorry. I like you too much to suffer through this miserable in-between shit you're insisting on. You won't be seeing me again.*

I expect sending it to hurt. And it does, just a little. But mostly I just feel a swell of bitter clarity crashing over me like waves along the shore. I don't check for a response. I'm not expecting one. I'll delete him from my client roster later.

I walk the shoreline as the sun sets, until the light's gone.

Finally, only when the darkness wraps around me, thick and salt-heavy, do I tap on my phone's flashlight, pick my way back up the path, and start the walk home.

Chapter Twenty-One

Nate

Everything is under control.

That's the lie I whisper to myself every morning as I dive into work, hoping it can drown the rest out.

I churn through assignments. Hit and exceed all my targets. Nod and do whatever I'm told like a model employee. Since coming back from suspension, I've filled every inch of free time with work. I've posted my best numbers in months—premium terror, immaculate harvests. Krell's practically salivating.

Turns out heartbreak, however self-induced, is fantastic for productivity.

I tell myself if I stay productive, maybe I won't notice the part of me that misses Mia. That's still reaching for her, and yearns toward her dreams each night when I know she's asleep.

It mostly works.

Krell compliments me every few days on my "return to form." He doesn't realize I'm not back—I'm gone. Buried so deep in forced routine I can almost pretend there was never anything else but this, working and resting and doing it all over again.

Almost.

Some indeterminate day later, I stumble from the nightmare chamber to take my lunch break. Flush from back-to-back feeds, my limbs buzz and tingle, and my shadows ripple off me in frantic bursts like one of those flailing inflatable dancers on street corners.

The last time I felt anything like this after a session in the chamber was with Mia. But that can't happen again. And even though the flush of power I feel now is the same, it's flat—just buzzes through me without filling me up.

But it's all I have, so I learn to stomach it.

I shut the stall door, roll my shoulders to dispel some of the tension, and let my shadow form melt back beneath my human glamour. It's effortless, with this much power in me.

The day-shift tech blinks as I emerge.

"You—uh—" He checks his tablet. "You've been in-chamber since 2am?"

The clock on the far wall tells me it's just past seven in the evening. "Correct."

The tech's mouth flops open. "Wow. Impressive. You good, bro?"

I nod. "Fine. Could you please verify that each dream I visited was logged correctly?"

"Of course." He taps rapidly around on his tablet, nodding, his tongue sticking out from his lips in concentration. "Yeah, I'm confirming fourteen separate dream visits, each with an average harvest of 87 fear units."

"Excellent, thank you—"

The sound of loud, slow, and obnoxious clapping echoes through the room. Director Krell himself glides over from another station in the corner as Kelly, our resident clown-faced revenant—full greasepaint, rictus grin, red wig and all— ducks her head and hurries from the room in tears.

"Alston. Did I hear that right?" A glance at the tech for confirmation, and he returns his beady gaze to me with something resembling a father's pride.

"Yes, sir, you did."

Krell beams. It's an eerie expression on him, to say the least. His smile is all teeth and rot, crooked like a row of gravestones in a swamp.

He claps a hand on my shoulder. "You're on a roll, kid. Who knew all it would take to get you back on track was a temporary suspension?"

I don't have the heart to tell him it wasn't the suspension or the threat of job loss that improved my metrics recently—it was pure desperation to avoid thinking of a hazel-eyed human girl. Luckily, he seems to be talking to himself more than to me.

"Listen, I've got a proposition for you. Walk with me down to the cafeteria and let's talk it out over food."

Before I can think of a polite protest, he's already set off toward the hallway, leaving me no choice but to follow. With a quick thank-you to the tech, I trail after Krell. It's a short walk from the chamber room to the main elevator for this floor.

As the doors close behind us, my very unhelpful mind conjures up the image of Mia pinned against the wall in my apartment's elevator, her legs around my waist, whimpering into my ear.

I shake the memory off. Try to pretend it wasn't the last time I felt alive.

Besides, it's not like she'd ever allow me that close to her again—emotionally or otherwise. During her scheduled cleaning shifts, she's all business now. Exactly as I asked.

Only, I wasn't anticipating it to hurt so much.

Krell keeps up an amiable flow of light chatter as we take the elevator down two levels and emerge into the bright white expanse of Obscura's cafeteria. Long rows of tables and chairs stretch out before us, with the buffet area along one wall. Being a company full of nightmare creatures, some who eat and some who don't, and some who eat *very strange things*, the assault of smells in this room is overwhelming.

It's quieter than usual, most day-shift staff already gone. This is my third "lunch" this week around sunset. Time barely matters here anymore.

Krell and I join the line and slide our trays along. I skip over the ash-rubbed venison, the shadow broth, the rare beef tongue, and the screaming mushroom stew, and go for human junk food instead—waffle fries drenched in salt and hot sauce. The salt and the sting are exactly what I crave right now. Next to me, Krell interrogates the sushi chef, then orders fugu sashimi.

I raise an eyebrow, but keep quiet. It's not like the fish—notoriously deadly if prepared incorrectly—can actually kill him. Being a wraith, he's already dead. Still, I've watched enough human cooking shows to have absorbed their level of risk tolerance by osmosis. It's a bold thing to eat in general, and bolder still to eat raw.

We settle at a table in the corner. Classical piano music trickles faintly through the speakers.

"So," says Krell, and tucks a paper-thin slice of fugu fish into his mouth. He does a little shimmy in sheer pleasure. Grins at me with the satisfaction of a dead man who cannot be poisoned. "The opportunity I mentioned. We've had our eye on a new initiative. Cutting-edge stuff, really, fresh out of R&D. And given your numbers lately…"

I drag a waffle fry through hot sauce, not looking up. "Sir?"

He leans in, his voice dropping conspiratorially. "Field work, Alston. But not the usual passive harvesting. This is implantation. Direct fear-seeding. Go in during the day, plant a little something—a flicker of unease, a visual that won't wash away. Leave it behind to marinate, and come back later that night to reap the results. Cleaner harvest, higher yield. Early tests show thirty percent improvement in energy extraction. We're calling it Project Harrow."

I stop chewing.

Krell grins, and I shudder at the sight of all his teeth. "It's still in the pilot phase, but we want you on it. Top performers only. You'll get clearance to bypass ethics review temporarily—we can't have those committee types slowing down innovation, not yet. I need to see what we can do first, how far we can push it, before asking for permission."

My appetite dies. "So we'd be... manufacturing human fear now. Not just harvesting it."

"If it works long term, yes." He waves his chopsticks. "We've always influenced dreams. This is just more efficient. Focused. Think of it as curating terror. Like premium content."

So this is my future: handcrafted misery, tailored to algorithmic taste.

Every nightmare I built before was a commission, temporary by design. Harrow is different. Worse. It's planting nightmares in unsuspecting civilians, letting them fester until they can't tell what's natural and what we put there.

I've always needed fear—it doesn't keep me alive the way food keeps humans alive, but without it my shadows turn inward, eating me hollow. Chamber work fills the hunger, dulls the edges. But this—manufacturing fear to order—feels like crossing into something uglier. Not sustenance. Exploitation.

I stare at my plate. Even salt and hot sauce can't cut through the heaviness in my chest. This twisted "reward" of Krell's only highlights how out of place I feel here.

"It's not mandatory," Krell adds lightly, popping another piece of fugu in his mouth. "But I'd think hard before saying no. A spot like this could put you in line for a true promotion next quarter. I think it would make your father proud."

I manage a nod. "I'll consider it."

"That's all I ask," he says, wiping his fingers on a black silk napkin. "Take your time. You've earned it."

He segues into more idle chatter, but I've lost both the desire to be around him and my capacity for meaningless small talk. I pick at my plate until I can't stand it any longer. Then I rise with a muttered thanks, my tray feeling suddenly leaden, and head toward the elevator.

My mind is buzzing, shadows twitching erratically at my back.

Curating terror. Bypassing ethics. Promotion.

I don't want any of it.

But I can't think about that now. I need to get back in the chamber. Back to distraction.

The elevator doors slide closed. My phone vibrates in my pocket. Annoyed, I snatch it out—then my heart leaps.

It's from *Mia*.

Without scanning the preview, I click into the message, dizzy with foolish excitement. Which quickly deflates as I actually read her message.

I reread it. Then again.

And again.

And I go still, thumb hovering over the screen like maybe I can undo it. Like maybe if I just don't read it again, it won't be real.

But it is, of course it is.

Because what else did I expect? I pushed her away. Over and over. Until she got the message. Until she finally believed I meant it.

A rush of heat slams through my chest, sharp and blinding. For a split second, I think I'm dying—some buried magical failsafe I didn't know existed, detonated by her rejection.

My throat closes. My limbs tremble. I can't breathe.

The elevator keeps climbing. It's only a few floors, but it feels infinite, far too fast, making my head spin.

I grip the rail behind me, fingers digging into the cold steel, and try to track the symptoms like I've seen humans do in dreams. Shaking hands. Racing heart. Vision tunneling like the world's collapsing inward.

Panic.

No—anxiety. That's what this is. I've felt it radiating off them a thousand times, seen it pull their dreamscapes into spinning loops of stairwells and impossible hallways. I just never expected to feel it like this. In my own skin.

And it's not from fear. Not exactly.

It's loss. I pushed her away to protect her—now she's gone, and I don't feel clean or noble or selfless. I feel hollow.

The elevator dings and spits me out onto my floor. The dream chamber door stands straight ahead, mocking me. I step out into the hallway like I'm sleepwalking. The power-flush from earlier has long since faded, and my glamour is slipping, my shadows trailing me like smoke from a dying fire.

You won't be seeing me again.

She's gone.

And I don't want to be here anymore.

Not at Obscura—here. In my body. In my mind. In the grief I carved out for myself.

I need to get out.

Out of this building. Out of this skin. Out of this version of myself I can't stand. So I run—before I shatter somewhere public.

Chapter Twenty-Two

Nate

I don't remember going home, but the apartment is dark when I get there. I don't bother turning on the lights. My limbs feel full of lead and static.

I'm riding the high from a dozen dreamfeeds, my numbers are perfect, Krell is thrilled—and I've never felt more like a ghost in my own skin. I fumble my keys, drop them, curse.

Even the silence in my apartment feels sharp enough to cut.

I kick off my shoes, throw my coat somewhere it doesn't belong, and collapse onto the couch with the remote.

Noise.

That's what I need.

Just enough sound to keep the thoughts at bay. I flip through channels, hunting for anything but silence—but all I find is a roar of pain in my own head.

Molly jumps up next to me and curls up against my side, a warm mass of fur and sulfur breath. I lay a hand on her, trying to ground myself with the thump of her rapid hellhound heartbeat.

It doesn't work.

I flip through channels faster. Just need something to keep me from spiraling—

There. A soaking-wet brunette teenager in a blue hoodie arrives to a fancy party, clearly late, and begins giving a speech. I have no idea what this is—some human movie called *The Princess Diaries* playing on cable—but I'm captivated.

I watch as the girl, apparently a princess, speaks eloquently about accepting an unexpected royal title she wasn't sure she wanted.

As the speech comes to a close, she says, "...I choose to be forevermore, Amelia Mignonette Thermopolis Renaldi, Princess of Genovia."

And...it hits me like a punch to the gut.

Because that's one of the first things Mia ever said to me. I didn't know at the time it was a movie quote. Now I do—and the realization makes my chest ache even worse.

She'd tossed it out in playful sarcasm to hide her nerves, but something in her tone made me think she believed it, too: that she could choose who she was, even if no one else believed in her. That line rolled off her tongue without effort, so it must matter to her.

And now, hearing it again, the more the ache of *missing* her floods me in a visceral, helpless way.

The ache turns into pressure. A horrible, collapsing sensation in my chest, something vital caving in. Like I can't get enough air, even though I don't technically need it.

I press a hand to my sternum. Try to shake it off.

It feels like dying.

Is everything I see going to remind me of her, now?

My phone buzzes, and I'm so keyed up I nearly jump off the couch. A quick glance reveals it's a message from Krell.

I really need to get work apps off my phone.

Obscura Group Internal Chat – 10:05 P.M.

Carlton Krell: *Alston—know we said we'd discuss the promotion next quarter, but I just left a very promising board meeting. Thought you'd want the heads-up: it's likely coming sooner. Nice work lately. Really proud.*

Proud.

Like I'm a well-trained dog. A good little monster. The word makes my stomach turn.

My metrics are perfect, my technique flawless. I've become the exact version of myself they always wanted. The numbers-driven creature my father designed this place to shape me into. Legacy fulfilled, even if it tastes more like ash than victory.

And yet I've never felt more monstrous, more wrong, or more alone.

I shut off the TV and sit there in the dark, shaking. Sensing the shift, Molly stirs at my side. Noses at my hand. Whines.

"I'm fine," I lie. The words don't even sound like mine.

But I can't sit here anymore. The walls are closing in. I need air—the sensation of it, at least.

Before I know it, I'm on the balcony, the wind snapping against my skin. This high up, it's brutal, hitting me like icewater to the face. Crisp, biting, painfully clean.

Distant and uncaring, the city glitters below. The beach is a sparkling blue vision several wide streets away. Sunset smears overhead like melted ice cream. From here, the view seems to stretch on forever.

But tonight, it brings me no comfort.

I step closer to the edge. My hands curl around the edge of the railing, tighter than necessary.

The street far below is a landscape of tiny cars and blinking lights. Somewhere, a siren wails. The wind pulls at my hair.

It would be so easy to just—

No.

But the thought is already there. Insidious. Persistent. Soft.

Maybe—maybe just to feel something. Just to prove I still can.

Not because I want to die. I can't. I'd dissolve mid-fall and reconstitute. But sometimes I think falling might feel like shutting off the noise—like suspending the ache for just one impossible second.

Just to see if I can leave myself behind.

My father used to call it a gift—the fact that we don't die, not like mortals, not by traditional means. He said it with disdain, like he couldn't imagine anything worse than being fragile, temporary, human. But I watched what really happens.

He didn't keel over. He unraveled. His shadow thinned piece by piece until there was nothing left to tether here. No grave. No body. Just...gone.

And all that legacy he tried to beat into me—numbers, discipline, dominance—it dissolved right along with him.

The truth of immortality isn't forever. It's just endurance.

And I'm tired of enduring.

I want this endless gnawing inside my chest to go quiet. I want the noise in my head—every scream I harvested, every dream I twisted—to shut the fuck up.

I want to not be *this* anymore.

Because what am I, really? I'm not human. Not a person Mia could love. Just a tool. A product. A monster wearing skin who will only ever exploit and hurt her, and she deserves so much more.

I lean forward slightly. Just enough to feel the pull. To imagine letting go.

Would it feel like floating? Would there be a moment of silence, of weightlessness, before the reassembly kicks in and I'm spat back into myself like nothing happened?

Would it give me a minute's peace?

I keep leaning, tipping forward. Until I'm staring straight down, bent at the waist. The wind kicks up, colder now and yet more intimate. As if the night knows what I'm about to do and is holding its breath.

I whisper into the dark, "Just one breath without this ache. That's all I want."

I'm so tired of being made of edges. Of sharpness and hunger and wanting. I want to be nothing, just for a moment.

Then I pitch forward and let go.

The world spins. Wind rips past my face, deafening and disorienting. The colors of the sunset, lights shining in apartments below, the distant ocean—it all blurs together as I fall, tumbling toward the pavement.

The rush of falling and the brief thrill of weightlessness lasts only briefly, and then—

Oblivion.

Everything goes black.

Half a second later, and I snap back. I'm on the balcony, on my knees gasping, shivering like something dragged out of cold water. My shadows whip-crack back into me. The impact of reassembly hits like a migraine behind my ribs. I retch and nothing comes out.

And Molly is there. Whining. Shaking. I left the door open—she must've followed me outside.

She stands frozen near the open doorway, hackles raised, her three heads locked on me with an expression I've never seen from her before. Not fear exactly. Not anger. Something heavier. Like she's seen something wrong in me—like she doesn't recognize who I am anymore.

That realization shatters me. Shame crashes through me in a hot, sick wave.

I brace myself on trembling elbows.

"Molly," I croak. "It's okay. I'm okay. I'm sorry, I—I just needed it to stop for a second."

At first, she keeps her distance. One of her heads gives a low, uncertain whine. Another inches forward to sniff the air around me like she's trying to check if I'm real.

Then—slowly—she pads across the balcony. Her claws click against the concrete. Her middle head presses against my ribs as she folds her body down beside me. The others follow, nuzzling and nosing until I'm surrounded by the warmth and sulfur-sweet scent of her.

I bury my hands in her fur and let myself cry silent, aching tears that burst forth from nowhere. She licks them away with her tongue and settles more firmly against me.

That shame burns brighter now, almost unbearable.

I'm all Molly has. She probably thought I was gone forever.

"I don't know what I'm doing," I whisper into her fur. "I don't know how to be this anymore. I miss her. I miss her so much it hurts to breathe."

Molly curls tighter around me, a barrier between me and the rest of the world.

And that's when it hits. A jolt, lightning behind my sternum. Sharp. *Wrong.*

My whole body jerks upright, heart slamming into motion. But what I'm feeling isn't mine.

It's *hers.*

Something's wrong with Mia. I don't know how I know—I just do. A connection yanks tight between us, panic scuttling rapidly across.

Molly jumps to her feet at the same time I do, all three heads alert.

"This shouldn't be possible," I mutter, breath short.

No tech, no chamber, no tether. But after everything we've shared—after weeks of feeding on her dreams, of letting our boundaries blur—a part of me stayed lodged with her. A thread tied too tight to sever.

I *feel* her panic as if I was standing at her side.

She's falling like I just did—only deeper into herself, drowning somewhere I can't reach.

And if I'm the only one who can sense it, I can't waste another second.

I dash back inside with Molly at my heels, grab my keys, and together we bolt.

This time, I'm not waiting for a dream to take me to her.

Chapter Twenty-Three

Mia

MERCURIAL//"Your shadow work is paying off. We love a meltdown with main character energy."

The second I close the door behind me, silence surges in like a riptide.

Not even Reika's apartment knows how to welcome me after the emotional whiplash of the night I just had.

Dropping my key in the bowl is almost offensively loud. That sound wakes Kiki, who opens her eyes from where she's curled in a hanging bucket in the cat tower in the corner, gives me a brief look, and goes back to sleep.

I should feel...better, right? Victorious, even. I turned down Imani's ridiculous offer. I told Nate I'm done with his back-and-forth shit. So there shouldn't be a hollow in my chest, or anything gnawing at me like the suspicion I might've made a mistake.

I wasn't expecting peace, exactly. But this isn't quite what I thought freedom would feel like, either.

A hot shower doesn't fix me, and as I go through the motions of getting ready for bed—things that usually bring me comfort—it all feels like someone else's choreography, like a part I'm only miming. Out of habit, I check my phone as I brush my teeth. No missed calls or texts, no unread emails.

It's like I've dropped off the face of the earth.

I shake it off. It's fine. Imani was drunk by the end of dinner and probably went home to sleep it off.

Nate is...well, Nate, and I probably won't be hearing from him again tonight, if ever. Whatever.

But then, as I'm crawling into bed, my phone buzzes with an incoming call. A glance at the screen reveals the worst.

It's Selene. Truly, she takes the award for world's worst ex.

"*Fuck,*" I mutter.

She must've found out about Imani meeting with me behind her back. I shouldn't answer. I should just decline the call, put the phone on Do Not Disturb, and try to forget about all of this until I've had a good night's sleep.

But apparently, I'm a glutton for punishment and an absolute idiot, so I pick it up.

"What do you want, Selene?"

"Just who the fuck do you think you are?"

The venom in her tone spears me like a thrown knife.

"Excuse me?"

"I'm working my ass off, staying late to get everything ready for a new feature rollout, and I have to find out via the fucking grapevine that you went to Imani about getting your old job back? What game are you playing, Mia?"

A slow coil of anger and unease unfurls in me.

"Let me stop you right there. I didn't go to Imani—she came to *me.*" Selene gasps. Good. So she didn't know that. "She all but begged me to come back to try to keep you in line. She told me you're terrorizing the entire company, Selene. Making everyone miserable. So I'm not sure why you'd accuse *me* of being the one playing games."

Selene scoffs. "You know what, it doesn't even matter who contacted who. You took the meeting, entertained the offer. Which means you've always been planning on coming crawling back."

"I didn't know why she wanted to meet! She ambushed me—"

"Let me just make something very clear to you. You don't belong here. And you're not welcome, at least as far as I'm concerned. You think just because you managed to string a few coherent thoughts together at dinner and get back in Imani's good graces that you're fixed? You're not. You're still the same mess you were when you bailed. And I cannot have someone incompetent, unstable, and unreliable in our C-suite."

Selene and I didn't implode because of one bad quarter, or because she hated me. We broke because she hated not *owning* me. My forecasting mistake gave her cover, but the rot started earlier—the nights she'd "fix" my slide decks without telling me, take credit for my models, tell me I was too "soft" for C-suite unless I hardened up like her.

Loving her meant shrinking, and there's only so much you can shrink before you disappear.

She continues. "Listen, I don't know what Imani told you, but I wouldn't believe a word of it. You think she wants you back because she values you as an employee? A friend? She wants someone to balance me out. To absorb the fallout so she can focus better herself—that's all. And she's dumb enough to think she could convince you to do it."

Selene's words hit like an elbow to the gut—unexpected, sharp, and nauseating. I know they're not true. Imani wanted me back to *help* her with Selene, not so she could offload that responsibility entirely.

I should hang up—this is going nowhere good—but I can't. It's the same fucked-up curiosity that keeps my attention pinned to true crime documentaries for hours.

I don't know if I'm more stunned by what Selene's saying or how easily it's all flooding back—those same accusations from months ago, the way she'd stare at me from across the kitchen counter in our apartment like she didn't recognize me anymore. Like she *didn't want to*.

"I didn't say yes." I'm aiming for confident, but my voice sounds weak, pointless. "I turned down her offer."

She laughs, short and bitter. "Of course you didn't. Not yet. You're dragging it out. You want us all to squirm. That's your favorite part, isn't it? When we're afraid of what you'll do next? Wondering what's going to happen to poor Mia and if she'll still be around when the storm clears?"

I go cold.

I...had no idea they thought about me that way.

I never wanted anyone to squirm, or to worry about me. What I wanted was small: for someone to say I was doing a good job, that the work mattered, that *I* mattered. For Selene to look at me across a table and say, "You're right," just once. For someone to make me feel heard and seen. It's pathetic, maybe—but that tiny mercy would've kept me standing.

I pull a blanket around myself like it'll shield me from her voice. It doesn't.

"I defended you, you know," she continues. "Back when you disappeared. When you left us all mid-product launch to go have your *Bell Jar* moment. I was the one who assured everyone you were going through something real. That you'd come back stronger. But you didn't, did you? And you're *not* coming back."

My eyes start to sting something fierce. I stare hard at the ceiling, willing the tears not to fall.

I should have something to say to this—a fiery retort, a volatile *fuck you*—just *something* to cut her off at the knees like she's doing to me. But I've got nothing. Her version of events will always differ from mine, but the sentiments are true.

I *did* disappear. I *did* fall apart.

She's right.

Selene goes on. "You just vanished. And now you expect us to, what, give you a standing ovation for answering your phone again? For being stable enough to go to dinner and listen to Imani bitch about me?"

I swallow hard and try to force iron into my voice, but it doesn't work. "That's not fair. You don't know what I've been through."

"I don't care." Selene's voice is suddenly flat. Cold. Final. "You always said I didn't see the real you. But maybe I did. Maybe you just didn't like what I saw. Maybe, just maybe, *that* is why we broke up. Maybe it had nothing to do with Mercurial at all. Your complete and utter fucking shitshow of an exit from the company was just a bonus."

That lands like a blade between my ribs.

I can't speak. I can't even breathe. I'm too stunned to move. Too gutted to close my jaw around any kind of reply.

Kiki jumps down from her tower in the living room, no doubt on her way to comfort me. I hear it all very distantly, as if I'm trapped at the bottom of a well.

Selene exhales like she's bored of the whole thing. "Do us all a favor, Mia, and if Imani calls you again, don't answer. There's only room for one overly sensitive, backstabbing bitch on the team, and she's got that covered."

The line clicks dead.

I stare at the screen, blinking at my own reflection in the black glass. My throat aches. My hands are shaking.

She didn't just call me a disaster. She made me believe it again.

Kiki's claws patter across the floor. The hum of the refrigerator grows louder. The walls press closer. My chest constricts, tight as a belt. I press a hand there; it doesn't help.

Breathe.

I can't.

My vision tunnels. My heartbeat's too loud, too fast, crashing against my eardrums like a wave that won't recede.

She's right.

I left. I fell apart.

I made everyone's lives harder and then just *vanished*.

I thought walking away was brave—but maybe it was selfish. Maybe I've been selfish all along.

I drop onto my side atop the bed, curl up small.

The phone slips from my hand.

I didn't fix anything. I just ran. I *always* run. My breath comes in short, shallow gasps now—too fast.

The room narrows, tilts.

I can't do this again.

Not another ill-planned escape attempt. Not another hospital bed. Not waking up to that curtain pulled around me, the sound of beeping monitors and someone saying, "She's lucky someone found her when they did."

Kiki meows. Soft and uncertain. She nuzzles against my leg and I can't even lift a hand to touch her.

I don't know how long I sit like that—shaking, unraveling, silently screaming inside my own head—before something shifts.

The air thickens. Prickles. Static before a storm.

Something hums under the floorboards.

And then, I feel it. A pressure. A warmth. Not from within—but *outside*.

Something is coming.

My head jerks up. For one split second, I swear I hear shadows brushing against glass, my name whispered through a locked door.

The knob turns by itself. Maybe Reika's place has decided I'm not safe alone.

I don't remember unlocking it. I don't care.

Because it's *him*. Nate. Slick from a sudden downpour, pale, eyes wide and storm-struck. He fills the bedroom doorway like a question I don't know how to answer.

Three pairs of glowing eyes peer around his legs. Molly. She slinks in behind him, unusually quiet, ears flat. One of her heads whines. It sounds almost mournful. Kiki yowls in response, tail puffed, back arched. Molly ignores her and lies down in the doorway behind Nate as if standing guard. Kiki quiets, unsettled but not running. Even she can sense something worse is happening here.

And I don't ask how Nate got here, or why, or what he's doing. Somehow, I already know.

He felt it.

Felt *me*.

The tether in my chest pulls taut. I called, and the apartment let him answer.

I must look like a wreck—red eyes, tear-slick cheeks, hunched and trembling in bed. But he doesn't flinch. He moves toward me slowly, as if he's afraid I'll vanish.

"Mia—"

His voice cracks. That one word hits me harder than anything Selene said.

I shake my head. "*Don't.*"

He stops short. His shadows twitch and dance behind him—a nightmare made man, some uncanny, dark thing I tempted to my doorstep with the scent and promise of all my worst feelings.

I force myself up on an elbow. "If you're going to take anything from me," I whisper, "then take *this.*"

He frowns, confused. "What?"

"This pain," I choke out on a sob. "Take this. Feed on this. Just take it from me. Please."

He goes still.

"Mia," he breathes. "You're awake."

"I don't care." If he can't do this, if he doesn't—if he just *leaves* me to this on my own—I don't know what's going to happen to me. "Just do it."

For a heartbeat, he's horrified. "That's not how it works. It's not safe—"

But then he looks at me. *Really looks.* And the argument dies on his tongue.

Something else flares in its place. Grief. Understanding.

And hunger.

He drops to his knees next to my bed, reaching out with trembling hands.

"Okay," he says, voice barely audible. "Okay. I'll take it."

He leans in slowly, as if planning on touching a live wire. His hands hover at the sides of my face. His shadows roil high in a dark corona around him, some twisted angel of darkness come to my aid.

"This might hurt," he whispers.

I nod. "Good."

And then he presses his forehead to mine.

For a moment, nothing happens. Then, the world splits open. Our tether flares. Not a dream—a bleed.

My breath rushes out of me, and suddenly I'm outside myself—hovering in a memory I didn't call up.

I'm holding a jug of bleach. The cap is on the counter. The colors on the label are too bright beneath the kitchen lights. I skim over the warning language at the bottom of the label, because really, why does it matter? I don't need first aid. I won't be calling poison control. That's not what I'm after, not even remotely.

I am just done with feeling misery like this.

I watch my own hand tremble as I lift the rim of the jug to my mouth.

Nate gasps. He's clutching my face now, as if he might kiss me, but the reality is so far away from that. His grip tightens.

The memory shifts—

I'm on the floor, staring blankly at a cobweb beneath the cabinets. I can't move, and I can't figure out why. Above me, my mother is screaming—she came to collect me from the apartment I shared with Selene, and found this instead.

So much screaming.

And then nothing, for a while.

Then pain, all over and especially from a tube in my throat, as I'm curled up in a hospital bed, being wheeled between rooms, with phrases like "corrosive ingestion" and "esophageal irritation" being tossed around me.

My mother's words are like razor blades in the ER hallway: "You don't get to fall apart. You haven't earned that."

"Is this what I raised you to do? To give up when things get hard? I don't understand you, Mia. Why'd you do this to me?"

She stayed just long enough to tell the nurse I'd be "fine." Long enough to say I wouldn't be moving back in with her.

I flinch. Nate's shadows wrap tighter around us, trying to contain it, to shield me, but it's all right there. Too big. Too loud.

And he's seeing *everything.*

The shame.

The aftermath of my desperate, half-baked decision—less of a plan and more of a thought that grew teeth when no one was looking. The doctors warned me about what bleach could do on the way down—scar tissue, swallowing problems. Luckily, I dodged most of that. Now it's just the occasional random metallic taste, like pennies under my tongue—a reminder stamped on me anyway.

The numbing quiet of the days that followed, filled with soft-voiced psych doctors and my limited visitors—never Selene. My mother, just that first night, just long enough to be sure I'd live. Imani, once or twice, when I was asleep. She left cards and candy.

Mostly Reika. Always Reika. My one and only true friend outside the Mercurial bubble. Without her—my small but mighty support system—I don't think the doctors would've felt comfortable releasing me at all. And without Reika giving me a safe place to land afterward, I never would've started to put myself back together.

I feel Nate *break* under it. A silent shattering. His breathing goes ragged against my cheek.

But I'm not the only one unraveling. This bind isn't just one-way. A bit of Nate's mind bleeds into mine, the strangest sensation.

Suddenly I see *him*—

He walks outside onto the balcony at his apartment. A fierce wind tears at his clothes, his hair, but he doesn't notice. He approaches the railing, hesitates for long moments, then leans dangerously far over—

I gasp. "You—"

"Don't," he murmurs. "Don't look—"

But I'm more than looking, I'm inside the memory. His grief spills into me like dye in water, and then I'm falling with him.

Because whatever this tether is, it cuts both ways.

I feel the wind shear his skin, the weightlessness, the flicker of peace right before—

Oblivion.

And when I feel his split second of remembered relief, it's so darkly sweet I could almost weep with it.

Then comes the reassembly. The agony. The shame—knowing he can't die and was desperate enough to try anyway. Seeing Molly's three terrified faces as he pulled himself back together afterward.

But it doesn't stop there. I fall again, into another memory of his. It feels older. Worn around the edges and grainy like a '90s movie.

Nate's bedroom. A woman with him—laughing, teasing, tugging him close. And before the jealousy can fully take root, the memory shifts. Nate in shadow form, a cloudy wisp stretched between them. He feeds gently from her sleeping form, with adoration. It shifts again. Morning. He goes to wake her—

She doesn't move. A thin line of blood trails from her nose.

She's still.

I feel his horror, yawning through me now, as it did him then.

A mistake—an awful, awful mistake.

Nate tries to pull back, cut the vision short—but it's too late. I see what he's done. The body. The silence. The ugly shame drowning him whole.

And the wretched, inhuman sobbing that shatters the whole recollection.

We break apart like we've both been electrocuted. Nate curls inward, cradling his head in both hands.

"Oh my god," I whisper. "Nate—"

He doesn't answer. He's trembling.

Still, I slide off the bed and crawl toward him.

Because now I know.

He's *not* okay. Not even close.

His voice is hoarse. "You weren't supposed to see that."

"You weren't supposed to see *me*," I say softly. "But now you have."

He lifts his head just enough to look at me. On a choked exhale, he reaches for me, and I collapse untidily against his chest. Then I'm crying again, tears streaming fast and hot down my cheeks and over my lips, caught up in grief for the both of us and the parts of ourselves we tried to kill off.

Molly lies beside us, three heads down, keeping vigil.

Nate holds me until the tremble in his limbs ebbs away. Until I realize how much I missed him, missed *this*—his steady, grounding presence. A lighthouse against all of my darknesses.

Finally, he exhales. It sounds like his first real breath in years.

"I didn't want to hurt you," he says.

He doesn't need to explain. I've already seen it all, felt his legacy of pain.

"I know."

I don't say anything else. I just let myself stay there, curled against him in the hush after the storm, where we're both still here—fractured and afraid, but not alone.

The silence stretches. Breathes. And somewhere inside it, the smallest piece of me starts to believe I might survive this after all.

But survival is a beginning, not an ending. Nate's arms feel like safety right now, but we both know safety is temporary. He still has to decide what kind of monster—or man—he's willing to be when he feeds. I still have to figure out what kind of life I want when surviving isn't the only goal.

So for now, we just hold on: fragile truce in the dark, a pause before the words that still need to be said.

Chapter Twenty-Four

Mia

MERCURIAL//"Your next chapter requires a softer kind of power. Wear something silky and ruin your situationship's worldview."

We stay on the floor for a long time. Long enough for my tears to slow and my breathing to even out, for Molly and Kiki to both slide into sleep.

In the aftermath of the panic attack that raged through me, I'm hollowed out.

Our bodies are magnets drifting toward each other—exhausted and fragile. There's nothing left to hide, no masks left to wear.

Eventually, we talk.

Softly at first, as if testing the shape of words again, I tell Nate about Mercurial—the rush and chaos of its founding by idealistic, volatile college grads, and the slow erosion of myself under the pressure of success.

The way that, after a while, Selene stopped seeing me as a person and started seeing me as a spreadsheet error.

How Imani meant well, but was too wrapped up in her own perfectionism to be of much use to the rest of us. How one mistake of mine gave a viciously insecure Selene the ammunition she needed to push me out of the company and our relationship.

And how it all came to a head the night I drank bleach because I was just so, *so* tired of bending over backwards to do everything right and getting shit on in return.

"And your mother found you?" he asks, pained.

I nod against his chest. The fabric of his hoodie is cool and soft against my cheek. "I told her to come get me from Selene's because we'd broken up and I had nowhere else to go, but when she didn't immediately respond, I spiraled. Panicked." I swallow, tasting a phantom memory of charcoal from having my stomach pumped. "I'd be dead if she hadn't found me when she did."

Nate makes a pained noise in the back of his throat and urges me to go on. He listens intently as I tell him the rest—my mother abandoning me in the hospital, and Reika stepping in to help keep me safe for a while before she had to leave to deal with her own family emergency.

I fast-forward through me picking up the cleaning job, meeting him, and spiraling in a different way entirely.

After I tell him about turning down Imani's offer to return to Mercurial, I go quiet. There's nothing left to tell.

Nate runs his fingers absentmindedly along my locs and begins to tell me his own story—the death that wasn't supposed to happen. The way his work for Obscura slowly turned him into something hollow. The helpless rage he carries from living forever, without ever really *living*.

"What happened to her?" I ask, gently.

His jaw clicks shut, but he grinds the words out anyway. "I...fed from her too deeply. Too often. Her body couldn't handle it. Her doctor said it was inconclusive whether I caused it, but... I've never been able to shake the thought. That's why I always checked your pulse, why I hesitated when you first offered. I couldn't bear the risk of breaking you too."

He falls quiet, and I fill in the blanks. He might not have actually killed her, but he internalized it as if he had. I think back to his sudden coldness with me after the endless hours of his heat. To his reluctance to even touch me in the first place.

It all makes so much sense now. He'd been burned before, and badly. And I naively begged him to jump back into the flames.

We trade pain like confessions, each offering up our worst moments in quiet absolution. Not out of obligation, but because I think we both sense that this moment between us feels too sacred to leave untouched. That if we don't speak all of this now, neither of us will ever be brave enough to say it again.

When we've both run through the worst of our traumas, Nate sucks in a breath. "Earlier, I—I sensed you. I'm not sure how. I wasn't even thinking—I just ran. I'm sorry for showing up unaccounted."

"I'll give you a pass," I say with a soft smile, tilting my head up to look at him. "I thought I'd pushed you away for good. I thought that was what I wanted. But you came anyway."

Nate's deep blue gaze pierces mine. "I did. I needed to see you, make sure you were okay, even if it broke me." A pause. "What about your text message?"

"I meant it in the moment. I was just tired of feeling like you didn't want me. But now I know..." My voice hitches. "Then you showed up and—and I remembered how it feels. Being held like this. Being wanted."

Nate exhales, his body softening as if for the first time in days. "I missed you," he whispers. "But I also hurt you, and I'm so sorry. I treated you like you were disposable, even when you were the only thing I wanted. I thought pushing you away was protecting you, but it was cowardice. You deserved better than that—than silence and half-truths."

The words land heavy. But they're also exactly what I've been needing to hear. An admission that I wasn't crazy, that he really had been running scared.

"You deserve so much more," he continues. "More than a creature like me."

"Stop saying that." His thumb traces the edge of my cheekbone. I lean into the touch, eyes fluttering shut. "Because actually, I think you might be exactly what I need."

When I open my eyes again, he's watching me. The quiet between us hums soft and steady, a gentle thread pulling taut.

He presses his forehead to mine again, gentler this time. Less desperate. A promise instead of a plea.

"Are you sure?" He cups my face like I'm something fragile, something holy. "I could hurt you, Mia. You know I could. You've seen it."

I half-laugh, half-scoff. "You can't kill me, Nate. I already tried to do that myself." I drop my eyes to his lips. "And yes, I'm sure."

And for once, I don't feel like I'm lying to myself.

I close the distance.

My lips brush his first—just a whisper of contact, not even a kiss yet. I'm testing, checking. Letting him know he can pull away if he likes.

But he doesn't.

He meets me halfway, his mouth soft and reverent. And I *melt*. I thread my fingers through his hair, anchoring us both, and deepen the kiss slowly.

"I'm not going anywhere," I whisper against his mouth.

His hands tremble on my waist, like he was half a second from pulling away again, retreating back into his fear. My words seem to anchor him in place. He kisses me again—still slow, still careful, but with heat blooming beneath. And I meet him at every point. His mouth on mine is the grounding I need—tethering me to the present moment.

His hand slides from my cheek to my neck—protective more than possessive—but warmth pools in my core all the same.

I swallow and rest a hand over his heart. With my voice quiet, but certain, I ask, "Come to bed with me?"

Half a smile quirks his lips before he nods.

We move together, scrambling up from the floor in a tangled, heated silence, broken only by our breathing. I'm still in just a T-shirt, and Nate's eyeing me like I'm the only thing in the world. With his focus on me, his grip on his shadows seems to have loosened. They unfurl from around him, reaching toward me. His human glamour shimmers and I glimpse the true nightmare beneath.

"Molly's gone," I murmur, noticing the empty spot by the door.

"She knows when to give privacy," Nate says, amused. "Kiki too, apparently."

"Excellent. So I have you all to myself."

Instead of pulling him on top of me, I give his chest a shove in the direction of the headboard.

"Lie back. Over there."

His half-smile widens into a grin. "As you wish."

Licking his lips, Nate arranges himself as I've ordered, slouching against the headboard. I crawl over to him and settle between his legs.

"Take your hoodie off," I tell him. "I want to watch you while I suck you off."

"*Fuck*," he whispers, and immediately obeys.

I curl my fingers around the waistband of his sweatpants, and he lifts his hips to let me wriggle them off.

As his clothes fall away, so do the last pieces of distance between us. His shadows dance along the walls, slow and sinuous, like smoke curling through candlelight. I can feel them responding to me—mirroring the reverence in his eyes, the hunger that's more emotional than physical.

Running my hands up his chest, I map the rise and fall of each breath, then lean in to kiss just below his collarbone. I drag my tongue lower, trailing open-mouthed kisses down past his belly button. As I do, his shadow tendrils multiply around us, pulsing, some tentatively reaching for me. Curious. Gentle. One wraps loosely around my ankle, another curls around my wrist like an embrace.

Remembering how those same shadows felt inside me, I shiver.

"You can touch me," I whisper to them as much as to him.

A few shadows shiver, then ease closer. One brushes along my thigh, oddly reassuring. Another curls at the back of my neck, warm and velvety and almost shy. They weren't this tender the last time—they were hungrier, more demanding, but there were decidedly fewer of them then.

I glance up at him. "Have you been holding them back this whole time?"

"I didn't want to scare you," Nate says, voice wrecked. "But they've always wanted you. They're an extension of me. What I want, they want. And I've wanted you more than I should."

I kiss his hipbone. "Let them want me, then. I'm not scared."

And it's true—I'm not. For the first time in weeks, maybe longer, I feel like I belong somewhere. Like I'm safe. Wanted. Worshipped.

I let spit pool in my mouth and lower my lips messily around his length.

He's thick, heavier than anything I've taken in my mouth before, and lined with ridges that pulse faintly, as if his hunger has a heartbeat. It's half him, half the dark, and it feels alive in my mouth in a way that shouldn't be possible. Shouldn't be bearable. But it is, and I moan around it like it's everything I've ever wanted.

His whole body tenses, then melts. To my left, one of his hands fists my bedsheets. His other hand, curled by my right shoulder, has gone fully black with shadow; the fingers are too-long and too many.

His glamour is fraying, and it's fucking *hot* to know I'm the cause.

I suck his cock with care and intention, with long, slow bobs of my head that leave him hissing above me, his chest heaving. Every few seconds, I glance up, and a little more of his true form has taken over—first an arm, then half of his chest, then his neck—

Until finally, I look up and his human form is entirely eclipsed.

And the shadows—God, the shadows are everywhere now, brushing, curling, fluttering like moths against my skin. I've lost track of how many are touching me. One slips beneath my oversized T-shirt and ventures into my underwear, lodging itself persistently against my clit. Lips wrapped around his cock, I moan deep in my throat.

Nate's hips start to buck beneath me. Once, twice. Then a shadowed hand brushes my cheek.

"You're going to make me come," he says, his breathing gone ragged. "But I want to watch you ride me first."

I slide my lips from his cock with a sloppy noise and nod, spit dribbling down my chin. As I sit back on my hips, I reach to remove my shirt, but his shadows beat me to it. Quicker than I can process, they shift and move and re-form in a sinuous, writhing mass of long, barely-there tentacles. Two or three of them yank my shirt off my head, and as I crawl forward on Nate's lap, they slide my underwear off and down my legs.

A deep chuckle echoes from Nate's chest at the shock on my face. "Come here, little mouse."

My breath catches. He called me that once before—Halloween night, half-teasing, half-feral. Hearing it again now, softer, feels like being claimed in a way I didn't know I wanted.

I straddle him, but take my time, rolling my hips against the length of him. The tip of his cock grinds against my clit and I whimper.

"Mia," he says, a hint of warning in his voice now.

With a laugh, I finally tuck him inside me, and with slow, deliberate movements, sink myself down onto him. We both gasp.

"God—*fuck*—"

"If it's too much, tell me—now," he murmurs.

"No. This is perfect."

My mind goes blank with pleasure. I put my hands on the headboard for leverage and start to ride him in earnest, bouncing up and down on his cock and feeling every inch of him mark every inch of me. His hands find my hips in a bruising, punishing grip, his fingers so long they brush my lower back.

His shadows go *wild*. They twine around my legs, my arms, my torso, until I'm bound completely. Because they're an extension of Nate, I feel his frantic pulse echoing in them, urging us faster. One tendril curls firmly around my neck just enough to restrict blood flow, while another writhes in the *exact* right spot against my clit. Combined with the rigid length of him filling me up inside, it's too much.

I cry out. "Nate, I—"

My words scatter into a whining moan as a sudden orgasm rips through me. My body convulses uncontrollably atop him. But the shadows don't relent, and neither does he.

"Not yet," Nate says. "I'm not finished with you yet."

"Oh my *God*," I sob.

He gives me maybe ten seconds to recover, and then, while my legs are still quivering, my walls still clenching around him, he shifts his hips beneath me and starts to thrust up into me from underneath.

No sooner do I collapse forward onto his chest than a litany of shadows haul me back up. They wrap themselves around my waist, between my breasts, around my neck and my arms and my wrists—until I'm trapped there, my arms suspended above me like I'm hanging from the ceiling.

The shadows hold me aloft and helpless as Nate seizes my hips and fucks me from below with a punishing sort of mindlessness.

There's a sense of utter trust and abandon in it that robs me of all coherent thought. His cock, his shadows, they're all one insistent intrusion of pleasure I couldn't escape from even if I wanted to. And that pleasure coils higher and higher into something dangerously intense. All I can do is gasp and pant and moan as Nate and his shadows work me toward a glimmering, golden edge.

The words rip out of him, ragged, rough with need. "You're mine, Mia. Every inch of you. You always were."

"Yes, yours, I'm *yours*—"

Three more thrusts and he buries himself in me, *hard*. The shadow tendril nearest my clit gives the slightest of undulations, and that's all it takes.

I break. If I thought the previous orgasm was intense, that was nothing. This one wipes me from the planet. My vision goes white. Nate's cock twitches and trembles inside of me, which only makes me flutter harder around him. I'm incoherent, making noises I can't describe, just trying to ride out this endless, unrelenting wave of pleasure. That one shadow on my clit wrings every last drop of pleasure from me until tears are streaming down my cheeks.

For a few seconds, neither of us breathes.

Then, and only then, do Nate's shadows go slack, losing their frenetic energy, and release my upper body. He lifts me off his cock, and the shadows help lower me gently onto the bed. I'm limp, boneless, an easy target for his long, shadowed limbs to gather up against him. My heart beats its frantic staccato in my throat. My legs and my core still tremble with aftershocks.

For a long time, we don't move. My cheek is pressed to his chest, sticky with sweat, and his arms are a cage around me—tight, protective, grounding. His heartbeat, steady now, thuds a slow rhythm beneath my ear. One hand strokes up and down my spine.

"You okay?" he asks, his voice low and hoarse.

The shadows have gone quiet and still. Draped loosely over my thighs, coiled at the small of my back, they feel almost like a blanket now—warm, comforting, spent.

"Yeah. I think you melted my brain."

He lets out a half-laugh.

I shift a little, trying to get my legs under me, but Nate murmurs, "Stay."

So I stay. I drag the back of my fingers lightly over where I imagine his collarbone is.

After another moment, he adds, voice quiet, "I wish I could feed from this. This moment. It feels so much better than fear."

I tilt my face up to his. "What do you mean?"

"This," he repeats, his face turning toward mine. Movement flickers in those black depths, right where his eyes should be. "Desire. Wanting, and its aftermath. It's...cleaner. Don't think it would rot me from the inside out."

"Maybe you can," I murmur.

But he's already drifting away into sleep. I fight it myself, trying to cement the inkling taking root in me. And something clicks into place inside me. An idea. A possibility.

Nate said before that Obscura has always only valued fear. Fear is the metric, the currency, the commodity. Desire was never even in the equation.

What if fear isn't the only energy worth collecting?

What if it never was?

What if Obscura's whole premise is wrong? What if fear was never the most potent fuel—just the most exploited?

I tuck that thought away, folding it into the warm, exhausted stillness between us like a seed dropped into soil. Someday soon, I think, it might bloom.

For now, I just snuggle closer to Nate, breathing in his scent, and let sleep finally claim me—safe in his arms, and safer still in the hope that there might be another way forward.

For both of us.

Chapter Twenty-Five

Nate

I may be going slightly insane—Mia's been distant, and I'm worried.

It's been almost a week.

I wanted to see her again, immediately. This thing between us feels too fragile to leave alone. But she claimed she was busy with work. Then she said she wasn't feeling well. Earlier this morning, I offered to meet her somewhere for lunch in between her cleaning shifts, and she had yet another excuse.

I don't know what it means. My brain makes it worse: "busy" turns into "avoiding," "not feeling well" turns into "not with you." I draft a no-pressure, "just thinking of you" text and delete it. Twice. If I push, I lose her; if I hang back, I might be losing her anyway.

I'm trying to be calm and not read too much into it. Trying to give her the space she clearly needs. We haven't put any official labels on this, after all, and the last thing I want is to chase her away by being too intense and affectionate.

It would be easier if she said she needed a few days. Silence is where my worst stories bloom.

"All right, 7 o'clock sharp, let's get started."

Krell's voice shatters the thread of my wandering mind and dumps me abruptly back into reality. Another workday, another boardroom. This time, at least, I'm not the sacrificial pig presenting my creative ideas for the board to shoot down.

This time, I'm *part* of the conversation.

I ended up telling Krell I was interested in joining Project Harrow, mostly because it's at least a change from my normal work. I still hate the idea. But it seems I can't get away from that stark fact of my work, can I?

My father's name is bolted into this place's bones. Walking out would be easy money-wise—and impossible pride-wise.

At Krell's signal, the drone of small talk in the room that I'd been tuning out trickles to a stop.

"Welcome to the very first official meeting of Obscura Group's newest initiative, Project Harrow."

A light smattering of applause follows. I force myself to participate.

Sitting up straighter, I clasp my hands together on the polished table, and pretend to care as Krell's agenda cycles into security briefings, NDAs, and risk analytics concerning the new project.

I'm supposed to be thrilled to be here, supposed to *want* this. Project Harrow is Krell's darling, a top-shelf restructuring of the fear-capture architecture—implant fear in an unsuspecting human during the day and return later that night while they sleep to collect the results, by then magnified and all the stronger for it.

It's like the worst kind of subliminal messaging you can imagine, and I want nothing to do with it.

I try to focus. On the spreadsheets. On the PowerPoints. On anything except the hollow beat in my chest that's been syncing itself to Mia's absence.

The inner mechanisms of the projector hum and whir, too loud, as the machine struggles to keep up with Krell's rapid-fire demands.

"...now that we've been through the basics, I'd like to invite my colleague to give a brief overview of our initial test proposal. Alston?"

Krell gestures towards me, and I jolt. He didn't mention this beforehand. I've seen the proposal the R&D department put together, sure, but he never indicated he'd ask me to speak. Is this some sort of test?

"Sure."

I grab for my tablet. Navigate quickly and desperately toward the document.

Then the sharp crack of the door slamming open slices through the room like a gunshot.

"Oops," says a familiar voice.

Every head in the room whips towards the intrusion—towards the Obscura security guard in a navy blazer who steps in first, scanning the room.

And towards the petite, beautiful human woman strolling in afterward like she owns the place.

It's *Mia.*

Mia, holding a large, glowing tablet of her own, and marching right up to the table.

Mia, wearing stylish glasses and a pantsuit in a rich, arresting red color like a smear of blood, with a Visitor badge swinging from a lanyard around her neck.

My brain short-circuits. She's not supposed to be here. She's not even supposed to know this room exists. For a second, I'm sure she's just a hallucination conjured by how much I've been missing her.

"Director Krell," the guard says evenly, "Ms. Williams is here as an external ethics liaison. Cleared and escorted from reception."

Groans echo throughout the room. Even Krell can't hide the irritation on his face. But he can't exactly refuse an ethics liaison entry.

I'd half-forgotten Obscura even had a human ethics advisory board. It's PR cover, more than anything—the board likes the optics.

"Fine." He waves the guard off, and then it's just Mia. "Ms. Williams, would you like a seat?"

"No, I won't be staying long," says Mia. "Forgive me for barging in, but I have an alternative idea you'll want to hear—I believe it can increase your net yield twenty to thirty percent without raising attrition or liability. I did slightly similar work at a company called Mercurial, and I'm prepared to tell you more."

With the pantsuit and glasses, and her shoulder-length locs tucked into a neat bun, she looks every inch like the sort of poised businesswoman who might work at Obscura. She *fits* in a room like this.

Except she's human, she shouldn't be here, and I have *no* idea how she even knew about this meeting.

I'm frozen, half-standing without realizing, my tablet forgotten in my hands.

I must look like an idiot, gaping at her. Part of me wants to drag her out before Krell notices, and the rest of me is just floored—because the distance, the excuses, all of it suddenly tilts into focus. She wasn't avoiding me. She was *preparing this.*

I thought she was slipping away. Instead, she's storming the boardroom. And I don't know whether to be terrified or in awe.

My too-long stare and silence are all it takes for the murmurs to start.

"Is she yours, Alston? You bringing your little human pet to meetings with you, now?" someone mutters down the table.

A few execs chuckle—mean-spirited, indulgent. Krell doesn't stop them. But he doesn't immediately kick Mia out, either. Instead, his focus only narrows on her, sharpening with interest.

Mia doesn't flinch. "That was rude," she says, calm and unshaken, with a wave of her hand. The chuckles trail off into silence. "I know I'm not supposed to be here. But you're missing something big—and I think you know it."

"I thought you were from the ethics board," says Krell.

"Technically, yes. But that's not really why I'm here."

With a few quick, confident steps, she joins Krell up at the head of the table, where he's standing near the projector.

"May I?" she asks, eyebrow raised. One short, amused glance at me, and he shrugs and steps aside. "Great, thanks."

Mia taps her tablet atop the projector to pair the devices. Temporary guest access—limited, view-only—flashes across the screen. The display behind Krell flickers, then seamlessly shifts as her projection replaces the company deck—sleek white type over a deep red gradient. It's clean. Stark. Confident.

"I read your Project Harrow brief," she continues. "The whole premise is implanting ambient fear to harvest more efficiently during REM cycles, correct? But you're thinking too small."

"Mia," I manage. My mind is racing. "How—how did you even get in here? How did you know about this?"

She shoots me a quick look. Warm. Steady. The ghost of a smirk playing at the corner of her mouth. Her response addresses the whole room, not just me.

"Relax. I didn't hack your servers, I signed an NDA, and my clearance as ethics liaison included review access. I came here to show you how to make Harrow work *better*."

When no one stops her, she goes on.

"I'm the former CFO of Mercurial, where I focused on financial modeling but also trained in emotional behavior tech. Obscura collaborated with us on an early behavior-modeling pilot. My colleague Imani Brooks led the behavioral science on that project—it was shelved, but Imani now serves on your human ethics advisory board."

Krell nods along at that. Meanwhile, I'm reeling. I'd completely forgotten about the human ethics advisory board, lost in a sea of meaningless committees in the back of my mind. When Mia told me she used to work for Mercurial, I knew the name sounded familiar, I just couldn't remember why.

Mia goes on, "When I told her I had an idea to present and asked about connections here, she said it was good timing and shared a redacted project summary. She cosponsored my clearance as a one-time ethics liaison. That's why I'm here."

My jaw drops.

While I was pacing my apartment like a wreck, worried I'd scared her off, she was out there wielding her old connections like surgical tools. Mapping a way in.

I thought she was pulling away. Thought her distance meant maybe I'd overwhelmed her. But no—she wasn't retreating.

She was *preparing*.

I'd told her once—quietly, in the safety of a dark apartment and tangled sheets—how much this job hollowed me out. How I hated what it asked of me. How I stayed not because I believed in it, but because I couldn't see another way out.

And now here she is.

Standing in front of the Obscura board with fire in her voice and blood-red power on her shoulders, demanding attention the way I never have in this room.

She's seen what this system does to people. To her. To me. And she's done letting it win.

But I'd be lying if I said it didn't feel like she just threw me a lifeline, too.

I want to tell her how much it means.

I want to stop the meeting, shut the whole place down, walk across the room and—

"This is absurd," Bowen, one of the execs says with a dismissive wave. "You say you're with ethics, Ms. Williams, but you've clearly got some other agenda, and we're not here to indulge civilian or human fantasies."

"Good," Mia retorts. "Because this isn't a fantasy." She steps closer to the table. Eyes sharp. Voice clear. "You don't need to harvest fear, not really. People walk around every day pulsing with wanting. You've been tagging those signals as noise, not bothering to tune in."

Silence. Then a mutter: "Where'd she even get the data?"

Another scoff: "Wanting? We've modeled it. Too volatile. Too hard to quantify."

And then—just the faintest shift. A glint in Krell's eye. The lean of one VP toward the table.

I've never seen anyone command this room like that.

Not Krell. Not the board. Not even the founders, my father among them, whose names are etched into this company's bone structure.

I'm sure someone, somewhere, has explored this angle before, discarded it over profitability concerns.

But Mia has their attention. She said the magic word: *wanting*.

Want is a market.

And every executive in this room is trained to smell potential revenue like blood in the water.

The moment settles over me like gravity shifting.

She isn't here to prop me up. The fire in her voice makes it obvious—she's daring them to want more than people's fear.

I thought I understood her completely. Watching her now, I realize I only ever scratched the surface.

I'm not just undone. I'm not just grateful.

I love her.

Not with the frantic need that's always haunted me, nor with the restless ache I've carried for years.

With awe.

With a quiet, steady certainty that's been waiting for me to notice it.

"Let me show you what I mean," Mia says, gesturing toward her projection. The screen updates—comparative graphs from public emotion-mapping studies, overlaid with a simple theoretical model of dream-state feeding. Two signatures appear: one fear-based, one desire-based.

"Desire is less volatile, but more consistent. Less corrosive, less metabolically damaging to your feed targets. And with the right alignment—"

A new graph appears. The yield spikes.

"—you get a cleaner, longer-lasting feed."

The room leans in.

"You're talking about replacing fear," someone says. "With lust?"

Mia doesn't falter. "With *want*. Lust is one expression. But there's also ambition. Craving. Curiosity. The ache of unfulfilled dreams. You've been tapping into the nervous system's emergency response. I'm suggesting you shift to its reward circuitry, or at least explore that option."

Another exec mutters, "Jesus."

I glance at Krell, expecting fury. But he's studying her like a chessboard.

"Wait a minute," The woman near the end of the table—Laramie, Strategic Risk—steeples her fingers. "You're showing us a model based on *proprietary* infrastructure. How the hell did you even generate this without access to our systems?"

The room tightens again, a reflexive recoil.

Mia doesn't flinch.

"That behavior-modeling pilot I mentioned? You gave Mercurial limited systems access a few years ago. The agreement is technically still active. Since the project was shelved, no one used it—until I asked Imani for help."

She swipes to the next slide: a timestamped simulation interface, annotated in meticulous detail.

"Imani has been running Mercurial's behavioral models for years. I just dusted off the old framework, plugged in your published updates, and asked a few informed questions."

Laramie sinks back, lips pressed thin. Around the table, a few glances flicker—quick recalculations as they register the open door she just exposed.

The floor seems to tilt beneath me.

Mia didn't just come in here with a bold idea—she came with proof. And receipts. And just enough technical fluency to back up her claims.

How did I never know how brilliant she was?

How is it I never thought to ask?

Krell's gaze sharpens. For one long, dangerous moment, I can't tell if he's impressed or planning to call that guard back to escort her out.

"Fascinating," he says at last, mildly, breaking his silence. "This model you've built is outstanding—grounded, persuasive, data-rich." He steeples his fingers beneath his chin. "But it makes me wonder where your interest comes from. Conviction like this isn't usually born from theory."

I tense.

He knows.

"Ms—"

"Williams. Mia Williams."

"Ms. Williams," Krell continues, tone still neutral, "What's your personal stake here? Why would the difference between sustained fear input and emotionally charged desire matter to you? Why go to all this trouble?"

The room shifts again. A dozen eyes pivot to her, then— inevitably—to me.

Mia's attention flicks my way but doesn't falter. "I know what it's like to be a feed target—told that only the worst parts of me have worth. I'm done being measured by fear alone. People are more than their nightmares. Humans have more to offer than terror, if you'll give them the chance."

"Interesting," Krell says. "And I'll assume you're referring to an incident outside of sanctioned channels."

I open my mouth—to defend her, to deflect—but Krell doesn't let me.

"Alston." He turns to me at last, a slight smile curving his mouth. "Since you clearly know this clever woman. In your professional opinion... is there merit to her claim?"

I go still. Every eye in the room is on me. They want data. They want *spin*. Control. But I'm looking at her—*Mia*, who walked into this lion's den armed to the teeth with knowledge and dared to offer me a way out of my suffering.

I draw a breath.

"Yes. There's merit." I pause, neutral, then let the words spill. "We already tag non-fear spikes, but don't build product on them. Desire-based feeding is less volatile and easier to stabilize. Yield's not always higher, but it's cleaner—less degradation for the subject—and it doesn't hollow the operator the way fear does."

The room goes quiet. Still waiting for the *real* answer.

I shouldn't acknowledge this. But how else do I prove it?

"I fed off her desire, on accident." My voice is steady, deliberate. "And for the first time in my immortal life, I felt alive."

A ripple moves through the room like static.

"Not just powerful. Not just functional. *Human*."

I let that sit. Watch Krell's eyes narrow, his curiosity turning surgical.

"You think what we've been doing is sustainable?" I continue, turning to face the table. "It isn't. Fear doesn't build—it corrodes. It breaks people down, and eventually it breaks us too. If we were smart, we'd be exploring backup options."

My hands clench on the table's edge, but I don't hide it.

"This model—this approach—it's not just more ethical. It's scalable. It's stable. It's the *future*."

Another beat of silence.

Then someone exhales. Another mutters, "Shit." A third scribbles something into their tablet.

Krell leans back, smile razor-thin.

And the room fractures into debate.

"There's no infrastructure for it," someone snaps. "We've spent decades optimizing *fear-based* sync."

"And billions in pipeline development," another adds. "You want us to toss that because your *girlfriend* gave you a boner?"

"You saw the projections," a third cuts in. "Even half of what she's modeled would expand our harvest base twenty percent without the same attrition."

"There are liability issues. Desire is intimate data—different risk class, messy consent frameworks."

"Consent's not easier to manage," someone argues. "Fear we spin as passive stabilization. Desire's harder to cover."

"She has a point," another interrupts, scrolling through Mia's deck. "Reward centers track closer to craving than panic. That's measurable."

"Reward-circuit priming failed in 2018," comes the rebuttal.

"Because we trained on panic, not craving. Wrong features, wrong cohort."

It's chaos—but the hungry kind.

Mia stands motionless in the storm of it, letting the numbers work for her.

Krell doesn't move. Not until the noise crests to a fever pitch. Then, he raises a single hand. And the room obeys.

"That's enough."

Silence falls again, this time heavy with the weight of possibility.

Krell studies Mia like a new acquisition. "This was unexpected," he says. "Unorthodox. Bold. I appreciate your creative entry point."

He nods once. "We'll explore it. Validate the model. Run simulations. Identify barriers and potential implementation strategies." A pause. Then, without even glancing at the others, "Alston, I'll expect your collaboration."

I nod—mutely. There's nothing else to say.

Krell returns his attention to Mia. "Ms. Williams, do you have a current employer?"

She lifts an eyebrow. "I'm...freelancing. Taking some time to decide what comes next. So no."

"Mm. Well." A small, cold smile. "We'll be in touch. I've never hired a human before, but assuming the board votes to continue this exploration formally, we may need a subject-matter expert. Advisory only. No system credentials. Your deliverables would be models and memos."

"I'll consider it." Mia inclines her head—perfectly poised, just a hint of a smile. "Should I expect the offer through your acquisitions department or recruiting?"

A few execs laugh—sharp, surprised.

Krell doesn't. "That depends on how you'd like to play it."

"I prefer clean boundaries," she says. "And good contracts."

"Noted."

He *offers her his hand*. Mia takes it and shakes, and if Krell's strange, undead wraith skin bothers her, she doesn't show it. She powers down her tablet, tucks it under one arm, and sweeps her gaze across the room.

"Thank you for your time," she says simply.

As she turns to go, her eyes meet mine, steady and certain, just for a second. And then she walks out with every eye still trailing her, her presence still ringing in the air.

I can't move.

Because somehow, she just rewrote the rules of my world—and made it look *easy*.

Chapter Twenty-Six

Mia

Mercurial//"Congratulations! You've survived another transformation. Update your profile to reflect your evolved self."

I exit the boardroom in a daze.

It takes my body a few moments to catch up to what just happened. I walk fast at first, like I'm being chased—though by what, I couldn't say. Adrenaline? Regret?

My tablet's still clutched tight to my chest like a shield.

I make it maybe halfway down the hallway, which is lined in plush eggplant-colored carpet, before reality sets in, and by the time I reach the elevator, I'm trembling despite the two anti-anxiety pills I popped on the way here.

Holy *shit*.

Did I really just pull that off?

At Mercurial, walking out of a room like that usually meant I'd said too much, or not enough. Or the wrong thing in the wrong tone to the wrong person. I used to replay every meeting like a court transcript, searching for the moment I lost—before anyone even told me I had.

But this time?

This time I stood at the front of that room, took control of the projector, and said exactly what I meant. I didn't bother to soften my intent to avoid pissing anyone off. I was just me, real and honest and raw. And they listened.

For once, it was enough. *I* was enough.

My body doesn't know what to do with success that isn't followed by punishment. It keeps bracing for the backlash—for someone to storm down the hall, tell me I misunderstood everything, that I made it worse, that I'm not qualified, that I should sit down and stay quiet.

But there's only the gentle beep of the elevator as it approaches this floor. And I'm standing here alone, heart hammering against my ribs.

It wasn't perfect, or as polished as I would've liked. Even if they rip the idea to shreds tomorrow, even if they decide I'm a joke—

It won't change the fact that I walked into a room full of nightmares and gave them something new to dream about.

I pull out my phone and send a quick message to Imani, who I'm supposed to meet for dinner across the street. *It's done. Be there in 5.*

The elevator dings. Before the doors open, a hand slips into mine. I'm tugged gently but firmly around a corner, through a door marked EXIT, into a brightly lit stairwell.

"What—"

Nate scrubs a hand through his hair and paces, eyes wide, his human glamour flickering.

"Nate, what are you—"

"I couldn't just let you leave."

He stops pacing long enough to really look at me. Something wild flickers in his expression—stunned, a little feral, like he's not convinced I'm real.

"If you're about to tell me I crossed a line," I say, forcing my voice even, "don't. I didn't come here to embarrass you. I wasn't trying to hijack anything, and I'm sorry for dropping off the face of the earth for a few days—"

"Mia."

"—I just saw a chance to shift the conversation, took it. You told me once you hated what you did. I didn't think you'd want me to sit back and watch—"

"Mia."

"—and if you're worried about Krell, or optics, or whatever fallout might—"

"*Mia.*" This time quieter. More urgent.

His voice cuts straight through my spiral.

I fall silent.

He steps closer. Gently takes my hand again.

"I'm not mad," he says. "I'm in awe."

I blink. "You're what?"

"I watched you walk into that boardroom and tear the place down. You changed the temperature of the room. You made Krell stop and listen." He shakes his head, eyes burning into mine. "I've never seen anyone do that. You were phenomenal." Another step closer, pressing me back against the wall, my heart thudding. "And I love you for it."

I let out a laugh. He's got to be joking. Because the truth of that would be *too much*. Too big. Too impossible to hold all at once.

"You're sure this isn't just some post-meeting stress hallucination?" I say, trying to keep it light, chill. "Your glamour's flickering. You look like a light bulb about to go out."

He grins, but doesn't back off. "I mean it."

I search his face, waiting for him to backpedal, to second-guess, to reframe it as a joke. But he doesn't. Instead he's steady, grounded, looking at me like I personally strung the sky with stars.

Does he...*actually* mean it?

I don't know what to make of that.

"I wasn't trying to impress you," I murmur, softer now. "Wasn't even doing it for you, not really. I just...saw a problem I might be able to fix. At Mercurial I always had ideas, but I learned fast to keep them caged if I wanted to survive. This time I figured, go big or go home. I already bargained my nightmares away to a shadow creature; what's one more gamble?"

"I know," he says. "That's why it worked. You finally bet on yourself."

It hits then—sudden, quiet, absolute.

With a terrifying clarity, I realize that I love him. That I've probably loved him for a while now. Not the whirlwind, crash-and-burn kind, but the kind that grows patient in the corners. I love him the way someone loves the lighthouse that keeps a ship from running aground: quiet, necessary, obvious only when it's absent.

The confession rearranges me entirely.

I love him for the way he looked into the face of my nightmares and didn't flinch. For the way he listened to me like I was saying something holy, even when I was really just rambling about nothing.

For the way he looked at me across that boardroom moments ago, like he already trusted I could do the impossible—and didn't even need to wait for proof.

I wasn't ready before. Not for this. Not for him. But now I feel steady. The old impulse to bolt—to be small and safe—is gone.

I meet his gaze and let the truth rise without shame. My breath hitches.

And then, inevitable as the tides, I say, "I love you too."

It comes out quiet. No fanfare, no theatrics. Just the truth, clean and simple.

Nate's expression changes. Something breaks open behind his eyes. Suddenly, I'm looking deep into the core of him, and for the first time, he's *letting* me—and I feel it all over again, how close I came to missing this. How far I've come from the version of myself who would've run the second someone looked at me like this, because it meant they now had the power to hurt me.

His human form flickers and vanishes. He reaches for me like he's afraid I'll disappear.

I don't.

I don't. I step forward, close the distance, and slide my hand up the side of his neck. His skin is warmer in this form—velvety, shadow-edged, humming with the magic just beneath the surface.

We melt into each other, mouths meeting, the firm, solid presence of his nightmare form caging me against the wall. This isn't sweet; it's hungry. All that tension—the misunderstandings, the aching pauses—ignites between us like a fuse finally, desperately catching. His mouth opens under mine with a sound that's half relief, half need, and suddenly we're devouring each other in this too-bright stairwell like it's the only place in the world that exists.

It's a grounding point in the chaos, a thread anchoring us both to something solid.

His body hums with heat and something darker, the scent of ozone and something older, more ancient, curling through the stairwell.

I press into him, feeling the ripple of power just under his skin, the way his magic flares every time I kiss him deeper. His hands find my hips, anchor there like he's trying to memorize the shape of me through layers of fabric and restraint. Then his arms circle around me, pulling me in like he's still afraid I'll vanish if he lets go.

But I'm still here.

And for the first time in a while, I actually *want* to be.

When I break the kiss, we're both breathing hard. The lipstick I spent way too long applying is probably ruined, and I don't care. I glance down at my tablet, which is now on the floor. The clatter must've echoed like a gunshot, but I didn't notice.

"That's expensive," I say with dismay.

"Is it broken? I'll buy you a new one," Nate says dismissively, and kisses me again.

The second kiss leaves me dizzy. One of Nate's shadows wraps itself lovingly around my ankle, and it snaps me back to reality. I can't let this go any further here in this stairwell, and I need to leave now, or I won't be able to resist.

I pull back and fight for the thoughts slipping through my fingers. "You can't keep me here," I murmur teasingly. "I'm supposed to meet Imani across the street. She's already ordered cocktails and will definitely murder me if I leave her waiting."

Nate nods. Moments later, with a visible breath, he pulls his glamour back into place. He's smiling—soft, a little dazed.

"Can I walk you over?"

"What about your meeting?"

"It's adjourned until tomorrow. Krell couldn't keep everyone from sniping at each other; they're all too excited about your idea."

The thought of a room full of nightmare executives arguing over how to implement an idea I gave them brings me no small amount of joy.

I huff a laugh, breathless and smug. "Good."

We leave the stairwell hand-in-hand, and I let him lead me back to the elevator like nothing just happened—like I didn't completely derail his day, his team, his *company*.

The elevator dings again as we reach it, and this time I don't flinch. My heart's still racing, but the rhythm has changed. Momentum, not panic.

Down on the ground floor, the lobby is mostly empty. Massive glass doors gleam ahead of us, sunset's light spilling in like creamy gold.

Nate's hand in mine as we walk out into the evening makes me feel like the most powerful woman in the world.

We're halfway across the street when he asks, "Are you nervous?"

"About dinner with Imani?" I raise a brow.

"I meant about what comes next. With Obscura. With... everything."

I think about that. About the look on Krell's face when I walked out. The way the room turned on itself. The model I built in a caffeine-fueled haze, finally projected into the world.

"I should be," I admit. "But I'm not."

Nate hums in response like that answer makes sense to him.

The restaurant comes into view—an upscale Asian fusion place, cozy and warmly lit, with a little patio strung in fairy lights. I spot Imani immediately, sitting at a corner table just inside, one leg crossed elegantly over the other, sipping a tall pink drink with a slice of lime.

At the sight of me, she raises her glass. Then she sees Nate.

And smirks.

"Well, well," she says, sipping from her drink without breaking eye contact. "I'm assuming you're the tall, dark slip of shadow I met on Halloween? Nice to meet you in your human form."

Nate slides into the chair across from her, utterly unbothered. "Nice to see you again, Imani."

"Be nice," I tell her, lowering myself into the chair next to him. "He came willingly."

Nate rests a hand lightly on my knee under the table. Not possessive or posturing—just *present*. Grounding, in a way that puts me at ease in the face of so much that's changing.

Imani grins, warmth flickering beneath her amusement. "I was always going to be nice, Mia. Did I not just help you put together that entire presentation?"

"That's true, you did. And I still can't thank you enough."

When the idea hit, I'd called Imani. I wasn't sure she'd help—I'd just turned down her offer to return to Mercurial and run interference on Selene. But to my surprise, she was eager. She said it was the first time in ages she'd been asked to work on an interesting problem, and she was happy to lend me her science-oriented brain. Somewhere between cocktails and commiseration, she admitted she'd been on Obscura's ethics board for years—something I was apparently the last to know. Back at Mercurial, all I saw was Obscura's glossy corporate face. Courtesy of an old fling, Imani was the only one who'd been invited deeper.

If Director Krell does offer me a job, I'll need weeks to deep dive Obscura's dream tech so I don't make a complete idiot of myself.

Luckily, I have my own personal nightmare consultant at my side.

Imani's expression softens. "You good? After the presentation?"

"I think so." I lean my tablet—mercifully unharmed—against the table legs. "Still processing. But... good."

She studies me a moment. "You look it. More than okay, actually." Her gaze flicks to Nate. "How'd she do?"

Nate beams at me. It strikes me all at once that I so rarely see him smile. "She was spectacular."

His whole energy feels lighter now. I can't help wondering how much of that is me, or what I just pulled off. I can't shake the feeling that I might've given him hope about his work for the first time in a while.

The way he's looking at me just about melts my heart.

"God, I am so single," Imani laments, and drains her drink in one long sip. "Well, glad you survived. I hope it was at least marginally more tolerable than the usual Mercurial presentation gauntlet."

"It absolutely was."

"Excellent. Anyway. You brought your nightmare boyfriend to dinner, so technically, this is a celebration."

Imani flags the waiter.

Dinner is delicious and slightly chaotic. Imani orders too much food and makes us try everything. Nate listens more than he talks, but when he does it's to land a jab that makes her choke on her drink—especially when she starts interrogating him about his career in emotional piracy.

"So let me get this straight," she says at one point, picking up a dumpling with her chopsticks. "You've been feeding off people's fear and other dark shit for centuries, but never even considered desire as a viable energy source?"

"In my defense," Nate says, deadpan, "Mia's dark shit is unusually potent."

"True," Imani agrees, flashing me a grin. "And now she's weaponized it."

The phrase sticks with me.

I'm used to being underestimated. Overlooked. Wrung out for other people's benefit. But this—this feels different.

They're not laughing *at* me. They're laughing because *I did something impossible and it worked*. For the first time in a long time, I feel not just wanted—but wanted *here*.

I catch Nate watching me, quietly, like he's seeing all of this land inside me in real time. Watching me rebuild my own foundation from the inside out. He doesn't interrupt. Just laces his fingers through mine under the table.

We linger longer than we mean to, ordering dessert we don't need and stealing bites off each other's plates like old friends. Imani teases Nate mercilessly. Nate takes it in stride. I bask in it—the ease, the joy, the strange, warm feeling of being *known* in a way that doesn't make me shrink.

When the check comes, to my shock, Imani insists on covering it.

I am *really* starting to like this new version of her.

"For being my favorite agent of chaos," she says, sliding her card into the folio with a wink. "And for *finally* getting laid."

Finally since Selene, she means. Which is mortifying enough without her announcing it across the table.

"*Imani*," I hiss, but Nate just laughs.

By the time we leave, I'm more than a little tipsy from too much wine. Outside, night has fully fallen, and in true South Florida fashion, the air is hot and wet like the mouth of some great dragon. Imani hugs me tight, whispers, *I'm so proud of you,* and disappears into her car with a promise to call tomorrow. I watch her go with an odd ache in my throat I'm not sure how to handle, my heart too full to speak.

When I turn back to Nate, he doesn't say anything either. Just offers his hand again.

We walk in silence.

Back at my apartment, I half-expect it to feel too small after the day I just had. But when I open the door, it smells like eucalyptus and lavender and the faint trace of magic that's always lived in the walls. Still mine, even if I don't know for how much longer. This place has always felt like borrowed armor—protective, familiar, but never really mine.

I'm only renting its steadiness until I figure out my own, and I think I'm finally starting to do that.

Kiki trots out from under the couch, tail high, twining around my legs, then Nate's, then meowing at him like he's an intruder. We laugh as she scurries off.

After I change into more comfortable clothes, we settle onto the couch to watch *90 Day Fiancé.* I curl into Nate's side, my legs tucked beneath me, the warmth of him soaking through every layer. He brushes his thumb over my knuckles, gaze sweeping slowly across the apartment.

"How long is your lease here?" he asks after a while.

"Technically month-to-month, depending on how long Reika's in Japan," I say. "Why?"

He shrugs. "Just wondering if you're...open to other living arrangements. Eventually."

My heart skips a beat. I glance up at him, and he's too casual, staring straight ahead, which tells me that my suspicion is correct—that was an offer to move in with him, if I want.

I can't fight the slow smile that steals across my face. "I'll take it under consideration."

"Fair enough," Nate responds, grinning.

We sit like that for a while—quiet, cocooned, the evening folding around us like a soft blanket.

Then my phone buzzes.

It's a text from Reika. Multiple texts, actually.

REIKA TSUKINO:

> Apartment says you've got company

> Are they hot?

I'm not sure what it is—maybe the fragile, lingering hope after the day I've had, the newfound self-confidence buzzing in my veins like the first shot of liquor, Nate's presence, or some combination of all three. But I push aside my usual instincts to lie and deflect, and finally, for once, tell Reika the truth.

MIA WILLIAMS:

> Yes. Very. Boyfriend material.

Another flurry of texts follows instantly.

REIKA TSUKINO:

> HELLO?! Are you joking? Since when?

> OMFG

> YOU HAVE A BOYFRIEND??

> IS IT MR. SHIFTY AURA DUDE?

> TELL ME EVERYTHING

I huff a laugh and toss the phone face-down on the coffee table without replying.

"What was that?" Nate asks.

"Nothing important," I say, burrowing closer to him. "Just the apartment being a snitch."

He kisses the top of my head. "Good to know it's looking out for you."

"Yeah," I whisper. "I'm glad it is, too."

I let myself be fully still—no running from the past, no panicking about the future. Just this moment. Just *us*.

Exactly where I want to be.

Epilogue

Nate

Three months later

The gentle crash of ocean waves is so soothing it almost lulls me right back to sleep.

I've lived a lot of places in my immortal life, and I've been in Coral Key the longest. Sneaking out here barefoot to watch the sunrise, I finally understand what I've been missing.

In my peripheral vision, a long strip of pale, white sand stretches endlessly to the horizon, and before me, the ocean is a rich turquoise that nearly takes my breath away. A light breeze shoves the waves toward the shore, where they crash, foamy remnants nearly reaching my feet.

I close my eyes and just *breathe*. I feel so calm here. Settled. *Right*. Content.

We've only spent one night here so far, sleeping on an air mattress while waiting for everything else to get delivered, but I'd say trading my penthouse for some new surroundings was absolutely the right idea.

"Nate?"

I look over my shoulder to find Mia weaving unsteadily towards me across the sand, wearing a giant T-shirt that falls to her knees. She's sleep-rumpled and radiant, the sight of her bringing an instant grin to my face.

Behind her, our small beachside bungalow sits like something out of a landscape painting—weathered teal shutters and whitewashed walls, fairy lights strung along the porch, sliding glass doors reflecting the sunrise. It's a short walk from the back porch down to where I sit on the beach. As she approaches, I reach up for her, and she tumbles down against me with a small *oof*.

"You're up *so early*," she whines, her voice still husky with sleep.

"Sorry. I tried not to wake you. I wanted to see the sunrise." I gesture toward the riot of color slowly rising above the horizon. "Also, Molly needed to go out."

"Hm." Mia glances around. "Where'd she go?"

As if on cue, a fountain of water gushes skyward a few hundred feet offshore. A dark form breaks the surface and starts paddling quickly back toward shore. Steam pours off of its large back as its superheated skin turns the water to vapor around it. Moments later, Molly trots out of the water towards us, sopping wet, all three heads wild-eyed with excitement.

Mia bursts out laughing, sounding much more awake now. Molly comes over for a quick check-in, nuzzles one of her faces to each of ours, then tears off in a bout of hellhound zoomies before sprinting full-tilt back into the ocean.

"So glad this is a private beach," I mutter, which makes Mia laugh again.

She curls up against me with a sigh, her cheek resting against my shoulder, and we watch Molly disappear into the surf again. We sit like that for a while—quiet, peaceful, in awe of the sunrise and wrapped in the kind of stillness neither of us used to believe we'd ever get to call ours. Eventually, Molly reemerges, and we all trudge back inside.

Since we're in the middle of moving, we have no food and no pans in the kitchen. We get dressed and walk to a bagel shop down the road, returning with coffee and sandwiches that instantly catch Molly's attention. Then we eat on the porch, our legs tangled under the table, listening to the distant crash of waves and the sounds of seagulls overhead.

The rest of the crew, and the moving truck, arrives around lunchtime. And slowly, the bungalow fills with our closest friends.

First is Reika, Mia's half-siren friend, recently back from Japan. She arrives in cutoff overalls and a cropped tank, her glossy black hair tied up in a glittery scarf, carrying a reusable cup of cold brew in one hand, and she tosses a longing look at the ocean.

"This place is cute," she says, squinting at the fairy lights. "Too cute. What are you two hiding?"

Mia just laughs and throws her arms around her. Reika accepts the hug without protest, but glares at me the whole time, sizing me up.

"You're the nightmare boyfriend?"

"I am," I say.

"Hm." She eyes me a moment longer, then nods like she's made some kind of decision. "Okay. But if you hurt her, I know people who can drag you into the ocean and make you disappear."

"Got it."

Then Tulgan shows up—Mia's former security driver when she worked for the cleaning app. He's an orc who towers over all of us, carrying a toolbelt like it's an extension of his soul. His tusks gleam when he grins, and the moment he spots Mia, he lifts her clean off the ground in a hug that knocks the breath out of both of them.

"Brought you a cursed bottle opener and a cooler full of meat," he announces. "Didn't know what your freezer situation was."

He turns to me next, one thick brow raised. "After...well. After what you pulled—" He waves a hand in a vague gesture, and I wince. It's a fair assessment, and I deserve it. Mia warned me he might not exactly be the warmest toward me as a result. "Mia must really like you a lot to give you another shot."

"I really hope she does," I offer.

"Good." He claps me on the shoulder hard enough to shift my spine. "You look like you need sunlight and friends. We'll fix that."

Imani arrives next, fashionably late and dressed like she's running for office. She kisses Mia's cheek, waves at me, and immediately starts opening boxes and organizing our spice shelf. Ever since Mia opened the door for her to leave Mercurial for Obscura, she's been a different person—now heading our scientific ethics program, while Mia consults on the desire-based feeding spinoff.

She smirks at me. "Organic spices and real wood cabinets? This looks expensive, shadow boy.

"It was."

"I knew Mia had good taste."

The last to arrive is Beck. I haven't seen him in weeks—he's been off on a research trip in the astral labs. Now, finally returned from California, he grins at me from the front porch. Wearing board shorts, a tank top, and flip-flops, like he's never known a single hardship, his human glamour ripples faintly.

"You look like you swallowed a surfer bro as a snack," I tease, and let him in.

Beck rolls his eyes. "Who knows? They're everywhere out there. Different vibe than the Florida ones. Maybe I did."

Slinking inside, he casts his gaze around with unfiltered curiosity and a bit of judgment. "So this is your new lair."

"It's a bungalow."

"It's...offensively charming. I hate it. But it suits you."

Mia appears from the kitchen—hair tied back beneath a bandanna, wearing a bright yellow crop top and athletic shorts, her colorful tattoos turning her arms into living artwork.

"Did you tell him we have snacks?"

Beck gasps. "Ah. Changed my mind. Love this place." Eyes crinkling as he shakes her hand, he says, "You must be Mia."

"The one and only," she jokes.

After a few minutes of chitchat, she goes to supervise Tulgan, who's volunteered to hang our wall art. Beck watches me watch her go.

"Look at you, dude," he remarks. "You're glowing. It's disgusting. And particularly impressive for a shadow entity."

"Shut up," I mutter, but I'm smiling.

The afternoon unfolds into a sweaty blur of laughter and controlled chaos.

Imani takes charge of the kitchen. Tulgan refuses to let anyone touch his power tools, and dutifully reassembles all of our furniture on his own. Reika assembles a shelving unit without instructions and threatens to drown anyone who fills it with "ugly mugs," saying she'll send us a box of some handmade ceramics that are worthy of display. Beck, naturally, makes a show of installing a singular curtain rod, then complains that manual labor builds *too much* character.

There was a time I would've avoided all of them, turned inward to stay safe. Now they feel like orbiting moons in a small, chaotic galaxy I never knew I needed.

Slowly, boxes get unpacked. Snacks get devoured. Molly, thoroughly exhausted from her ocean sprints, conks out in the hallway like a demonic speed bump, and no one has the heart to make her move, so we all just step over her. Mia floats between us all, bright and steady, gently glowing with happiness. She steals chips from people's plates and kisses my shoulder in passing.

Somewhere around golden hour, when we've retrieved all the boxes from the moving truck and the entire house is a mess, everything slows down. The furniture is roughly where it belongs, boxes are mostly opened, and no one has the energy to pretend we're still being productive. There's no edge to brace against. Just softness, laughter, warmth.

I don't know if I've ever been this full without feeding.

Beck collapses onto the couch with a groan. "I am, officially, never helping you move again."

"Even if we bribe you with tacos?" Mia asks, grinning down at her phone.

Moments later, the doorbell rings, and I answer it to find a delivery driver bearing an ungodly amount of street tacos.

Of course, this reanimates Beck almost instantly.

Within minutes we're all scattered across the living room, sitting on the floor or half sunk into pillows and mismatched chairs. The table's still buried under packing materials, so Reika balances her plate on a stack of Mia's old college textbooks. Tulgan eats three tacos in a single bite. Imani eats hers delicately, like she's judging the structural integrity of each one. Molly snores on, blissfully unaware of the feast happening around her.

And Mia—Mia is cross-legged at my side, gushing about her carnitas taco, glowing with the kind of ease I see in her more and more every day.

I take a breath. Let the moment settle.

Not so long ago, I was standing in a glass tower, harvesting fear and convincing myself it was fine. That *I* was fine. Turns out this is what a harvest can be too—sunlight, tacos, love. No fear required.

I'm barefoot in a cozy house with our hellhound, a bunch of friends, and no cutlery because we can't find the box it was packed in.

And the human woman who made me believe in love again—who made me want a *life* again.

And it's not just fine; it's perfect. Loud and messy and complicated, but bright and real. All mine to keep.

I look over at her, and she's already watching me.

Her smile softens when our eyes meet, like she can feel the shift in me—like she already knows exactly what I'm thinking.

I hook my pinky around hers, greasy with pork residue. She leans into my shoulder without a word.

This is it, I think.

This is actually what I've been hungry for all along.

***

To read an exclusive bonus epilogue, sign up for my newsletter!

If you enjoyed the book, consider leaving a review!

In the mood for another small town monster romance? Click here to read the first in the series, SASQUATCH SUMMER.

Acknowledgements

This book took more out of me—and gave more back—than I expected.

Mia's story came to life during a strange, hard, in-between chapter of my own. I started writing it when I wasn't sure what came next, when everything felt a little heavier than it should. Her journey—messy, hopeful, darkly funny, and full of stubborn survival—helped me find my own footing again. If you've ever been there too, I hope this story reminds you that even brutally dark times, you're not alone.

To my beta readers—Chrissy, Victoria, Luna, and Ella—thank you for your insight, encouragement, and chaos. Your live reactions had me wheezing, and you made this book so much stronger (and much more fun to finish).

Thank you to my husband, Josh, for your eternal support.

And finally, thank you to anyone who gave this book a chance and enjoyed it. Stick around! There's so much more to come.

Also By

Also by Talia Greer

Monster Romance | Wild Wanderings (Standalone Series)
Small towns. Big monsters. High heat.
Sasquatch Summer
Alder King Spring
Hat Man Harvest
Standalone monster romances that blend paranormal heat with emotional depth. Expect high heat, strange creatures, and protagonists who discover love in the unlikeliest places.

***

Romantic Fantasy | The Ardor Magic Cycle (Trilogy)
Elemental magic, forbidden power, and tangled loyalties.
A Cure for Magic
Book Two (2026)
A dark, character-driven fantasy trilogy set in a dangerous world of legacy and rebellion. This series centers fantasy first, with romantic subplots that grow across the arc.

***

Dark Fantasy Mystery | Standalone

Dark secrets, a captive demon, and a poison-brewing nun out for revenge.

Poisoner's Vengeance

A gothic fantasy mystery about revenge, and buried secrets. This standalone features a slow-burn romantic subplot and a morally gray heroine navigating a world of manipulation and power.

Αbout the Αuthor

Talia lives in the mountains with her husband, two chaotic cat children, and a stubborn corgi. When she's not writing, she's drinking iced coffee or watching truly terrible horror movies.

Want to stay in touch?

Join my newsletter:

https://www.taliagreerbooks.com/newsletter

Visit my website:

https://www.taliagreerbooks.com/

Follow me on socials:

@taliagreerbooks or TaliaGreerBooks on the following platforms.

instagram.com/taliagreerbooks/

tiktok.com/@taliagreerbooks

amazon.com/stores/author/B0C5467N5V

bookbub.com/authors/talia-greer

goodreads.com/author/show/35989564.Talia_Greer